STONED IN CHARM CITY

CHARM CITY DARKNESS
BOOK 1

KELLY A. HARMON

Pole to Pole Publishing
Baltimore

Other Stories by Kelly A. Harmon

Blood Soup
Selk Skin Deep
On the Path
The Dragon's Clause
Sky Lit Bargains
To Live by the Sea
Lies

STONED IN CHARM CITY

ISBN-13: 978-1-941559-00-0
ISBN-10: 194155900X

For Tim

The immortals know no care, yet the lot they spin for man is full of sorrow; on the floor of Zeus' palace there stand two urns, the one filled with evil gifts, and the other with good ones. He for whom Zeus the lord of thunder mixes the gifts he sends, will meet now with good and now with evil fortune; but he to whom Zeus sends none but evil gifts will be pointed at by the finger of scorn, the hand of famine will pursue him to the ends of the world, and he will go up and down the face of the earth, respected neither by gods nor men.

~ Homer - The Iliad

STONED
IN
CHARM CITY

CHAPTER 1

D o my numbers."

A filthy hand slapped a twenty-dollar bill onto the table beside Assumpta.

The filthy hand was attached to a tanned arm. He wore a faded yellow T-shirt, stretched over full biceps and a flat stomach. Green eyes bored into her brown ones. He tried to hide a stitched laceration with black, tousled bangs over his forehead. "Please."

Assumpta closed the *Baltimore City Paper* in her lap, with a finger inside to mark her page, and set down the mug of Charm City Brew, a light roast of coffee that she drank black. She brushed her long, auburn curls out of her face and looked up at him. "I don't do that anymore."

True. She had promised her mother. Strict Catholic. Assumpta didn't see a conflict with reading numbers and keeping the faith, but sometimes it was just easier to do as Mom bade.

"Please," he said, laying another twenty on the table.

Assumpta stared at the cash. A promise is a promise—but she was late on the rent—and tuition was due in six weeks, not to mention that she still hadn't found a job. She didn't have enough cash on hand to pay for either, nor to pay her father his extortionist monthly reimbursement, and every little bit helped. Her dad had made it clear she was on her own once she turned eighteen. There'd be no help from that quarter, not even a pass on what she owed him this month. *Bastard.*

She nodded and reached into her huge purse for a notepad and a felt-tip pen. She turned to a blank page.

"Name?" she asked.

He sat, drumming his dirt-lined nails on the table. "Can't you do this without my name?"

She shook her head. "It doesn't work that way. I'll need your full name."

"Greg LaSpina."

"Greg or Gregory?"

"Gregory."

"Middle name?" she asked.

He hesitated. "I never use my middle name."

"Doesn't matter. I need to know what it is in order to run the numbers. If you want, I'll work it both ways, with and without your middle name, and by both Greg and Gregory. But it will be more accurate with all your given names."

Still, he hesitated.

"It's just a name," Assumpta said, though she knew what a crock that statement was. Try going through life with a name like Assumpta Mary-Margaret O'Conner. *Ammo.*

He nodded, tight-lipped, his long dark lashes shadowing his green eyes. "Claude."

She would not laugh. Ill-named folk must stick together. "Claudius?"

"Just Claude."

She nodded. Claude wasn't bad at all. She'd expected much worse.

Assumpta turned the notebook sideways and wrote Greg's name in block letters across the page. Beneath each letter, she wrote the corresponding number.

"And your birthday?" She held the felt-tip poised over the paper beneath his name.

"April 23, 1985."

Assumpta wrote the number, and then she began adding. It was a simple process: the birth date was reduced to a single digit by adding all the numbers and substituting the number four for April.

Each letter of the alphabet also corresponded to a number. Assumpta added those that matched the letters in Greg's name, reducing until only a single digit remained.

The day of his birth revealed his soul number. The number of his full birthday revealed his destiny, or path. His name would divulge his talents, abilities, and shortcomings—even his heart's desire—if she parsed it out and did all the calculations.

She didn't know what he expected to find out by this, why it was worth so much to him. Most folks treated numerology as a lark, but Greg seemed intense. What did he expect to learn?

Once she began her work, he relaxed.

"You've been doing this for a while," he said.

She nodded, adding the numbers again. She really didn't want to talk. The conversation being made over the music in the small coffee shop was loud to her ears. She didn't feel like shouting while she did this.

"How long?"

She looked up from the paper. "Long enough. Years. How did you hear about me?"

"Caroline Paulson."

Assumpta smiled. Caroline was her on-again, off-again best friend. They must be on again if Caroline was sending people her way. Her smile flattened. Unless she sent Greg this way in order to make her break her promise to her mother. *Bitch.*

She hurried, but it was still going to take a while. She would give Greg his money's worth, she decided, providing him with all the information she could. And then she'd get rid of him as fast as she was able.

And then she could finish looking through the want ads. The precious few jobs requiring little skill would be filled by tonight in the poor Baltimore economy. She needed to knock on some doors this afternoon in order to have a chance.

She finished adding the numbers and didn't like what she saw. To make certain, she pulled out the reference chart she'd made for herself and scanned down the list of words associated with the numbers in Greg's name. She definitely didn't like what she was seeing. A loss— but nearly everyone lost something now and again. The rest of the numbers pointed to trouble: the kind that got out of hand fast and had tendencies to create collateral damage just by being near it. The numbers couldn't reveal specifics, but she was certain she didn't want to know. Mr. Greg LaSpina was currently in deep shit.

"I need help," Greg said.

"I can see that from your chart." She ripped the pages out of the spiral notebook and pushed them toward Greg along with a photocopied description of what all the numbers meant. Normally, she spent a few minutes going over everything with the person, but she reserved the photocopies for times like these: when she wanted someone to go away.

"Caroline said you could help me." He was angry, but didn't seem like the type to hit a girl. Still, she hurried to pack up. "Please."

Well, *crap*. Assumpta didn't like where this was going. "Did Caroline say why she thought I'd help you?" She put her marker and notebook back in her voluminous purse and wondered why she even asked. She did not want to get involved in anything with Greg LaSpina.

"She said you used to be friends," he said.

Off again.

Well, that cinched it. Caroline was sending trouble her way and she really didn't need any more right now.

"Look, no offense, Greg—"

"Whenever someone starts a sentence with 'no offense,' it usually means they're going to offend," Greg said. A smile flickered.

"What I meant was," she started again, "don't take this personally. After all, I've never met you before today, right? I hardly know you, but if Caroline sent you in my direction, it's either because she wants a little fun at my expense—or yours." Assumpta picked up her newspaper and stood. "And I'm not in the market for any more trouble these days."

Reluctantly, she pushed his twenties back toward him. "Keep these. Numerology isn't going to help you with your problem. Good luck."

He stood and gently grabbed her wrist. "Caroline said you could help me find things." His voice was soft. The pleading look in his eyes stopped her from ripping her arm from his hand.

"Caroline used the word *find*?"

He nodded.

She stopped. He had her there. That's what she did: *find things.* Maybe he'd lost a watch or something. Or keys. Something he wouldn't mind paying a few more bucks to locate. Maybe she was wrong about his numbers and the loss she noted there was nothing more than what he needed found.

On the other hand, bad number mojo and Caroline did not a coincidence make. Assumpta had meant what she'd said earlier: she didn't need any more trouble right now, *especially* if it were coming from Caroline. Still, Greg was awfully quick to hand out the twenties, and she could use a few more—more than a few more, in fact—this month. Rent was due.

"What else did Caroline tell you?"

"She said you do numbers for folks; that you have a talent to help people find things they've lost."

"And did she explain this talent?"

"I thought the numbers were the talent."

She let out a breath. Who knew how that conversation went? Especially if she and Caroline were off again.

"What have you lost?"

"It's not—" He paused, a confused expression crossing his face. "Is there any way you can help me find something, without me telling you exactly what it is?"

"The more information I have, the easier it is to find something," she said.

"What if I can't tell you *exactly* what it is?"

Assumpta set the rolled paper back on the table and watched it unroll. She sat down again. "Why don't you tell me everything from the beginning?"

Greg sat down across from her. "It's more case of what I've let escape, rather than simply lost." He reached into his knapsack and pulled out a clay pot and lid, together about the size of a large cantaloupe. Blue and gold paint dotted the circumference of the pot, but in such poor condition she couldn't make out whether the marks formed pictures or just designs. The pot certainly looked old, and had a nice big crack running from the lip to about halfway down the side.

Assumpta looked at the pot and wondered what could have survived living in such a cramped, dirty space. She hoped it wasn't mice, or rats. A snake she could live with.

"I'm not sure I'm following," Assumpta said. "You've lost a mouse?"

"Worse."

"A rat?"

He gave her a look that said they were getting nowhere fast. "Hear me out, okay? I don't want you to think I'm crazy."

"I'm already not liking the sound of this."

She stared at his forehead, letting her eyes blur a little, and searched for his aura—a talent she withheld from her mother. What her mom didn't know, she wouldn't forbid Assumpta to do. And she could do this and appear to be paying attention. Words could lie, but auras didn't. The talent came in handy.

She finally saw Greg's aura. It was bright turquoise, with a purplish haze around the edges. She breathed a sigh of relief; he couldn't be a serial killer with such a bright aura. But the purple denoted fear. He was scared…scared enough for it to manifest itself physically.

"I'm getting my PhD in archeology," Greg said, turning the clay jar over in his hands. "For several summers I've worked in Virginia at Morven Farm, digging pits and searching for early American settlers and Indians." He looked at her. "Are you familiar with the dig?"

"I've seen the Jamestown exhibit at the Museum of Natural History in Washington."

Greg nodded once. "Similar. But that's an anthropological study of bones found in those settlements. There are some artifacts, too, but nothing like what's found at Morven Farm. Some of the items found there on the farm date back twelve thousand years. Like this clay pot." He set it down on the table between them.

"Jamestown settlers arrived in the sixteen hundreds," Assumpta said. "There's no way things date back more than a few hundred years."

"*English* artifacts found there only date back to the early seventeenth century, but ten-thousand-year-old stone tools have been found in the same soil. That land was settled and resettled for thousands of years before John Smith sailed into the Chesapeake Bay."

"So what's your point?"

"Dr. Tim Arnold is an archeologist affiliated with UVA, but he's spending a summer working with anthropology students at Johns Hopkins. Because I know the area, and I've worked with the Morven Farm for six years—"

"They trust you."

Greg nodded. "Right. They trust me." He picked up the clay pot again, turning it over and over in his hands. "I was asked to bring the pot from UVA to Johns Hopkins so it could be reviewed by Doc Arnold before it was x-rayed and then unsealed. But the seal broke before I made it to Dr. Arnold."

Assumpta could see Greg's aura flare a deep purple. The memory was strong enough to trigger a strong negative reaction in his aura. He'd been scared—was *still* scared.

"What happened?"

"Traffic was bumper to bumper on 695," Greg said. "I had to brake hard or rear-end the guy in front of me. When I hit the brakes, I heard a pop, and the car filled with thick, black smoke. It got really hot. Sweat poured down my face. I heard a shrieking so loud, I thought a freight train was careening to a stop behind me. I thought I was dead."

"Wait—" Assumpta said, giving him a questioning look. "If this urn was so valuable, why wasn't it more protected?"

"It couldn't have been more secure," Greg said. "The urn was tissue-wrapped, surrounded by foam peanuts, and held in a sealable polyethylene storage container."

"So how did it break?"

He shook his head. "I'm not certain. The container did slide forward when I hit the brakes, but it didn't hit the back seat hard enough to break it. Yet, the container was cracked, as though someone had taken a sledgehammer to it from the inside. The tissue was burned away from the urn, and most of the peanuts had melted.

"So you heard a shriek, and you thought you were going to die. Then what happened?"

"The shrieking got louder and louder, and the smoke started to spin in the car. I felt a coldness, then a burning sensation on my right shoulder. That's when I realized it wasn't smoke. It was something... *alive*. It was alive, and it had bitten me. I opened the door, thinking to escape the car, and it shrieked out of the opening in a single mass. It lifted into the sky and broke into a hundred pieces, each going in a different direction."

He looked into her eyes. "The shrieking stopped, the temperature returned to normal, and horns blared everywhere. I'd brought traffic to a halt. My shoulder was killing me; I couldn't drive. I let off the brake and moved forward, moving right through two lanes of traffic until I could get onto the shoulder and stop the car.

"When I got to the shoulder, I turned off the engine, leaned my forehead on the steering wheel and closed my eyes. I don't know how long I sat there. Long enough for rush hour traffic to pass me by. Long enough for the sun to go down. It was dark when I finally opened my eyes. I may have dozed, but I'm not sure. My right hand felt sticky. So I turned the dome light on to look at it. Blood soaked the sleeve of my T-shirt and ran thick down my arm. That scratch I felt—"

Greg put the clay pot back onto the table and reached for the collar of his shirt. He pulled it away from his neck, bending to show Assumpta what lay beneath: four raw scratches, long and wide, ran over the side of his neck and down his right shoulder. The skin surrounding each scratch flared red, as if infection had set in.

A tremendous, mouth-shaped bruise purpled the skin so far left of the marks, it sat almost on the back of his neck. Individual teeth marks, each the size of a quarter, could be seen in the outline of the bruise.

"If I hadn't opened the door, it might have bit my neck right off my shoulders," Greg said. "I know it sounds crazy…"

"You know what it sounds like to me?" Assumpta asked.

"Pandora's box."

She nodded. That's exactly what she'd been thinking. But she couldn't believe what she was hearing. She looked at Greg's aura again. It burned bright turquoise. He was telling the truth, at least how he saw it. She latched onto the first thing she could think of to refute his idea. "Pandora opened a box, not a clay pot."

Greg smiled. "Actually, that isn't the case. The original Greek translates that Pandora opened a jar, or urn, something much like what I've got here."

Assumpta took a deep breath. "But this can't be Pandora's box— *urn*," she said. "Those evils were never captured. All that was left when they fled was hope."

"Then we've got a bigger problem on our hands," Greg said, "because there's no hope left in this jar. There's nothing left at all."

CHAPTER 2

WHILE THE WATER BOILED IN A SMALL POT IN her equally small apartment, Assumpta grabbed her checkbook, box of receipts, and account book and laid them on the table for her monthly appointment with herself. Dreading the reality, she made the tea, letting it steep for a long time before carrying it to the table, black. There wasn't any sugar—and likely not to be any for a while.

She sat, then wrote checks for the back rent she owed and the phone, thankful that gas and electric were included in her rent. There wasn't much left in the account.

Then, she opened the ledger, looked at the numbers, and felt like crying. How was she going to pay all this money back? How could her father do this to her?

Well, she knew the answer to that. It still burned a hole in her gut, but she was learning to get over it. And once she paid him off, she could write him out of her life.

The figure popped off the page: $163,642.68. It was more money than some folks spent for a mortgage, and they had thirty years to pay it back. She didn't want to know her father for thirty more minutes, let alone thirty more years. She had to get this paid off.

At least she was no longer reeling from the shock of it. She remembered her eighteenth birthday like it had been yesterday.

Her mother had baked her favorite cake—double-chocolate, dual-layered with raspberry filling in between. Her gifts had been practical: a microwave, bed linens, towels. It wasn't until she'd opened her father's gift that she understood why. After all, she hadn't made plans to move out. She'd enrolled in University of Baltimore and intended to live at home for a few more years.

Her father had other ideas.

"Now that you're an adult," he said, "It's time for you to pay your share." He handed her a pink, green, and brown striped bag with matching tissue shooting out the top. Assumpta glanced at her mother who smiled at her with watery eyes. She'd known then she wouldn't like what was hiding in the bag. Neither did her mother, if the tears were any indication, but still her mother was willing to take her father's side. Just like she always did.

Why am I surprised? she thought. Shouldn't the sheer amount of money inspire some sort of sympathy from her mother? Maybe it did, but her mother couldn't afford to show it. She had to live with the man, after all.

Assumpta pushed her hand through the tissue and clasped a book, tearing it from the festive bag and spilling the tissue to the floor. Not just any book. A ledger.

She opened it to the first page, saw her name emblazoned on the inside cover in her father's handwriting. Underneath her name, he'd written the date of her birth. The first entry in the ledger read:

August 15, 1988 - University of Baltimore Hospital, Assumpta born - $5,287.62

She flipped through random pages and noted several entries: August 11, 1994 - Sears, Back to School Clothes - $64.32. October 23, 1994 - University of Baltimore Hospital, Broken Arm, $987.42. She turned to more recent pages. March 18, 2006 - Hit or Miss - Prom Dress - $165.13.

She remembered that prom dress. The satiny hem brushed the floor and belled out when she spun, but hung in graceful lines when she stood still. Its price was way more than her mother had wanted to spend, so she'd steered her toward the plainer, less expensive options. But Assumpta had stood her ground. Now she realized why her mother always watched her pennies. Why hadn't her mother said anything to her then? Would it have made a difference? Probably not. What teenager listens to her mother when it comes to prom gowns?

A November entry caught her eye. Wilson's Leather Company: backpack and matching purse. She'd received those for Christmas!

She had slammed the book closed and looked up at her father. "You're asking me to pay you back for every penny you've spent on me since the day I was born?"

"As soon as possible."

"Every birthday present? Every Christmas gift?"

He nodded.

"I didn't ask for any of those things. They were gifts!"

"I didn't ask for you," he said shortly.

Assumpta took a step backwards, feeling the blow to her chest as though her father had punched her. Her face must have reddened, she felt the heat of blood rushing to her cheeks. Her eyes burned, but she refused to let the tears fall.

Her mother started crying. "He didn't mean that, Assumpta."

"It certainly explains a few things," she had said, realizing then what she'd taken for reserve had actually been dislike on her father's part. The fact is, her father had never wanted her.

"I'll give you a few days to find an apartment," he said. "After that, you're on your own."

"And if I decide not to leave?"

"Then you'll find your things on the front lawn at the end of the week. I'll call Goodwill to come pick them up."

"You can't make me pay this," Assumpta said, shaking the ledger at him. "No court will uphold this kind of debt."

"You'll pay. Or I'll toss you out today and your mother with you."

There was a tense silence while they stared at each other. Assumpta's mother wept quietly beside her. "I'm so sorry," Assumpta heard her whisper.

There was no way she could do that to her mother. Her mother was in worse shape than she was: married at eighteen, no work experience. She couldn't support her mother and herself.

Assumpta ground her teeth together. "I'll pay. But I want all the corresponding receipts."

Her father smiled. "I thought you'd never ask." He left the room, but returned shortly with a cardboard box—the kind reams of paper were sold in—and handed it to her. "I've already copied these," he said. Then, he produced a contract and a pen. She could tell he'd typed the contract himself. It was a single line. "I agree to pay all sums noted in this ledger." There was space for her to sign her name. The remaining bottom two-thirds of the "Contract" was blank.

She looked him in the eye. "I won't pay for anything that doesn't have a receipt. And I won't pay for gifts I didn't ask for." How she was going to prove that, she didn't know, but at least it was something.

His face darkened, but he nodded tightly.

Assumpta wrote, *Addendum*, beneath her signature, then printed:

1. Assumpta M.-M. O'Conner does not have to pay any expense for which there is no corresponding, legible, receipt.

2. Assumpta M.-M. O'Conner does not have to pay for any gifts she received which she did not ask for.

"I'm adding a few more," she said, continuing to write.

3. In the event of Assumpta M.-M. O'Conner's death, any remaining debt is canceled.

She knew it was going to take her decades to pay off this debt.

"No," her father said. "If you die, your children need to pay me back."

"I'm not saddling my children with any of my so-called debt," she shot back.

The look in her eyes must have quelled him, because instead of disagreeing, her father said, "Then we've got to agree to a payment schedule, with interest, compounded monthly."

"Yearly," Assumpta said.

Her father crossed his arms across his chest and leaned against the arched doorway separating the dining room from the living room in their cramped Eastern Avenue row home. "All right. But you'll pay two hundred dollars a month on the loan to start."

"Are you kidding me?" Assumpta said. "There's no way I can pay you two hundred dollars a month, pay for school, and pay for an apartment, too. I can't work enough hours."

"Then drop out of school until you pay off the loan."

Frustration so fierce it made her want to scream clawed at the edges of her throat. But she knew she had to keep it under control. Her father wouldn't listen to reason, but maybe he could see the logic of her continuing school.

"If I get my degree, I'll be earning far more than minimum wage in four years," she said. "If you give me some leeway now, you stand to earn back more of the total amount and in shorter time, too."

"Then we'll escalate it," her father said, pulling the pen from her hand, then writing and speaking at the same time:

"4. Good-faith payments of no less than $50 dollars will be paid monthly until Assumpta M.-M. O'Conner graduates from college. Upon graduation, payments will be $100 monthly. If at any time Assumpta M.-M. O'Conner obtains a job paying—" He looked her up and down. "Twenty-two thousand dollars a year or more, payments will increase to $200 per month."

She snatched the pen out of his hand.

"5. If Assumpta M.-M. O'Conner becomes unemployed at any time, payments are suspended."

"No. Payments can revert to fifty dollars a month."

"How can I pay you if I don't have a job?"

"Where there's a will, there's a way."

"You want me to turn tricks? I can't believe you're trying to make money off your own daughter."

"I'm not trying to make money," her father said, "I'm just trying to get back what's owed me."

"More than that. You're charging me interest."

"For everything I've lost by not being able to invest this money in the market."

"Two percent."

"Five."

"Five!" Assumpta yelled. "There's no guarantee that's what you would have made in the market. There's no proof that you would have even invested any of this money. Who says you wouldn't have spent it on more booze?"

He slapped her, open-handed. Still, her head snapped back and she fell to the floor. God, that hurt. He'd never done that before. Her eyes burned. She blinked away the beginnings of tears, not wanting to give him the satisfaction.

She picked herself up, burning with fury. "One percent. And if you ever hit me again, I'll call the police and press charges for assault. Even at one-percent interest, it will be decades before I pay this off. You're going to have more money than you'll know what to do with."

He nodded tightly, while she wrote.

"I'm not paying for being born," she said.

"Well, *I'm* certainly not."

"You already have," Assumpta said.

"If we disagree on that," he said, looking at his still-crying wife, "then you'd better pack your bags now, dear."

Assumpta took a step toward him and said, "If you want to risk over a hundred and sixty thousand dollars on a measly five, that's your prerogative. But I guarantee you that if you toss Mom out over that sum, you'll lose a lot more: we'll get a good divorce lawyer who will force *you* out of this house and get half your pay in alimony. Do *you* want to risk all that over five grand?"

"Assumpta, no—" her mother started to say, but quieted at Assumpta's harsh glance.

She turned back to her father. "Do you?"

He shook his head.

"Then I think we've finally come to an agreement."

She wrote the remaining details on the sheet, turning it when it ran out of room, then drew lines for both their signatures and the date.

"I'll take this," he said, pulling the page away almost before she'd finished signing her name.

"I want a copy."

"I'll see that you get one."

"We can do it now with the scanner on the computer," she said. "I'm not leaving until I get a copy."

She took her copy and the receipts, packed up her stuff, and left the house she'd lived in all her life. She'd never been back. And as long as her father lived there, she never wanted to.

Now she had to pay off the damned loan and its godforsaken interest.

In four years she'd managed to pay her father back only twenty-four hundred dollars, but even simple interest on the loan meant that after paying on it for four years, she was in the hole an additional forty-five hundred dollars. She hadn't been able to attend college, either, except for a class or two each year, so there was no high-paying job anytime in the future.

The only saving grace about owing a family member nearly a hundred and seventy thousand dollars is that it didn't appear on her credit report somewhere. She could still qualify for student loans in the fall.

But everything was moot if she didn't find a job soon.

CHAPTER 3

B LESS YOU, MOM, ASSUMPTA THOUGHT, PULLING the Christmas list she'd made when she was five from the box of her father's receipts. Mom had given her the Sears catalog and told her to cut out and paste all the things she'd wanted Santa to bring.

She hadn't gotten a single item on the *list*.

When she had asked her mother why Santa hadn't brought her even one thing she wanted, her Mom had told her that Santa probably thought she would like the things she got a whole lot better than her impulse wishes.

"I do, Mom, I surely do," she said reaching for the ledger to remind herself of what she'd gotten instead.

Barbie dolls, a magic set, several books, and a lot of spring and summer clothes. God, how she'd hated getting clothes for Christmas, but she couldn't help but smile now as she tallied up the entries.

Many of the gifts she'd gotten over the years made more sense now, like the ten-speed bike she'd gotten when she was eight. She'd asked for a hula hoop and a pogo stick, according to her list, and had been crestfallen when she realized she wouldn't be able to ride the bike until she'd grown at least two more inches.

Smart, Mom, she thought, *thinking ahead...giving the gift long before I could think to ask for it.*

Assumpta sighed, looking over the edge into the box at thousands of receipts she hadn't looked at yet. Once a month for four years she'd been dutifully writing her father a check, digging through the box every once in a while, looking for something she could cross off her father's list, and then carrying on. Denial is a wonderful thing.

It's not like I'm going to be able to pay it off tomorrow, she thought.

"But it's time to get organized," she whispered. She closed the ledger and put it aside, then grabbed a handful of receipts from the box and started sorting by year. Why hadn't she done this sooner?

CHAPTER 4

HOLY ROSARY CHURCH RAN THE LENGTH OF THE block, its steeple rising above the surrounding row homes on S. Chester Street. The bell tower rose high, the stone dark against a darkening sky. As Assumpta approached the granite staircase at the front of the church, the bell began to toll the 6 p.m. *Angelus.*

The bell pealed three times. Out of habit, Assumpta whispered the words to the Ave Maria. *Hail Mary, full of Grace, the lord is with thee...* The bell rang three more times, paused, pealed another trio, then fell silent.

Beside the church, the Holy Rosary Rectory was as unimposing as the church was grand.

Assumpta reached the top of the third granite step and knocked on the plain wooden door of the rectory.

A minute later, Father Tony Devericks, her spiritual mentor since grade school, opened the door and stepped back to wave her in, holding the door wide. Assumpta crossed the threshold of the door and crumpled to the black–and–white tile as pain erupted in her right shoulder. Father Tony stooped to help her up, but Assumpta waved him off, easily getting to her knees, and then standing.

"Are you all right?" he asked, lifting a plump hand to sweep back a lock of graying brown hair that fell into his eyes when he'd bent to help her.

She put a hand to her shoulder, rubbing the stinging muscle, and nodded. "I felt a sharp pain in my shoulder, but nothing now." As quickly as the pain had come, it had gone.

"So good of you to see me, Father," she said.

"You said you needed to talk. When have I ever turned you down?" He smiled and gestured to the stairs. "Let's talk in my office. The chairs are more comfortable."

Assumpta followed him up the stairs, their footsteps muffled by a swath of burgundy colored carpet running down the center of the treads. At the top of the staircase, the bathroom door stood open, the smell of talc and shaving cologne drifting into the hallway.

The door to the first office on the hallway stood closed, the glass dark.

Father Tony's door, in the center of the hall, stood wide open. Inviting, just like Father Tony.

He walked in ahead of Assumpta and took a seat behind his large, cluttered desk. Assumpta sat in the chair on the left in front of his desk and dropped her purse to the floor.

"Your mother is worried about you," he said.

"She always worries."

"It's a mother's curse," said Father Tony. "But in this case, I think she's worried more about your immortal soul than your physical self." He raised a questioning eyebrow.

Assumpta looked down at her purse at her feet. What could she confide in Father Tony? He was her spiritual confessor, but outside the confines of the confessional, he had no obligation to keep his mouth shut. Inside the confessional, she had nothing to say. She didn't believe her abilities were sinful.

She reached down and pulled her pendulum from her bag: a teardrop-shaped crystal with the wide end tied to a thin gold cord about fourteen inches long.

"Have you lost anything recently, Father?"

"That's an abrupt change of subject," he said, smiling. "Not ready to talk?"

"Humor me. I want to show you something."

He tilted his head as if considering, then said, "I can't find my glasses. They've been gone since last week. Had to print out my homily in really big type so I could read it at Mass Sunday morning. They'll turn up."

"Have you looked?"

"Everywhere," he said, smiling again.

"Apparently not," said Assumpta, pinching the cord between thumb and forefinger, and running it from the crystal to the knotted end to get the kinks out of it. She moved her purse to the side of her chair and dropped the crystal down on its string between her knees.

Once it hung motionless, she said, "Are Father Tony's glasses in the church?"

The crystal remained still for a moment, then began to swing to and fro, building momentum, and then began a counterclockwise swirl.

She shook her head back and forth to indicate *no* to Father Tony.

"Are his glasses in the rectory?"

The pendulum continued circling counterclockwise. She shook her head again.

"Are they in his office?"

The crystal dropped abruptly, then began a clockwise circle. Assumpta smiled. "They're here in your office, Father. Where haven't you looked?" She glanced up and caught his eye.

He stared at her for a moment. "My office is the most likely place for them to be found."

Assumpta looked at the pendulum again. It continued to swing in a lazy circle. "But you've looked everywhere," she said. "And yet, you haven't found them." She said toward the circling crystal, "Are the glasses *under* something?"

The pendulum dropped abruptly and began a to and fro swing, eventually achieving enough momentum to circle counterclockwise.

"Are they *on top* of something?"

No change.

"Are they *inside* of something?"

The crystal jumped, and circled clockwise. "What have you been digging in, Father?"

"Desk drawers," he said, and the pendulum dropped and began to swing. Assumpta shook her head.

"The supplies cupboard."

No change in the swing of the pendulum.

"The old church photos!" he said.

Before the pendulum began its clockwise circle, Father Tony jumped out of his seat and reached for a stack of boxes parked on the left side of his desk. "I was digging through these last week, scattered them all over my desk, and then I remembered an appointment. I piled them up and put them all back in the box unsorted."

He reached for the top box, removed the cardboard lid and rifled through the contents. When he didn't find his glasses, he returned the lid, settled the box on the floor to his left and reached for the second box in the stack. He pulled off the lid and shuffled through the photos.

"My glasses!" he said, sitting back into his chair with a thump. He put them on, blinked, and then sobered.

"I remembered where they were," he said to Assumpta.

She wrapped the pendulum's cord around her hand, then tucked it back in her purse. "Not without my help."

"I would have remembered eventually," he said quietly.

"I'm sure you would." Assumpta grabbed the handle of her purse and stood.

"You're leaving?"

"I see no reason to stay." She saw a tinge of orange appear in the bright blue of his aura. Blue was the reason she trusted him; it proved his spirituality. The orange told her he felt confusion on this issue. Confusion is good, she thought. It meant he had an open mind about it, even if he didn't think so.

"I think you have a fine sense of intuition," Father Tony said. "You can read people well. It's probably that skill which leads you to believe you can find things for people. As for an alternative to intuition—"

"Let me prove it's not just about intuition," Assumpta said. "Ask me to find something else. Something that would take more than intuition to find. Something someone hasn't been able to find for years."

CHAPTER 5

"THERE IS ONE THING YOU CAN FIND," FATHER
Tony said, "that will make me believe you speak the truth."

"I do speak the truth," Assumpta said, her hands fisting. She tensed
for a fight.

"I know you believe that." Father Tony busied his hands in his desk
drawer, pushing paperclips and pushpins together.

Meaning, Assumpta thought, that he was either being kind by
saying so and humoring her, or he thought she was crazy.

She unfocused her eyes a bit to see his aura. Not seeing anything
but the usual blue and the slight yellow of his calling around his head,
she relaxed.

"What *else* have you lost?" *I'll be confessing that little jab later,* she
thought, schooling her face to complete innocence.

Father Tony raised his eyebrows, but didn't call her out.

He knows I'll be confessing later, too, she thought.

"I'm not the one who lost this object." Father Tony rose and walked
to a high bookcase near the window, and took down what looked to be
an old photo album. He returned to his desk, pushed aside several piles
of paper, and laid the album down, flipping over the pasteboard cover
and turning to the middle of the black construction-paper pages. He
kept turning until he found the page he sought. Then he turned the

album around and pushed it to the front of his desk so Assumpta could see it: a newspaper clipping from 1976.

"You can't breathe a word of this to anyone," he said.

Assumpta nodded. "You know you can trust me."

He looked into her eyes, compressed his lips, and nodded. "I know."

He pointed at the headline: *Polish Cardinal from Vatican Visits Holy Rosary.* Beneath it, a subheading read, *Pope Bestows Relic upon Miracle Church.*

"I didn't know we had a relic here," Assumpta said.

"Because we don't talk about it anymore," said Father Tony. "Not since 1978, when it went missing."

Her eyes widened. "Missing? How can you lose a relic gifted to the church from the Vatican? What was it?"

She could only imagine what might have been considered holy: a finger bone from Saint Elizabeth Ann Seton, a Baltimore-area resident? A centuries-old icon, liberated from the Holy See? Lord knows what lay stockpiled in the Vatican archives after all these years. It probably cost them nothing to gift it to a church. The publicity would have been fantastic at the time.

"A shard from the lance of Longinus."

She blinked. It hardly seemed important, but he'd said it in a voice so filled with awe she knew she was missing something.

"So?"

"*The* spear, child," Father Tony said reverently. He ran a finger across the bottom of the grainy photograph of the biretta-capped Cardinal holding an ornate, gem-encrusted reliquary, about the size of a shoe box. "A piece of wood from the handle of the spear that pierced Jesus's side as he hung on the cross."

Really? A fragment of wood didn't seem all that, well, *holy*, to her. She looked at the box in the photo. The box looked holy. Well, it looked gaudy; maybe that was how the church perceived *holy*. Still, she could only imagine the embarrassment to Holy Rosary Church to lose something of such significance. No wonder they didn't talk about it.

"What happened?"

"The story goes—"

"You don't know for sure?"

He shook his head. "Way before my time. I was still in seminary when all this happened. But from what I've been told, and what I've read in the old pastor's journals, after Cardinal Karol Wojtyla left—" Father Tony put the clipping away. "You do know he was later elected as Pope John Paul II, right?"

"I didn't know that."

"No, you probably wouldn't. We stopped teaching the succession of the popes because we didn't want to answer too many questions. Cardinal Wojtyla became Pope John Paul II the same year the relic disappeared."

"Where was the relic between '76 and '78?"

"Father Michalski displayed it in the Sacred Heart Chapel." He stood. "Let's go there. I'll show you."

Assumpta grabbed her purse and stood, following Father Tony down the stairs and out the door of the rectory. The buildings were connected physically outside, but no doorway existed between the two. To get from rectory to church, or vice versa, one had to go outside and use the street entrance.

Assumpta climbed the front stairs to the church and waited for Father Tony to unlock one of the six large doors. He pulled it open and allowed her to enter before him.

Pain ripped through her right shoulder as she stepped across the threshold. Again, she fell to her knees, crying out. The hair at the nape of her neck felt as though someone yanked it out by the roots. Tears sprang to her eyes.

Holy water in the two marble fonts standing at either side of the entrance to the sanctuary boiled for an instant, releasing a hiss of steam to shoot up from the basins. Had Father Tony seen that? God, she hoped not.

She looked at her hands and unfocused her eyes, only for a moment. Her aura glowed a faint, sickly brown. Heart thumping wildly in her chest, she felt her gorge rise. Swallowing hard, she realized the problem.

Father Tony reached for her elbow.

"Don't touch me, Father," she said, shuffling away from him quickly and standing on her own.

"Are you all right?" he asked.

He looked hurt, but she'd had no choice. Hadn't Greg told her that his visit had cursed her? Would she curse Father Tony by being here? Would she bring trouble to the church? Surely not, she decided. The church could protect itself from evil, right? Especially within the sanctuary?

"It's not you," she said, holding up a hand as he stepped toward her. Would he believe her if she told him a loose tile in the foyer had tripped her? Probably not. "I've just figured it out," she said, and while they stood in the narthex, she told him about Greg LaSpina and the broken urn.

"The curse seeks to prevent me from entering the church," she said in conclusion.

"I'm not sure I quite believe you," he said.

"Can't? Or won't?"

She watched through squinted eyes as the edges of his aura flared an angry red, then calmed. Angry still, but not so much.

"It's not as if I don't want to believe you, Assumpta—"

"Then try," she said. "Ignore the words I'm saying and consider my pain when I entered the church. I'm not faking that. I couldn't fake it."

Father Tony's aura turned orange, marking his confusion. A thoughtful expression crossed his face. The orange dimmed, blue licked at the edges, then overlapped it, and he seemed to make a decision. He looked relaxed.

Maybe he found something comfortable in her words. He reached for the heavy crucifix he carried in his pocket, the same one he wore around his neck on Sundays. "There are some prayers I can say—" He dangled the cross over the holy water font.

Assumpta felt the pull on her hair again.

"I'm cursed, not possessed," she said. "I don't think your prayers will help."

He pocketed the crucifix. "Then what can I do?"

"I'm not sure yet. But when I figure it out, I'll let you know." She looked to the heavy swinging doors that separated the narthex from the Sanctuary. "Let's do this."

CHAPTER 6

THEY PUSHED THROUGH ANOTHER SET OF HEAVY doors and into the church proper. Cathedral ceilings rose sixty feet in the air, decorated with angels and saints painted in jewel tones and accented by gold leaf.

A white marble altar stood at the front of the church, nude of any cloth and bare of the accouterments of Mass: no chalice, no paten, no Gospel opened to the week's readings.

Marble pillars rose to the ceiling behind the altar. Between them, on a dais fifteen feet in the air, sat a life-sized statue of Mary, her infant Jesus seated on her lap and wrapped in her left hand. Her right hand reached out as if to supplicate attending parishioners. Someone had placed a large-beaded rosary in her hand, the crucifix dangling out over open space above the altar.

Father Tony chose the left-most of the three aisles and hurried toward the front of the church. He veered left, then down six steps into an alcove chapel: the Chapel of the Sacred Heart.

Assumpta followed him slowly, her feet dragging. She felt the pulling of her hair again, though she was almost used to it by now. It was the yanking she couldn't abide. But she felt as though she had a rope tied to her waist, pulling her back toward the narthex. Her steps slowed, and though she turned toward the chapel, she couldn't step down into the small room.

A larger-than-life portrait of Christ was painted on the wall. A red heart blazed from his chest with streaks of vibrant gold and yellow shooting out in all directions. The *sacred heart.*

Father Tony turned to her. "Aren't you coming?"

She cleared her throat. "I can't seem to make my feet move." She tried to take a step forward, and couldn't make it any farther toward the main sanctuary either. She stepped backward with no resistance.

"Something is preventing me from moving any closer to the shrine," she said.

Father Tony raced up the steps toward her and stretched out his hand. She held hers up, and he stopped.

"No touching, Father. I have a suspicion of what this is, and I don't want to transfer it to you. You need to be able to say Mass on Sunday."

He spread his hands wide. "What can I do?"

"Right now? Nothing."

He frowned. Assumpta chose her next words carefully. "There is something you can do once I find the relic."

"Yes?"

"Let me borrow it."

He looked to the burgundy carpet runner covering the black-and-white tile floor of the sanctuary, shaking his head. "I can't let you take it," he said. "If you were to lose it…"

She smiled. He'd more or less admitted that he thought she could find it. He was coming around to seeing her point of view. "You wouldn't be any worse off than you are right now. Besides, it's impossible for me to lose *anything,* Father."

"And if someone takes it?"

"I can still get it back," she said. "I'll know exactly where it is."

She let the silence drift between them. Stillness infused the hushed sounds of the Sanctuary. Hundreds of votives flickered in their ruby sconces and the portraits of long-dead saints peered down from the cathedral ceiling.

"You may not even find it…"

"I will, Father. You just have to let me try."

He frowned, looking down at the carpet again. Abruptly, he shook his head. "No. Not if finding it means you get to take it away again. To have it and then lose it again—I just couldn't bear it."

"I'll only be borrowing it," Assumpta said.

"I can't let you." He began walking to the rear of the church, away from the altar. Assumpta turned and followed, the geas, or jinx, offering her no resistance. It wanted her to leave. "How would I explain it to Rome?" he asked.

"How has its disappearance been explained so far?" asked Assumpta, her question rhetorical. And then, "I don't see what you have to lose. Think of how good it will feel to be the one to tell them you've *found* it again."

It was not the argument she should have made, she realized when he stopped and turned to her, a dark look on his face, his aura darkening around the edges, then flaring red in anger.

"*Pride goes before disaster, and a haughty spirit before a fall,*" Father Tony said.

"Proverbs," Assumpta whispered.

"You know your verse."

"Some of it," she said. "And I didn't mean that the way it sounded. But how can telling Rome be such a bad thing? Consider this: the Holy See knows that we lost the relic, right? Won't they be overjoyed to know that it has been returned? You wouldn't be telling them for the glory, but letting them know it hasn't been lost all along, simply misplaced."

"Now you tempt me."

"So, am I the devil, or the world?" she asked, referring to Christ's temptations in the desert.

"I'm not sure," he said, pushing open the door to the narthex and quickly ushering her across the short expanse of tile to the front door of the church, then opening that door as well.

"We'll talk again," he said, "After I've had time to think about this."

She lifted her chin. "You mean about me."

45

He was silent for a moment, then nodded. "See you Sunday."

If I can make it through the door, she thought. *I can't even make it down the aisle far enough to see the old chapel.*

CHAPTER 7

ASSUMPTA WAVED GOODBYE AND WALKED DOWN the front steps of the church.

She walked to the corner and waited to catch the bus home.

While she had conversed with Father Tony, dark clouds had moved over the city. Lightning arched across the sky. Fat globules of rain tumbled out of the clouds, drenching her in seconds.

A perfect night for the bus to be late, she thought, hugging her purse close to keep the rain from getting in.

She thought about the pain she felt in her shoulder when she entered the church, the pull on her body as she got closer to the altar.

She needed to know more. Would the library have the information she needed? No, but the Internet might…and the public library had computers and high-speed connections. But she'd wait for hours for a terminal…and be allowed only an hour of research time. Would it be enough? Probably not, but she'd bet Gregory LaSpina had a computer. He could let her use it, since he had infected her. It was the least he could do, but all that she would ask for. And once she figured out what she needed to make this go away, she'd call it quits.

The bus arrived in a hiss of steam and the whine of air brakes.

She'd go home, change, and dig out Greg's address. Then she'd pay him a visit.

* * *

47

S HE ARRIVED HOME AND FOUND AN EVICTION notice taped to her door. She tore down the notice and entered, then mechanically turned the knob on two deadbolt locks and hooked the chain. According to the notice, she had three days to pay two months of back rent, or she had to leave.

She felt that sinking sensation in her stomach, the same one she got when she looked at her father's lien book every month to see how much she still owed. Would it never end?

She dropped her purse on the chair by the door and leaned into the small mirror to see just how bad she looked.

And that's when she caught a glimpse of the thing on her right shoulder.

Black and white and gray, with a hideous, pointy face leering at her and pointing at her with one tiny, shriveled hand. It couldn't have been more than four or six inches tall, but it looked like stone, like a gargoyle she'd seen in pictures of Notre Dame. But it couldn't have been made of stone, because she didn't feel the weight of anything on her shoulder.

Was she hallucinating? Her heart beat wildly in her chest.

She looked away from the mirror and then turned back again.

No, she wasn't hallucinating. *Ohmygod,* she thought.

Though silent, it looked as though it were laughing at her, head thrown back and mouth wide open, sharp teeth dripping saliva.

She batted at it, felt nothing as she appeared to hit it, until she saw it reach for her shoulder, and she felt the pain of its claws digging into her skin, almost exactly as painful as they'd felt at the church tonight. Her knees buckled, and she grabbed the nearby chair to hold herself upright.

With one shaking hand, she tugged at the neck of her shirt, but couldn't see much in the small mirror. She ran to the bathroom, stripping her shirt away as she did, and turned her shoulder to the mirror.

The gargoyle-thing was gone, but blood red scratch marks, some still oozing, ran the length of her shoulder from her neck to the top of her arm. Amid the scratches on her shoulder were two sets of puncture marks, one much bloodier than the other. Teeth?

"Oh, my god," she said aloud. "What have I gotten myself into?"

While she stood there surveying the marks, she saw something bound from the floor to the sink, a gray streak and then a leap from the countertop to her shoulder.

It was back. And it didn't look happy.

CHAPTER 8

ASSUMPTA POUNDED ON GREG'S DOOR WITH her fist.

He opened it a few seconds later. Face drawn, one hand wrapped around a mug of steaming coffee. The aroma of a brewing pot wafted in her direction.

He smiled when he saw her. "You've changed your mind about helping."

"Not really," she said. "But I realize the need for me to do so. We need to talk."

Nodding, he stepped back and opened the door wider. "Do you want a cup of coffee?"

"Black, please," she said, stepping into his apartment and halting abruptly on the threshold. Her entire apartment could have fit into his living room, and half again into the dining area of the open floor plan. She'd known he lived in a swanky area of Baltimore from his address, but her imagination hadn't pictured this.

Black granite tile covered the floor. An overstuffed black leather sofa and two chairs flanked a chrome-and-glass coffee table in one area. A black-and-white diamond-patterned rug softened the austerity of the stone floor. The furniture hulked around a fireplace, in which a fire crackled with real wood.

Chrome chandeliers hung in the foyer and the other two areas.

She'd bet her parents' tiny row home that the Edward Hopper hanging over the mantle wasn't a print. How much money did you have to have to take this for granted?

Taking a deep breath, she walked into the living room and dropped her purse on a chair, breathing in the aroma of burning hardwood. Its pleasant fragrance reminded her of crisp fall days and hunting for pumpkins.

A waist-high bookshelf separated the space from the dining room. Books and artifacts filled the two low shelves. Three small pedestals squat on top, equidistant apart. One held a chipped clay vase with what appeared to be Greek figures chiseled on it. Definitely not the urn that started this mess. The second showcased two coins, made of metal, or maybe stone, she couldn't identify.

She walked to the third pedestal. A pie-sized plaster-of-Paris disc lay propped on a wooden plinth. A child's handprint flattened the top of it, with the name "Greg" scratched underneath in a child's penmanship. The entire piece was painted royal blue.

"This one must be worth a million," Assumpta said, as Greg returned with her coffee.

"It's priceless, according to my mother."

"Was it her idea to include it with the other artifacts?" Assumpta asked.

"Mine, actually," Greg said. "I had to beg her for it."

Smiling, Assumpta walked to the couch and sat. "I should have charged you a hundred bucks for the reading."

"I would have considered it money well spent," Greg said, handing her the cup of coffee. *Thank God it came in a real mug*, she thought, and not one of those demitasse cups she imagined the rich drank out of. Now where had that come from? *Stop making hasty assumptions*, she told herself. *It will get you tossed out of here quicker than you can say "High Rent District."*

"I thought you said you were an archeology student," she said.

"I am."

"So…you're staying with a friend? Your parents? You won the lottery?" She took a drink of the coffee and lowered the mug to her lap, letting the heat of it warm her hands. She turned an interested face in his direction, staring just past his left shoulder, looking for his aura. As she unfocussed her eyes, it came into view.

Turquoise—a highly energized person, organized—although flames of brown muddied the color at his shoulders. *No surprise there; my aura probably looks the same, since we've both got a creature hanging around our necks.*

Greg smiled at her, obviously not even irritated that she pried into his personal business. "None of the above," he said. "The place is mine."

She raised an eyebrow. "A little pricy for a grad student."

Greg smiled and placed his cup on a nearby table. His aura flared to a sulfur-yellow color about his head, then faded back to turquoise. "This isn't quite the conversation I thought you and I would be having when you finally showed up here."

Not unhappy about being questioned about his money, Assumpta thought, but not giving away any secrets, either. She said, "Finally?"

"Well, I told you you were cursed, too. I knew you'd have to come around sooner or later. You must have seen it in action. Gray and black? All claws and teeth and scaly ruff up over the neck?"

"Close enough," she said, then sipped her coffee, playing for a little time. His creature was different. *Is that important?* she wondered. "I think you may need my help more than I need yours."

"Probably," he said. "But I've got the information. You've got the skills. Between the two of us, we should be able to recapture these things. But first, we've got to get uncursed."

"And how do you propose we do that?" she asked, lifting her mug to her lips. Heat bathed her forehead as she sipped.

"We exorcise them."

She looked over the rim of her cup, raising her eyebrows, and sipped again. "You're assuming we're possessed."

"Possessed. Cursed. Same thing."

"Not at all. If we're possessed by demons, then some of our actions—maybe even our thoughts—would be controlled by the demon. A curse is simply bad luck, or misfortune. Has anything bad happened to you lately?"

"Nothing. What about you?"

"Nothing I can attribute to this," she said, thinking of the debt she owed and the eviction notice hanging over her head.

"Then what about the creatures? The demons in the mirror?"

"I'm not sure how they relate."

"How can you not be sure? You're the expert on the supernatural here."

She shook her head. "I don't know what gave you that idea."

"The numbers, your ability to find things."

Assumpta felt her face grow hot. "I don't consider those things supernatural. They're just things I'm able to do. I was raised a *Catholic*," she said, knowing that didn't quite answer his question.

"So you know about exorcism."

"Know of? Yes. Know how to perform one? No," she said. "And I'm certain I don't want to try without the expert help of a priest. But you may be on to something. My little hitchhiker—"

"Hitchhiker?"

"Might as well get accustomed to using a euphemism now. We don't want to be talking about demons—or whatever they are—in public."

Greg stood, nodding, and walked to the fire. He grabbed the poker and pushed at the bottom log, leveraging it up. A plume of red sparks erupted from the fire into the chimney. He placed another log on top, the dry wood crackling from the burn.

"My little hitchhiker did not like being in church," Assumpta said once Greg sat back down. She told him about her visit with Father Tony, what happened with the holy water fonts, and her inability to move once she got within thirty feet or so of the altar.

Greg whistled. "And Father Tony did nothing?"

"I'm fairly certain he's never encountered anything like this. It's not like being a Catholic priest automatically makes you a target—or beacon—for supernatural occurrences. I don't think he has any idea how close he's come to it. He didn't know how to react. He did offer to help."

"And that means...what?"

"Nothing, right now. But he's a smart man. He'll figure it out." She reached for her purse and pulled out her pendulum. "Unfortunately, I think that means he'll either shun me, forbid me to enter the church again, or want to perform an exorcism."

"So he's as close-minded as the rest of them." Greg's aura flared red around the edges.

"Do I sense a problem with Catholic priests in particular, or just clergy in general?"

"Not relevant to the discussion," Greg said stiffly.

The fire hissed and crackled in the silence raised between them, but only for a moment. She nodded. "Fair enough, she said. "Regarding Father Tony, I'm not sure if he's as bad as you think. I've known him all my life, and he's always seemed open." She dropped the teardrop pendulum and let it swing to and fro while she talked. "Of course, I've never challenged his beliefs before...and right now, he seems to be sticking pretty close to them. It could be he's taking the stance he'd know I'd expect of him. He might be more open if I can prove a few things to him."

"How?"

"By finding some items that have been lost in the church."

"Like what?"

She lifted her eyes to his. "I can't say. I promised not to mention it. Telling you that the church has even lost something is probably breaking my promise."

"Can I help?"

"Probably not. But you could tell me more about the urn, and what you think has been released from it."

She stifled a yawn, covering her mouth with her hand.

He smiled. "Let's talk in the morning, then."

"Can't. I'll be looking for work."

"The afternoon, then."

"I'll probably still be looking for work. We can meet the same time as tonight. Is here all right?"

He frowned. "A new job means more to you then getting rid of your *hitchhiker*?" His tone implied that money meant more to her than anything.

"I'm between jobs right now," she said, "and behind on my rent. I need to go job hunting tomorrow."

"I'll pay you for your help," he said.

"Of course you will," said Assumpta, wrapping the cord of her pendulum around her hand. "But when I'm done helping you, I'll still need a job." She shoved the pendulum inside an inner pocket of her purse. "And that doesn't help me with the rent right now."

Greg stood and crossed to an oak secretary by the door and yanked open a drawer. He grabbed a leather checkbook and opened it on the tabletop. "How much do you owe?" he said, rummaging for a pen. "I'll take care of your rent right now."

Assumpta felt her cheeks burn. There was no way she was going to accept a rent check from a guy she just met, regardless of the circumstances. She swung her purse up to her shoulder and walked toward him, reaching for the doorknob to let herself out, then stopped.

"I don't charge enough for my services to cover what I owe in rent. Besides, we'll settle up when the job is done."

"Weekly," Greg said, shoving the checks back into the drawer and slamming it shut. "I'll pay you weekly, regardless of what we accomplish."

She nodded and opened the door. "All right. Weekly."

Greg grabbed her arm, stopping her. "Move in with me," he said.

"Are you kidding?"

"It makes sense," he said. "We can work more closely together. You won't have to work."

"I know you're not stupid enough to be propositioning me," Assumpta said, "so you must be feeling desperate—"

"And you're not?" he practically shouted. "Doesn't the knowledge of some invisible creature—some demon—sitting on your shoulder fill you with desperation to have the business taken care of?"

She couldn't answer. She hadn't looked in the mirror since she'd noticed it the first time. What she couldn't see, couldn't hurt her. *Denial.* The word echoed in her head. She shook it, as if to erase the thought.

"I can't move in with you," she said. And she couldn't. She could name a hundred reasons why, starting with the impropriety of it and ending with the fact that she couldn't take advantage of his money. She'd feel like a slut. Her father would call her a whore. It would be too easy to get accustomed to living in such luxury. Then where would she be?

"I'll see you tomorrow," she said, slipping out the door.

CHAPTER 9

ASSUMPTA PUSHED HER KEY INTO THE LOCK AND entered her tiny flat.

She yawned, her mouth so wide it hurt her cheeks, and with a loud inhalation of air she would have attempted to stifle in the presence of anyone else. She dropped her purse to the wooden wine crate that served as an entry table and, covering her gaping mouth, headed straight for the tiny kitchen and a squat, wide-mouthed jar of oil.

She had an idea.

Oil in hand, she crossed the ten or so feet into the living room and knelt before her personal altar pressed against the east wall of the room.

Father Tony would probably have a conniption if he saw it. She knew she crossed the line with some of the rituals she performed here, but wasn't Mass itself a ritual? Turning bread and wine into the body and blood of Christ? Priests performed rituals on their altar in front of hundreds of people at church. One did not have to be ordained to formally ritualize. Why couldn't she perform her own rites here at home with only herself in attendance?

Was it blasphemy to even ask that question?

Mom had told her that in the sixties, the Church encouraged families to keep an altar in their den or family room. Not so much anymore. Mom said she didn't understand why, since having one in the home kept faith at the forefront of family life.

But Assumpta had her suspicions for why it was no longer vogue. Followers of voodoo, Wicca, and other non-Christian faiths almost always keep an altar in the home. And with so many following the path of Wicca these days, she was certain the Catholics wanted no reminders that their own faith once embraced those pagan rites as a means to bring nonbelievers into the fold.

Or, she thought, it could be that Catholicism at its roots was so damned controlling. Strike that. It wasn't Catholicism that was controlling, it was the men preaching the Catholicism. Maybe discouraging personal altars was their way of forcing people back into the church. Still, why shouldn't she practice her faith at home?

Her altar, made of another wooden wine crate turned on its side and covered to the floor in a green cloth to match the liturgical season, contained the usual Catholic items: a crucifix, a picture of Christ and a statue of his mother, Mary, a small dish of holy water and a second one of blessed salt, an incense burner, and Assumpta's numerous rosaries and candles. For simplicity's sake, she borrowed from Taoist tradition, and stood the altar candles upright in a bowl of sand. Much less messy when the wax poured down the candle into the grit, rather than onto the candlesticks. *Let's hope that doesn't buy me a place in Hell,* she thought.

In non-Catholic tradition, she kept her pendulum here to *recharge* it. Father Tony would probably accuse her of witchcraft because of that simple addition. But did he realize how many of these items could also be found on a witch's altar? The salt, the water, the candles, the icons… Pagan worship wasn't a bastardization of Catholicism. It was the other way around.

She put the jar of oil on top of the altar, then lifted the corner of the green cloth and reached for the box of wooden matches she kept beneath on the right. As she stretched for the matches, her fingers brushed across the top of her Bible.

A sudden jolt of pain ran up Assumpta's neck, then down to her fingers, and she fell back onto the floor.

The acute pain diminished when her fingers left the cover of the book, but she still felt the aftershocks. This she could tolerate. She sat up, clenching and unclenching her right fist as if the action could work the pain from her arm. She bent her head forward and side to side, stretching there to relieve the pain, too.

She'd touched the Bible and been rewarded with pain. *Why?*

Her little *hitchhiker*, of course, thought Assumpta. He didn't like her Bible.

With a shaking hand, she reached toward the Bible again, holding her fingers as close to it as she could without touching it. The hair on her scalp and her forearms rose. She could feel little jolts of pain against her fingertips. The longer she held her hand toward the book, the greater the pain escalated. When she could take no more, she moved her hand away. The pain dissipated.

Would anything else here cause her pain?

She moved her hands to the right and held them above a clothbound missal she'd purchased after her Confirmation a few years ago. Nothing, but her pinky moved close to her white-covered children's missal leaning against it. Pain lanced up the finger and to her wrist before she pulled back.

What was the difference between the two missals?

One was a gift; one was purchased. One was for adults; the other, for children. One was black-covered; one was white. She hadn't looked at the children's missal in years, with its large font and junior versions of Gospel stories accompanied by colorful pictures of Christ and children. Surely that was not enough to give a demon pause?

She'd give it more thought after she tested the other items.

Assumpta held her hands out over the stack of altar cloths to the right of the books. Closer and closer she moved toward them, until she nearly touched the fabric. She felt nothing. Then she considered that she'd touched the green cloth earlier and had not been hurt. Certain she'd drawn the correct conclusion, she dropped her hand upon them, resting the tense muscles in her arms for a moment. She took a minute to relax, closing her eyes and leaning her head forward.

She was tired.

She raised her arms over her head, crossed her wrists and threaded her fingers together, then stretched, trying to ease the tension out of her arms. Then she turned to the items on the top the altar.

She raised her hands to the icons, first the painting of Jesus (a tasteful version—not one of those *wandering eyes* paintings that always gave her the creeps) and then the small statue of Mary, her left foot crushing the head of a green snake.

Nothing.

The salt and the incense burner resided so close together on the altar that they nearly touched, and Assumpta could test them simultaneously. The incense had come from a dollar store, but the salt she'd purchased at the May Day festival at the church. Neither caused her any pain.

Nor the candles, she thought, floating her hands above them.

That left her rosaries and the holy water.

She reached for the beads, pooled together in a dish: a green stone rosary from her *very* Irish grandmother, a wooden one she'd picked up in an Episcopal church thrift store (what it had been doing there she didn't know; Episcopalians don't pray the rosary. She always felt like she had liberated it from the shop.), and an old, cheap plastic one she'd made in Vacation Bible School. There was also an ancient, butter-yellow, plastic glow-in-the-dark rosary, too. So old, she couldn't remember where it had come from. It used to hang on her bedpost growing up.

Her fingers tingled as she moved them above the dish, some jolts of pain stronger than others.

So, some of the rosaries bothered her hitchhiker, and some of them didn't. She turned to the last item on the altar: the blessed water, from straight out of the font at Holy Rosary. When she moved her hand over the shallow dish, the water churned on the surface, boiled, then spouted up in a cloud of steam, searing her hands.

"Ow!" she cried out, jerking her arms back.

She turned her hands over to see the damage. The palms were wet, scorched bright pink where the steam had seared them. Welts formed on her fingers where the water had touched. They hurt, but it wasn't unbearable. She wiped her palms on her pants, careful of her damaged fingers.

Blessed things, she realized. All the items that caused her pain had been blessed or sanctified. But why such a strong reaction from the water? Should she not attempt her idea? After all, she was about to bless something; or, at least, ask that it be blessed.

She blew out a breath, giving herself time to decide if it were worth it. She nodded once. She had to do this. She had to try.

Once more, Assumpta reached for the matches, her movements slow and exaggerated as she avoided all the blessed items.

She lit the candles, one on the left and one on the right of the altar, then bowed her head, clasped her hands together, and began to pray.

"Dear Lord," she said aloud, "I haven't always seen eye to eye with the Catholic Church, but I have always believed in You. Perhaps I've never bought into the Hollywood vision of what You're supposed to look like, and I've often considered that You might be female, but I've never doubted Your power. In fact, I like to believe that my divining skills are gifts from You, rather than Satan…and that makes me believe in Your power all the more: after all, You've given me the ability to help others.

"I'm sure there's a prayer in the missal I could be reciting right now, but I'm hoping a plea from the heart is better than the store-bought version. Also, there's this blessed-items-cause-me-pain issue right now, and I'm inclined to do this free-form as usual. So, if it is Your will, please help me rid myself of this creature—this possible demon—in my life. I cannot do it alone, and humbly request Your assistance."

She pushed the jar of oil into the center of the altar and laid both hands on top of it.

"Dear God," she said aloud, "imbue this oil with Your Holy Power so that I might cast this creature out of my life. I don't know what this...*thing* was sent to do, nor what its plans for me are, and I beg for You to protect me and keep me safe from its harm."

She felt her neck grow warm as she prayed, and felt a sudden weight on her shoulders, as if the invisible creature manifested itself as she spoke.

"Mother Mary, I request your intervention," she said. "On the off chance that Christ cannot hear my plea, please intercede on my behalf, and ask him to grant my prayers. I thank you for your help. Amen."

The weight on her shoulders grew heavier.

Standing, she grasped the oil in both hands and repeated the prayer more forcefully. Then she walked the few feet to her bedroom window—the one farthest from the front entrance of her apartment— and uncapped the jar.

She held her hand over the top. Did she feel tingling in her fingers, or was it only wishful thinking?

Better safe than sorry, she thought, getting a tea towel from the kitchen and walking back around the corner to her bedroom. She poured some of the amber liquid onto the towel and drew an unbroken line around the window frame. As she drew the line, she recited, "Dear God, bind this demon and remove it from my home. By the blood of Jesus, cast it back to Hell."

The entrance to her bedroom was a doorless archway; still, she rubbed the oil across the threadbare carpet, up the left side, across the top, and down the right, making certain to ensure the line remained unbroken.

Assumpta prayed. "Bind this demon, Lord. Cast him from my home and my life. Send him back to Hell where he belongs."

She paused. If she asked God to send a demon to Hell, was that a revenge of sorts? Wasn't she supposed to turn the other cheek? Did that count, for demons, or whatever *ungodly* being this was?

Would she go to Hell for wishing a demon there?

She shook her head. She couldn't give up. She took a few steps backward, then turned left to anoint the window in the living room. She repeated the process, and the prayer, hoping still that she wasn't out of line.

She anointed the kitchen window, and finally made her way to the front door of the apartment.

Assumpta laid the oil on thick on the doorframe, and then she prayed, begging God to send this demon back.

The entire procedure hadn't taken more than fifteen minutes, but she felt drained. She returned to her altar and snuffed the candles, licking her fingers first and squeezing out the flame. She fell to her knees and made one final plea for the Lord's intervention with her *hitchhiker*.

The weight on her shoulders grew heavier.

Finally, she breathed a deep sigh, and returned to her bedroom and tumbled into bed. Before she fell asleep, she made a mental note to take her blessed salt back to church to be blessed...because whoever did the job in the first place had botched it.

CHAPTER 10

FATHER JAMES HUGHES, PASTOR—AND THEREFORE leader—of Holy Rosary Church, took the cellar staircase in the back of the rectory and descended two levels to the sub-basement. Here, a narrow tunnel led him to unused storage rooms beneath Holy Rosary.

It was early morning and his white hair, still damp from a shower, was combed back off his balding forehead. He was clean shaven, except for a wide, white mustache. He wore a sport coat to combat the cellar damp over his black shirt and clerical collar, the pockets of which were filled with the items he needed for *prayer*.

He practically skipped down the shallow steps, eager to get started. He pulled the string on a single light bulb in the center of the room, and the bulb cast a harsh glow immediately beneath it. The far corners of the room remained dim.

Father Hughes would not be deterred. He drew a circle about six feet in diameter in the dirt floor with a yardstick he found propped in the corner, then withdrew a bag of blessed salt from his left sport coat pocket. He tipped the bag and traced the drawn circle with the crystals, making certain to leave no gaps in the ring.

The salt was merely precaution. The drawn circle should do the job, but he was taking no chances.

From the same pocket, he pulled four stubs of altar candles and a small compass.

"Michael, I call upon you to watch from the north," he said, placing one candle on the due north point of the circle and lighting it.

"Uriel, I call upon you from the east," he said, placing a candle on the east side of the circle and lighting it.

"From the south, I call upon you, Raphael, to guard this circle and protect me from your brethren." He placed and lit the third candle.

"Gabriel, archangel of *His* armies, guard me as I call upon those who will help me attain what I want." He lit and placed the fourth candle and closed his eyes, taking a deep breath.

Lord, grant me the strength to do Your bidding, he thought, then opened his eyes to the circle in the dirt.

From the other pocket he took a packet of index cards, rubber-banded together, the edges dog-eared and worn. He wondered, *Am I ready for this?*

With the edge of the yardstick, he drew several shapes in the dirt around the candles, pictograms meant to bind the spirit in the circle. Then, Father Hughes wrote the names of the four archangels in Hebrew beside each candle. Naming the angels wasn't part of the process—*the prayer,* he reminded himself—but names were for strength, and surely naming them would bind the spirits in the circle even more.

For luck, at his feet he wrote the name of his guardian angel, Saint Sealtiel, knowing himself to be doubly blessed, for Saint Sealtiel's name contained the word *seal,* proof to him that all would go well with this *prayer,* and that he alone was suited to this purpose. But also because Saint Sealtiel was the patron saint of the ordained. One couldn't have better luck, or better spirits, behind him, he thought. He walked to the edge of the circle, the toes of his shoes inches away from the salt and scored line.

He began to chant.

In the enclosed space of the basement, he felt the first stirring of a breeze as a cool touch on the hair at the back of his neck. His bangs stirred across his forehead. It swept in from the north, Archangel Michael lending his power.

Raphael cast his lot, and the wind breezed in from the south, stronger than Michael's. The two met in the middle of the circle, brushing aside a few grains of salt, but the circle remained whole.

Father Hughes felt the winds collide, bringing with them a smell of freshness, pushing aside the damp-earth smell of the cellar.

He continued to chant.

A small puff of breeze from the east pushed the flame of the corresponding candle toward the center of the circle. *Uriel.*

Finally, Gabriel sent his wind with the force of a storm, or an avenging army. The winds met in the center of the circle and spun, merging together like a mini cyclone, stirring up the loose earth and pulling it together until it danced in the center of the circle.

It ceased abruptly, the dirt cascading down into an anthill heap. Only the slight flickering of candles showed Father Hughes the spirits of the angels remained with him.

Father Hughes flipped to the index card referring to his plea, finding the words to the *calling prayer.*

"Banished spirits of the earthly realm, those..." he paused for the right words to fill in the description of the request "...those wrongly sealed within the *Urn of the Righteous,* hear my call for help and appear before me."

The candles flickered. A sweat broke out on Father Hughes's forehead. The sound of water sizzling in a frying pan thrummed through the basement chamber.

More than a dozen shadowy forms, long and lean like ferrets—or weasels, he thought—began to take shape in the center of the circle. The shadows took on detail, lightened; evolved into a stony appearance with claws and teeth and tiny horns like the decorative statues on the Cathedral of Notre Dame.

"Gargoyles?"

The largest one stepped forward. "If that isss what you want to call us..."

"Isn't that what you are?"

It laughed, the lips of the wide mouth thinning, the sound a high-pitched wheeze. Drool gushed over a thick tongue and dripped to the floor, steaming away when it hit the cool, damp surface.

"You are a fool, human. Playing with that which you have no conception of." It tilted its head, dog-like, to the north and addressed Gabriel. "You protect him?"

The large shadow paused the stretch of two heartbeats. Then snorted, and turned back to Father Hughes.

Father Hughes turned to the candle. *Had Gabriel responded to the creature?* He hadn't heard anything. How could this thing communicate with angels, when he had to go on faith that the angels were even in the room with him?

The creature danced to the edge of the salt ring and lifted its chin. "What do you want of ussss?"

"What are you?" asked Father Hughes, taking a step back. Perhaps he'd been hasty in performing this ritual just yet.

"We are those whom you have called."

"With whom do I speak?"

"Namesss are power, human. And they are of no consequence in this transaction."

"But I thought…"

A ghostly wisp of a human figure coalesced in the center of the circle, taking on only the substance of shadow. Father Hughes could see no features on the face of the being, which towered over him by at least a head. The smaller creatures moved to the back of the circle as the faceless being stepped forward.

"You have a request," it said in a mild voice.

"I did," said Father Hughes. He felt his lips tremble, all the muscles in his face spasming as fear took hold, and he had difficulty forming the words to speak.

"I did," he said again, more firmly, "But I'm not sure I want to do business with—" He stumbled. He didn't want to use the word *creatures* and offend them. Surely, they weren't *still* angels as Saint Patrick—who himself fought demons—stated in this ritual. Shouldn't angels be more, well, *angelic*?

"You didn't really believe you were calling upon angelssss when you started this rite, did you, Father Hughes?"

Fallen angels, yes, he thought, *beings not quite evil, but powerful enough to help.* "I'm no longer interested," he said.

He bent to blow out the eastern candle.

"I wouldn't do that, if I were you," said the figure. Its eyes had brightened in the shadow of its face, and Father Hughes could clearly see the hunger in the dark pupils. They cast a faint light on his face, creating the angles of a Roman nose and high cheekbones. "Salt only holds us back for so long, and without Gabriel's presence at the circle, a weak point will develop there." It smiled, and white teeth appeared in the gloom, surrounded by full, aristocratic lips. It grew more distinct by the moment.

"And we still have a bargain to discuss."

"As I said," Father Hughes started, "I want no part of it."

"Unfortunate," said the shadow being. "Once we're called, we can't depart until we've provided a favor."

"I want no debts on my conscience."

"Then release us from the circle and we'll be on our way." It folded its shadow arms across its chest. "You need only kick the salt away, and we'll make our own way home."

The wind kicked up, and the candles flickered. Though he didn't hear any voices, Father Hughes got the impression that the guardians at the flames were telling him that letting the creatures go without some sort of bargain would be tragic. He could not release them *unbonded* into the world to do as they pleased.

"Sorry," he said. "I can't do that, either."

"You'll have to decide soon, or we'll take the decision out of your hands." It waggled a finger at the salt on the ground in front of him and a few grains rolled away from the edge, thinning the line. "What is it you wanted, anyway?"

Father Hughes thought, *What harm could come of telling the creature?* It seemed hubris to discuss it with his fellow priests in the rectory, because they would think him ambitious. And he was, but for the church, not for himself. Yet, he knew human nature, and knew that though they might agree with him in person, behind his back they'd be calling him arrogant.

"Holy Rosary is in need of funding," he said.

"And so you want money," interrupted the creature. "Well, that's easy enough to come by. I could—"

Father Hughes smiled. "Easy for you, perhaps, but a sum of money would only get us so far. What this church needs is an income stream, a guarantee from the diocese to fund the needed programs, to make repairs on this nearly century-old building, to contribute more to the local food pantry."

"That's a bit harder," said the creature. "A windfall can be explained away: a wealthy donor, the sale of an artifact… A steady influx of cash is not so easy…"

"Not if Holy Rosary had a sympathetic bishop in the diocese."

There was a brief bit of silence—only the flickering of candles could be heard—while the shadow creature seemed to take the comment in.

"You have someone in mind," it said, lips curling up. It made the words a statement, not a question.

"I do," said Father Hughes, a leaden feeling in his belly. "Myself."

How could he convince people that good intention, not pride, motivated him to seek a position in the diocesan office?

"Of course, you want the promotion in order to help Holy Rosary. Furthering your own ambitions is the farthest thing from your mind."

Let them believe what they want, Father Hughes thought. He couldn't sway them, in any case. And what did this creature's opinion matter?

"Of course," he said. "In that position, I can direct money to the churches that need it the most. Holy Rosary's aging population makes us an ideal candidate. Diocesan leaders' insistence that bringing in new members to ease the cash flow is unrealistic. If I can divert funds from the parish as needed, I can accomplish much."

"And I can get your promotion to the diocese," said the creature.

"You've said as much," said Father Hughes, "but I don't know that I can now afford the payment."

Nor do I want to, he thought, looking the creature over from head to toe.

He sniffed. The smell of damp and stone permeated the small space. The four candles at the edge of the circle burned brightly, wavering in a small breeze that persisted. Was that the work of the unseen angels protecting him?

"But you don't even know what we ask for such a small service," said the shadow creature.

"Small?"

"Certainly," it said, moving even closer to the edge of the barrier, bending at the waist to lean closer to Hughes. As its head broke the plane of the salted circle, Father Hughes could see the creature's face—a man's face—much more clearly. Dark, curly hair swept away from his forehead. Blue eyes danced above an aquiline nose. Straight, white teeth graced the curve of his mouth as it said in a conspiratorial voice, "Why, the payment is almost nothing."

Involuntarily, Father Hughes felt himself lean even closer. He strained to hear the words the shadow man said.

"Almost…*nothing?*"

"Why, of course." It waved a finger and several grains of salt danced away from the inner edge of the circle. The shadow man pressed its toe closer to the outside. "It's not as though you ask us to kill anyone. It's not as if you ask for money—indeed—for *anything*, for yourself." It lifted its cleft chin toward Father Hughes. "We're not talking murder, or greed…"

Father Hughes felt himself nodding. Agreeing.

"I can help you," it said, brushing away a few more grains of salt. "You only need help me," it added.

Father Hughes was still nodding.

"Will you help me?" It held out its shadowy right hand to Father Hughes, crossing the boundary of the circle again. Clothing appeared on the portion of the man's arm outside the circle: a navy blue suit, a white shirt, the cuffs secured with diamond cuff links shaped like St. Peter's Cross.

"And what will I owe you?" asked Father Hughes.

"Your help," said the shadowy figure. "That is all."

"And what shape will this help take the form of?"

Even in the darkness of the circle, Father Hughes could discern the shadow figure's smile growing larger. "Nothing more than you're able to do," it said. "But we must shake on the deal to make it official."

Reluctant, yet wanting to do the most good for the church, Father Hughes held out his hand to the shadowy figure and grasped it.

A strong wind blew through the cellar room, extinguishing the candles, startling Father Hughes.

"What happened?" he asked.

"You've made your choice," the figure said, its voice sharper, less compelling. "The angels have gone."

"Gone? But they were my protection."

"They could do nothing once you made your choice," the figure said, brushing past the salt on the floor.

He moved closer to Father Hughes, pulling on his arm at the same time, bringing them closer together. Hughes tried to pull away at the last moment, heart racing, a sweat breaking out on his brow.

"No—" he cried.

And then they melded, and the two became one in Father Hughes's body, his clothes.

Then, *Father Hughes* smiled, his eyes no longer his own as he muttered, "*This* is how it was meant to be."

He waved a hand and the remainder of the salt disappeared in a dust devil, spinning off into a corner of the room. Sixteen ankle-high creatures, with bodies the appearance of stone gargoyles, danced at his feet for attention.

Father Hughes looked down at them affectionately, leaned to pat one or two as they vied for his attention. "If we're going to do this right," he said, "we need to preserve appearances." He wiggled his fingers and the stone creatures froze, rock solid, then each collapsed in a heap of stone dust.

He dragged a booted toe through the dust until he found what he sought, then bent to retrieve it: a rosary decade, heavy and masculine, with fifteen charms—one for each saint solemnized in portrait on the cathedral ceiling of Holy Rosary. Ten charms surrounded his wrist, five more hung down to a miniature golden cross, Christ hanging on it upside down.

Father Hughes snapped the rosary around his left wrist, then patted the stack of index cards in his left pocket and turned for the stairs.

CHAPTER 11

WHEN SHE WOKE THE NEXT MORNING, ASSUMPTA remembered the eviction notice. She stretched and closed her eyes again, covering them with the back of her hand. *What was she going to do?* Even if she did find a job today, no one was going to advance her the money she needed.

She should have taken the money from Greg, she thought, sitting up and putting her legs over the side of the bed. She toyed with the ragged edge of her childhood comforter. Well, she thought, standing, she was going to see him tonight. She would get a check from him then. And somehow try not to feel like a complete mooch.

But then she'd have another month to come up with the rent and get her dad a few bucks to keep him off her back, too. That peace of mind had to be worth taking money when you had too much pride to want to.

Baltimore is a thriving city, despite the current economy, she thought. *Why can't I find work?*

Because you're cursed.

The thought popped into her head unbidden. That stopped her in her tracks. "Really?" she said aloud, letting out a deep breath. "No. I am..." She searched for the right word. "I am bedeviled, but I am *not* cursed. I *will* find a job today."

Then she remembered the ritual of the previous night. She ran to the bathroom and looked in the mirror, searching for the creature.

It was gone!

She jumped, pumping her fist into the air, a wide smile on her face.

Then she felt the pain on the back of her neck, the gripping of claws at her nape, and then a painful slide of the claws, scratching from above her nape down to the small of her back.

Assumpta cried out and whirled around, putting her back to the mirror, turning her head to spot the culprit over her shoulder.

"No!" she shouted, batting at the creature as it ran down her back again and up. She could feel its weight upon her, like a heavy cat, moving up and down her torso. Unable to catch it, she finally stopped, hanging her hands at her sides, her breath raspy. It scuttled to her left shoulder and perched like a vulture, lifting one forepaw and pointing at her in the mirror. It opened its mouth in a grotesque parody of a smile. *Did the thing look slightly larger this morning?*

"Schee, schee, schee…" It laughed, the sound of dried, autumn leaves, rasping the length of a sidewalk.

"You can talk," she accused, batting at it again.

It laughed again, louder, and scampered across her shoulders, easily avoiding the sweep of her hand.

She turned her back to the mirror again, and pulled her oversized T-shirt over her head to survey the damage on her back. Eight streaks ran from her shoulders to the small of her back, angry red and puffing up, but they weren't bleeding.

Thank God for small favors, she thought.

The creature lifted a hand to her in the mirror, wiggling its lethal-looking claws at her, leering, as if there were nothing it would like to do more than rake those claws down the length of her body again.

Assumpta turned away, tossed her nightshirt in the corner, and shimmied out of her undies. They joined the shirt on the floor. She pulled back the shower curtain and turned on the shower.

Then she went back to the mirror.

The hideous thing perched again, vulture-like, on her left shoulder. She could feel the weight of it sitting it there, the tense grip of claws, feeling like a parrot might if one sat on her shoulder. She batted at it, and it scampered down to her waist, only the concrete-gray of its oscillating tail visible, until it clambered up to her right shoulder. Again, she felt the movement, the weight.

She turned her back to the mirror, and immediately felt the weight of the creature disappear. She stepped into the shower, letting warm water sluice down the front of her.

This certainly explained why she rarely felt the weight of it while she walked around all day. If she didn't see it, it didn't seem to have substance. But that didn't touch on why she began to feel its heavy presence when she blessed the oil last night. Or why she had felt it a few seconds ago. Perhaps it had something to do with her praying, she thought. She'd have to test that theory. But first, she had to find a job.

She adjusted the spray, then turned her back to the water and sucked in her breath, feeling a sting on the welts running the length of her back. She released it when the pain eased.

She'd tell Greg everything she'd learned when she saw him tonight, she thought, lathering her hair with shampoo. Maybe he'd heard some legend about such creatures. Didn't archeologists know a lot of legends?

Tilting back her head, Assumpta let the hot water beat on the top of her head, rinsing out the soap and relaxing her.

Almost as good as a massage, she thought.

Then she heard the grating laugh again, and she froze. A coldness formed in the pit of her belly and moved up to her chest. She could hear it, and she wasn't facing the mirror. She put a hand up to steady herself against the shower stall.

"Oh, God—" she said aloud. She drew in a deep breath and looked down at the water swirling around her feet. And she felt the presence of her hitchhiker on her back.

A gray and black tail snaked around her waist, then twitched back and forth like a cat's, only rough and pebbled like concrete. Two sets of claws settled on her hips and another two settled on her shoulders. It laughed again, and she felt something abrasive swipe between her shoulder blades and up to the base of her neck. The welts burned again. Then, she felt a cold, gritty hand slide to her shoulder and rub slowly back and forth. The tail uncoiled from her waist and slid down to the small of her back, the tip stealing down to stroke the crevice between her buttocks with a cold, hard, touch.

She squealed, and slammed back against the wall of the shower, hoping to hurt it, but instead banged the scratches on her back against the cold tile. She tensed with pain.

The smell of wet cement permeated the small shower stall. All sensation of the creature disappeared.

She turned off the water, yanked the curtain back, then reached for her towel, avoiding looking into the mirror. The less she had to see of her little hitchhiker, the happier she'd be. On shaking legs, she toweled dry as fast as she could, and set a record getting dressed.

She applied makeup as best as she was able without a mirror, omitting her usual mascara, and put on her only pair of shoes: a set of white, canvas tennis shoes that had seen better days. They wouldn't make a great first impression, but they were easy on her feet. And she needed that when she'd be pounding the pavement all day.

She grabbed her pendulum from the altar and shoved the non-blessed jar of salt into her handbag, then walked to the door. On a whim, she turned back to the altar and picked up the jar of oil. *You never know*, she thought.

She grabbed her keys and walked out, slamming the door behind her.

CHAPTER 12

ASSUMPTA RANG THE BELL AT THE RECTORY DOOR and waited for someone to answer it. A minute later, a nun she didn't recognize opened the door. From the pinched expression on her face, Assumpta knew there would be trouble.

"Yes?"

"I'm looking for Father Tony, is he around?" She hoped he wasn't out to lunch.

"Do you have an appointment?"

Oh, brother, she thought, gearing up for a fight. She sneaked a peek at the sister's aura. A bright yellow nimbus appeared around the sister's head.

Goodness, Assumpta thought, a light feeling entering her. She was in the presence of a true believer and, quite probably, a *chosen* one. She bit her tongue before she said anything rash.

"Father Tony is my mentor, Sister. He's been my spiritual advisor since I started catechism in the first grade."

"Father Tony is a very busy man, helping to run this parish," the nun said. "You'll need to make an appointment if you want to see him. An appointment at *his* convenience."

Assumpta couldn't help herself. "I wasn't aware that I needed to make an appointment when I am suffering a religious crisis."

The nun snapped out the words. "What kind of crisis?"

"That's between Father Tony and myself."

The nun straightened and stepped back slightly. "If you want to meet with Father Tony, you'll have to let me know what this is about so he can judge if an immediate meeting is necessary."

Assumpta nearly laughed. She thought, *Does she think there's something going on between me and Father Tony? What a hoot!* She'd love to carry on with that little charade, but it would get her nowhere. She needed to backpedal and soothe the beast at the door. She didn't know if she were capable.

"Sister," Assumpta said gently, "I'm sorry if my arriving has disturbed or upset what's going on in the rectory right now, but this is urgent." She raised supplicant eyes to the hard-faced religious woman. "But I can't tell you what my visit is about—it's between me and my confessor, and as you know, the bonds of the confessional are sacred."

Two ruddy spots of color appeared on the nun's unadorned face. "The confessional only binds the priest from speaking, not the penitent," the nun hissed. "If you truly desire to see Father Tony, then you will call the rectory and make an appointment." She stepped back again and began to close the door. "Now, if you will excuse me—"

Assumpta put her foot in the doorjamb to prevent the nun from slamming the door in her face. "Father Tony!" Assumpta yelled at the top of her lungs. "Father Tony, I need to see you!"

"Stop this," the nun said. "Stop this at once."

"I need to see Father Tony," Assumpta said. She gave the nun a determined look. "Father Tony!" she yelled again. She knew the nun was powerless to stop her. She couldn't so much as kick her foot from the door, since that would be a *grave sin*, a premeditated strike against someone else, and could cause her to lose her place in Heaven. On the other hand, maybe the Sister just abhorred violence.

"You must go!" The nun looked over her shoulder, then back at Assumpta, giving her a pleading look. She whispered, "Please, go."

Assumpta squinted. The nun's aura continued to glow a bright yellow, but purple licked the edges. She was scared. Assumpta wondered,

Scared for herself, or scared for me? Me, Assumpta concluded. Under other circumstances, she might like to get to know the nun, but she didn't have the time right now. She opened her mouth and took a deep breath in order to yell again.

But then Assumpta heard creaking footsteps on the second floor, heading toward the staircase.

"What's going on here?" someone yelled from the top. Father Hughes ran down the steps. Assumpta had never seen him look so immaculate before. Not a hair out of place, not a speck of dust on the lapels of his jacket.

"I'm having a spiritual crisis and I need to see Father Tony," Assumpta said. "Sister won't let me in."

"This creature does not deserve the grace of God," the nun said. Assumpta whipped her head around at the harsh accusation. "She nearly assaulted me."

"I didn't lay a hand on you," Assumpta said.

"You rushed the stoop and jammed your foot in the door. Had I not leaned against it, you would have pushed me away and entered this holy place through false pretense."

"I merely wouldn't let you shut the door," Assumpta said through gritted teeth. "Father Hughes," she said, turning to the pastor, "I have a fervent need to meet with my confessor."

"Let's be calm, Sister Michael," Father Hughes said, turning toward the nun. Sister Michael stiffened. "Did this woman actually hit you?"

"Nearly, but no," Sister Michael said.

"Then we've no cause to be grievous on that score," he said, smiling. The sister inclined her head to him, then looked down at the floor, clasping her hands together.

"You may go," he said to her, and turned to Assumpta.

Sister Michael nodded again, then raised her eyes briefly to Assumpta's. "Leave," she mouthed, giving her another pleading look, then turned back into the short hallway and entered the receptionist's office through the first door on the right.

Vibrant purple nearly obliterated Sister Michael's yellow aura, then disappeared. Did Sister Michael know something Assumpta didn't?

"What can I do for you?"

Father Hughes smiled at her, but she felt a chill of apprehension as she faced the priest. He was saying and doing everything right, and yet there was something she couldn't put her finger on. She darted her eyes above his left shoulder, looking for the edge of his aura, then snapped her eyes back to meet his.

He's studying me, she thought. *What is he looking for? Can he see the creature in my presence?*

"I need to see Father Tony," she said. "There's something I must discuss with him."

"Is he expecting you?" Father Hughes said, stepping toward her. She nearly cursed aloud. This close, she couldn't focus on his aura. She took a step back to see it more clearly, and he stepped forward again.

She said, "No, but he's never complained about me dropping in on him before." She shrugged the strap of her purse up higher on her shoulder, gripping it tightly between her fingers. "Is this a new policy?"

"Not at all," Father Hughes said, putting a hand out to her shoulder and gently guiding her toward his office. "But we've started a little campaign for the fall here at the church, and Father Tony is busy working on that project. Perhaps *I* can help you with your problem, *child.*"

Assumpta stepped out of his grasp and stood fast on the black-and-white checkered tile of the foyer. "No offense, Father Hughes, but Father Tony knows all my history already. I'd feel more comfortable talking with him."

"Then you'll have to come back another time," the priest said. His words were light, but there seemed to be an edge of steel behind them.

"Of course," she said, eager to be away. Then, "Oh, wait..." She reached into her purse and pulled out the jar of not-blessed salt. She held it toward Father Hughes. "Can you bless this for me, please?"

She held the jar toward him.

"What is it?" he asked.

"I'll take care of it," Father Tony said, coming down the stairs of the rectory. He gently took the salt from Assumpta's hands before Father Hughes grabbed it.

"Don't you have work to do?" Father Hughes asked.

"I completed the assignment," said Father Tony. "If you want to see my notes, I can have them on your desk this afternoon."

"Excellent," Father Hughes said. His smile was back, but so tight it looked like rictus. "We can discuss it before dinner."

"Then we don't have much time," Father Tony said, turning to Assumpta. "Good to see you. Shall we adjourn to my office where we can talk?"

"Certainly."

"Excuse us," Father Tony said to Father Hughes, and led Assumpta up the stairs.

When they were halfway up, Assumpta said, "Sister Michael burns with the glory of the Lord."

"Stop making fun."

"Oh, I'm serious," Assumpta said, "She's found joy in religion. She's one of the few people I've met with such a passion. I'm convinced she's one of God's chosen."

"You only talked to her a few moments," he said. "How can you know?"

"I peeked at her aura."

Father Tony turned to look at her sidelong. "Are we going to have another one of *those* conversations? You need to abandon your New Age ideas and stick with the faith you know."

"You need to broaden yours."

"Assumpta—"

"I didn't come here to argue," she said quickly. "I came because I need a favor. But I do like Sister Michael."

"Really?" he said, a dimple appearing on the left side of his face. "I got the impression from the shouting that the two of you weren't hitting it off."

They turned the corner of the little landing at the top of the stairs, and he crossed himself when they passed the statue of Christ on a short table there. Assumpta lowered her voice. "You heard all the commotion and you didn't come down?"

"I'd been given my orders," he said. "You'd best call for an appointment from now on. Or, at least until Father Hughes is gone."

"He's leaving?"

"He'd like to. He aspires to move up to a higher rank in the diocese."

"Ahh," she said. "Typical climber."

"Not quite," said Father Tony, entering his office and sitting down behind his desk. He set the jar of salt to the side. "James says he's interested in getting Holy Rosary the money she needs to survive. He can funnel more money to this church if he's involved at the diocesan level. He can support our outreach programs."

"And you believe that?" Assumpta sat in the right-side chair of the two facing Father Tony's desk.

He was silent.

Assumpta said, "I know you probably shouldn't be sharing your opinions with me, but who else do you have to talk with? I'll keep it to myself."

He fiddled with the paperclips on his desk. "Tempting as it is, I'll keep my own counsel."

"I'll take that as a *no*," Assumpta said. "I'll tell you this: he's acting strange. I didn't feel comfortable with him. He's not himself."

"His priorities have changed."

"It's more than that—" It was her turn to be silent.

"What?"

She sighed. "He wouldn't let me read his aura."

"Assumpta—"

"Well, you asked. He wouldn't let me read it. It was like he knew what I was trying to do. He kept moving closer to me, getting into my personal space. He deliberately tried to make me feel uncomfortable."

"I doubt that's the case."

"We'll have to agree to disagree," she said. "Can you bless the salt? Then I can get out of your hair so you can meet with Father Hughes."

Father Tony picked up the jar and looked at the label. "We sold this at the last May Day Festival. It's already been blessed."

"It's not."

"Yes, it is," Father Tony said. "See, here on the label: *Blessed Salt*. We import it from Rome, but we make the labels ourselves so that it has a picture of Holy Rosary on it. Amazing what you can do with a computer these days. When we bought the salt, they sent a template for making labels."

"But how do you know it's been blessed?"

"That's how it was advertised. The church takes the order, blesses the salt, then fills the jars and ships them."

"Who does the blessing? The Vatican?"

"Why does it matter?"

"Because you got taken. Did you pay extra for the holy benediction? This salt isn't blessed. You might as well have bought it from McCormick's down the road and put your pretty label on it. It would have amounted to the same thing!"

"And you know this how?"

Assumpta crossed her arms on her chest. When she didn't speak, Father Tony said, "You can prove it's not blessed?"

She almost smiled. "Would I ask you to bless it if I couldn't prove it?"

He looked away from her and muttered, "I can't believe I'm asking you to show me."

At that, Assumpta did smile.

"Show me something around here that you know is blessed," she said. "Preferably something you've witnessed being blessed, or you have blessed yourself."

He opened his desk drawer and pulled out a black rosary purse.

"Is the purse blessed, or just the rosary inside?" she asked.

"Just the rosary."

Assumpta held out her left hand and Father Tony laid the purse upon it. She clutched the purse in her hand, feeling the slight weight of it in her palm, then squeezed the spring mechanism at the top to open it. Taking a deep breath to guard against the pain, she opened her right hand and dumped the rosary into it, clutching her fingers closed.

The deep breath did not prepare her for the pain.

"Shit!" she cried. Even Father Tony could not have missed the sizzle, the sound of flesh burning, and the puff of smoke accompanying it. *Oh, my god,* she thought, *do I smell charcoal?*

Assumpta turned her hand over and dropped the rosary to the desk. She shook her hand, blew on it, trying to ease the pain. Then she looked at it.

The shape of a cross was burned sideways into her palm. A line of dots, the shape of the beads, flared across the fleshy portion beneath her fingers and another seared across the bottom of her thumb. She lifted it to show Father Tony.

"Most definitely blessed," she said, reaching for the salt. "Now, see what happens when I pour the salt in my hand."

"No!" He grabbed the jar from her hand. He was shaking his head, as if not believing what just happened. She watched a sweat break out on his brow. "*Sweet Mother of God,*" he said, crossing himself and pushing his wheeled desk chair backward, away from Assumpta. "What just happened is *not* possible."

"And yet, it happened," Assumpta said.

"The only explanation—"

"Is that I'm possessed." She laid the rosary purse onto the desk. "But, I'm not. I'm not speaking in tongues, I don't suddenly possess knowledge I didn't have before. I don't feel compelled to do evil things."

"*Now the Spirit speaketh expressly, that in the latter times some shall depart from the faith, giving heed to seducing spirits, and doctrines of devils...*"

"First Timothy," Assumpta said automatically. "But come on, Father, you've known me forever. Have I given up my faith? Have I embraced any doctrines of evil? Do I appear possessed to you?"

"You've always shown me a great predilection to read people, a fantastic analytical mind—if your high school science classes mean anything—greatly at odds, I might add, with this propensity of yours to believe you can find things by dangling a crystal on a string—"

"Father!"

"But you've never shown me before that blessed things can *wound* you, child." His voice softened, and he looked at her with such a hurt look on his face that Assumpta didn't know what to say. Suddenly, she felt defeated. Father Tony wheeled his desk chair closer to the desk and rested his elbows on the edge, steepling his fingers on the bridge of his nose. "Assumpta, there is something going on here."

"Evil, you mean?"

"Most definitely. What other force in the universe burns at the touch of something blessed?"

He bent to the bottom right desk drawer and pulled out a shallow silver bowl with a cloth-wrapped bundle inside. "Unfortunately, or maybe fortunately, I don't think you're possessed. I'm not even allowed to consider it until you're seen by a psychiatrist. It's a damning thing to accuse someone of possession."

"I'm not going to see a psychiatrist." She wasn't crazy! She'd seen what she'd seen. *Now, that does sound crazy,* she thought. But she knew she wasn't. Greg suffered, too. They couldn't be crazy together when they hadn't even known each other before this.

"I'm not suggesting you do," Father Tony said, unwrapping the cloth and revealing a slender volume bound in red leather. "I don't think you're crazy. But something's going on. Performing an exorcism won't work, but this little book might have just the thing we need."

The gilt-edged pages looked pristine, as though the book had never been opened. She couldn't read the Latin inscription on the cover.

"Your book looks brand new," Assumpta said. "You've never performed an exorcism?"

"Never had the need to." The spine on the book cracked when Father Tony opened it.

"What's the silver bowl for?"

"Oil, water. Sometimes salt. Whatever a priest feels is necessary."

"Why do you have it?"

"Lunch," said Father Tony, turning another page. "I sometimes have soup." He looked up from the pages of the book and smiled, then sobered. "If you tell me what you think is going on, I might be able to find something that will help."

Assumpta debated what to tell him, then decided that she didn't know anyone better who might have some answers for what was going on. She told him about meeting Greg and the broken urn, and why she wouldn't let Father Tony help her up that day she'd visited the church and fallen, for fear of cursing him.

He leaned back in his chair, listening.

"At first I could only see it in the mirror, Father, a gray-black thing with sharp teeth and claws, with rough skin, like concrete. Half-cat, half human with pointed ears and huge eyes."

"And now you can see it outside the mirror?"

Assumpta nodded and told him what happened in the shower.

"Demons often enjoy sexual congress with those they've possessed," he said. "But the possessed often lack the knowledge of the assault. What else?"

"I blessed a bottle of oil—"

"You did, did you?"

"Well, I'm fairly certain I did. Blessing it led to my discovery of my inability to touch things blessed." She told him what happened at the altar. "The more I prayed, the heavier the weight became on my back and shoulders. I'm certain it was the creature, but it didn't interfere with what I did, other than make its presence known. When I was done, I anointed all the windows and doors and begged God to rid me of the demon—or whatever this creature is.

"Unfortunately, God didn't answer my prayers."

Father Tony gave her a harsh look. "Well, *He* didn't," she protested.

"It hasn't been long enough for the Lord to do anything, in my opinion," he said. "Don't jump to conclusions. I'm willing to bet that the Lord had a hand in this problem somewhere." He thumbed the pages in the book. "I don't think I'll be needing this," he said, laying it down. "At least, not yet."

"What do you mean?"

"You've not described anything I can exorcize. I don't even think you're cursed, in the truest sense of the word. And I certainly don't think you're dealing with a demon, despite all the blessed craziness you're enduring."

"So what do you think is going on?"

Father Tony took the jar of salt she'd brought and poured it into the silver bowl, then stood. He made the sign of the cross over the salt, whispering a prayer at the same time. When the prayer ended, he crossed it again. Next, he scooped his hands into the bowl, drawing up a large portion of salt. He bowed over it, nearly touching his forehead to the grains, praying still, and let the salt run through his fingers.

Assumpta thought she heard the words "servant" and "plead" but she couldn't be certain, his words were so soft and quickly spoken.

When he was done, he dusted his hands over the bowl. "I'm not sure what you've gotten yourself into," he said, making a funnel of a piece of paper and dumping the salt back into the jar, "but I do believe you might be needing this." He sat it on the desk in front of her. "You didn't bring the oil with you, did you?"

Assumpta rummaged through her purse and produced the wide-mouthed jar.

Father Tony took it and unscrewed the cap. When he poured the oil into the bowl, he poured it over the fingers of his left hand as he bowed and said his prayers. Again, he made the sign of the cross over it several times, then wiped his hands on the cloth that had protected his prayer book.

"In any other instance," he said, lifting the bowl to pour the contents back into the jar, "I'd use this oil and salt to make the sign of the cross on your forehead and beg God to keep you safe. But I have a feeling that even if such a ritual did bless and keep you from harm, it's not worth the pain you'd suffer to endure it."

He finished, screwed the lid on, and then said, "I can't forbid you to enter the church, but I don't know what entering there would do to you. I'll do some research to see if I can find any such incidence of this happening before. Maybe there's a way we can rid you and Greg of your little hitchhikers."

"If they're not demons, and I'm not possessed, then what are they?" Assumpta asked, putting the jars of salt and oil into her purse.

"Minions, I think," Father Tony said. "Technically, they are demons—tiny demons—not very potent in their own right, but servants of another, more powerful, demon. The questions now are: who is their master, and, where is he?"

CHAPTER 13

GREG ANSWERED HER KNOCK IMMEDIATELY. HE gripped a cup of coffee in his hand and looked as if he hadn't slept at all last night. By the look of him, Assumpta just *knew* he had had a similar experience to her own.

"You can see it outside the mirror," she said, brushing past him and into the living room. She sat on the sofa, dropping her purse to the floor, and pulled her knees to her chest. She rested her chin on them.

"And that's not all," he said, slamming the door and sitting down next to her. "It—"

She raised her eyebrows, but she didn't say a word.

"Do you want some coffee?" he asked, standing again and walking toward the kitchen. Clearly, he wasn't ready to talk about it.

She nodded. She could use the caffeine. Her stomach rumbled, loudly.

He turned back to her. "Join me in the kitchen? I'll fry us up some eggs. I haven't eaten all day."

Assumpta believed him...but she was certain *he* didn't offer to cook just because he was hungry. He was doing the manly thing and providing for *her*. Normally, this kind of thinking raised her hackles. Tonight, she was hungry.

"How about an omelet?" she asked. At his nod, she said, "Do you have any cheese?"

"Top drawer." He pointed to the refrigerator. The, he pulled a skillet out of the bottom drawer beneath the glass-topped range and a grater from the middle one. He handed the grater to her silently, and placed the skillet on the stove.

Assumpta got the cheese, then took a peek in the crisper while Greg sprayed the pan with oil and turned on the heat. She found onions and mushrooms, but no green peppers or anything else she might like to toss in with the eggs.

She laid them on the counter and started opening drawers, looking for a knife to chop them with.

"Make yourself at home," Greg said, smiling. He reached for the cutting board and laid it on the counter in front of her. "Knives are in the drawer two to your right. Do you want toast?"

Assumpta nodded. "Wheat, if you have it."

She washed the mushrooms while he laid thick slices of whole grain bread in the toaster oven. Assumpta cooked, letting the onions and mushrooms simmer while she grated the cheese. Greg made fresh coffee.

It took only a few minutes for everything to finish. The bell dinged on the toaster oven just as Assumpta split the eggs onto two plates and carried them to the small table in the kitchen.

Greg stacked the toast on a small plate and put it in the center of the table, then retrieved ketchup and strawberry jam from the refrigerator, and picked up the butter from the counter where Assumpta had left it.

He poured fresh coffee for each of them, and then they sat.

Assumpta reached for toast, spread jam on it, and took a bite, savoring the burst of fruit flavor in her mouth. Nothing had ever tasted better than the strawberry jam did at this moment.

Greg upturned the ketchup and squeezed a crisscrossing stream of red all over his eggs.

She sipped her coffee, then said, "That's a waste of a terrific omelet."

"Can't stand scrambled eggs," Greg said, setting the ketchup down. "I was offering sunny-side up or over easy. If you'd have tossed green peppers into it, I'd have passed and had some cornflakes."

She laughed. "Why didn't you say anything?"

"You looked determined."

"Sorry." She scooped eggs onto her fork with the crust of her toast and savored the flavors.

They ate in silence for a moment, then Greg asked, "Good?"

Assumpta nodded, mouth full.

Greg picked up a slice of toast and, smearing it liberally with strawberry jam, held it out to her.

"Thanks," she said, taking it with her left hand and lifting it to her mouth. "Best meal I've had all day," she said, then bit into it. Again, she used the toast to push eggs onto her fork.

"I'm betting it's the only meal you've had all day," he said.

Assumpta stopped, her fork halfway to her mouth. She could feel herself color. Slowly, she lowered the fork back to her plate.

I'm making a pig of myself, she thought, embarrassed. *He's rich! He's not used to such manners. What must he be thinking?*

"I'm sorry," she said, trying to sound nonchalant. She lowered the toast and picked up a napkin, trying to dab the jam off her fingers with dainty motions. "It's just so delicious, I must look like an animal, shoveling it all in."

"Not at all," he said, taking a large scoop of ketchup-covered eggs and shoving it into his mouth. "Although you are eating a little fast."

Greg finished chewing and scooped up another large forkful of eggs. She'd just started to relax when he said, "Just how long has it been since you've eaten?"

"I had breakfast!" she said, laughing. *As long as a starlight mint counts for breakfast,* she thought, remembering the candy dish at one of the businesses where she had dropped off a résumé this morning.

"Liar." Greg took a sip of coffee.

"It's not nice to call someone you barely know a liar."

"It's not nice to lie."

Touché. Her mother would agree with him, she thought.

"So, it's manifested itself outside the visual of the mirror," she said. "Right?"

Greg laid his fork on his plate and crossed his arms, leaning forward to rest his elbows on the table. He took a deep breath. "I had just turned in last night, but I was exhausted. I fell asleep right away. It wasn't more than a few seconds later that I started having this incredible dream…"

"Pornographic?"

"More like erotic," Greg said.

She raised an eyebrow. "How could you tell the difference?" she asked, laughing.

"You can't?"

She laughed again. "Of course I can," Assumpta said. "It's *your* ability I'm questioning. Men usually have a hard time discerning."

"Watch it," Greg said. He pushed his empty plate toward the center of the table and leaned in even closer. "Your prejudices are showing." He waggled a finger at her.

"So how do you know?"

He raised his eyes to the ceiling as if pondering. "Pornography is those naked lady silhouettes on truckers' mud flaps. Erotic is the naked women depicted in the Kama Sutra or on ancient pottery."

"Like those big-bellied, big-breasted mother figures you often see in museums," Assumpta asked. "You consider those erotic?"

"Mmm-hmm," he said with dancing eyes. "Under the right circumstances they are. Satisfied?"

She was going to have to be. They could explore his mother fixations later, she decided. She said, "Okay. I'll allow that you know the difference. So you were having this erotic dream…"

"I was laying on my back, rock ha—very excited, and a woman was crawling up my body, rubbing herself all over me—"

"You're sure this isn't pornographic?" she asked, fairly certain she didn't want to hear any more of this.

"Yeah, well, it doesn't matter anyway."

"Why not?"

"Because that's when I woke up."

"And you found out it was all a dream?"

He looked away from her.

"No, that's when I found out it wasn't a dream at all. I really was lying in bed, and there really was something warm crawling up my body…"

"I know exactly where this is leading," Assumpta said. "You don't have to finish."

"But I do," Greg insisted. "It was my… *hitchhiker*, rubbing herself all over me. She…*it?* opened my pants and was licking—"

"Enough!" Assumpta said, throwing her hands up. "I really don't need to hear this. I had a similar experience with my own little hanger-on—"

"It undressed you?"

"I was in the shower—" She lowered her hands, dropped her toast onto the plate, and laid the fork on the edge.

Greg looked horrified. "Oh, my god," he said. "It didn't…"

She shook her head. "I don't know how it could have, with it only being about the size of a large cat—"

"Cat!"

"Well, it has grown slightly since it's attached itself to me. That's one of the things I wanted to talk to you about tonight."

"Assumpta," Greg said, his voice barely more than a whisper, "my hitchhiker is nearly as tall as I am."

"Oh, no," she said. *Father Tony was right.*

"*Oh, no* is right," he said. "We have to get rid of these things. Fast. I can't go to sleep knowing there's the chance that this thing will assault me again in my sleep and there won't be anything I can do about it."

"What did you do this time?"

"I pushed it off," Greg said, "Which wasn't easy. It's stronger than it looks. When it came at me again, I punched it. Felt like a damn brick." He showed her his knuckles. Bloodied scabs crossed the top of his right hand. "I couldn't believe how hard it felt, after feeling so soft against me." He shook his head. "But I rolled off the bed to the opposite side. Farther away from me, it appeared to shrink. I think we're somehow connected. Like, it's gaining size by feeding on me, or on my energy."

"So it's small again?"

"No. Not as small as these creatures were when we first encountered them. Only about a foot or so smaller. But then it rushed toward me, and I could see it regaining its stature. So I grabbed the first thing my fingers touched and hit the creature square between the eyes."

"With what?" She tried to think of the things she kept on her own nightstand. A book. A flashlight.

"A baseball bat. I keep one on the side of the bed just in case somebody breaks in when I'm here."

She thought about the gun her grandfather had given her when she graduated from high school. No telling what that would have done to these creatures.

"And?"

"Like hitting a cement post. Literally," Greg said. "Pieces of the demon broke off and hit the floor. And then it disappeared."

"So it's gone," Assumpta said.

"Just invisible. It's been talking to me today. Telling me all the lewd sex acts it wants to use me for." He leaned back in his chair. "It likes to whisper in my ear, when I least expect it. I think it enjoys surprising me...and grossing me out."

"And the pieces of it?"

He stood up, the chair legs scraping across the floor. "Here," he said, "look at this." Greg crossed to the open living room, picked up a tin can she hadn't noticed earlier, and brought it back to the kitchen. He dumped several lumps of gray stone matter onto the table. Assumpta reached for one of the pieces.

"Don't touch it!" Greg said.

"Why not?"

"It could hurt you," Greg said.

"It's already hurting me," she said, reaching for a broken shard. "This will be good practice for when I finally get my chemistry degree. We need to examine it."

When her fingers approached within a few inches of the pieces, the largest one sailed into her hand, slapping her palm with a loud *smack*.

Assumpta's eyes widened. "It was like a magnet," she said, smiling. "It just popped into my hand." She squeezed her fingers around it. "It feels like sandstone, or that rough cement they use on city sidewalks. The kind that rips open your knees even if the fall you take isn't so bad."

She lifted it to her nose. "Wet cement," she said, "just like I smelled in the shower."

Greg gave her a puzzled look.

"Smell," she said, opening her palm flat and offering Greg a whiff of the stone, like handing a sugar cube to a horse.

As she levered her arm toward Greg, she felt a tingling in her palm, then a burning sensation.

"Ow," she cried, shaking her hand to dislodge the stone. It wouldn't budge. She tried to pry it from her palm with her other hand. Her fingers burned where they touched the stone.

"It's shrinking!" she said to Greg. "It's melting, dammit, and burning my hand!"

Greg grabbed her by the arm and pulled her to the sink, where he turned the cold faucet on full blast and thrust her burning hands under it.

"It still hurts," Assumpta said, gritting her teeth, "but the cold water is helping. It doesn't feel nearly as bad."

Greg reached for her palm. "No, don't," she said. "You don't want this to happen to you. I can bear it." She pulled her hand from the spray to survey the damage. She imagined blackened skin and a bloodied wound in the center of her hand.

A pea-sized fragment of stone remained attached to her palm, which was now the same gray-black hue as the chunk had been when she picked it up. While she watched, the fragment shrank further, appearing to melt and run across her palm, which absorbed it as quickly as it melted. With a little puff of smoke, the fragment was gone.

Her palm, the pad of her thumb, the first joints of her fingers and the bend of her wrist carried the mark of the stone: they were grayish-black, and rough like sandstone. Her hand felt heavy. She looked at her

99

left hand. The pads of her fingers, which had touched the stone when she tried to pry it loose from her palm, also carried the mark. She turned it over and tapped them on the counter.

The flesh *clinked* against the marble countertops, stone against stone.

"Your fingers!" Greg said, reaching for her left hand. He grasped it before she could pull it away, and lifted her hand closer to see.

Not just the pads of her fingers were stone, but the entire first joint, and her fingernails, too. It looked like she had dipped them into a very thin cement and let it dry.

She tapped the fingers on the top of her right hand, imagining herself turning entirely to stone. Her left fingers stuck there, and she couldn't pull them away. Like the magnetic force of the shard that had flown into her hand, her left fingers were magnetized to her right. Unbearable pain shot threw her left fingertips.

"Ow!" She cried, feeling a powerful suction.

She watched as the stone was leeched from her left hand to collect on the right, smoothing and thinning, spreading, until it covered her right hand.

Assumpta got a lump in her throat. She looked to her right hand and slowly turned it over.

The entire hand, front to back, fingertips to wrist, appeared to be stone. It was grayish-black, like a cement statue long exposed to the elements, but perfectly detailed, an exact replica of her hand, as though she'd dipped it in stone, the earlier burn of the rosary standing out in bold relief.

CHAPTER 14

ASSUMPTA FLEXED HER WRIST AND MOVED HER fingers, gratified to find that they functioned almost as fluidly as they had when they were flesh. But she didn't like the sound of stone grinding against stone as she wiggled her fingers.

What was happening to her?

"Oh, my god," she whispered. "I'm turning to stone."

"We don't know that," Greg said, staring at her hand. "Maybe the small fragment has the power only to turn so much of you to stone. You said it was melting. Perhaps it can only melt and spread so far."

"But what if I am?" She spoke barely above a whisper. "The melted stone is inside my body! It's in my bloodstream." She could feel herself getting hysterical. The high-pitched tone of her voice wasn't normal. "How can I stop this?"

"I don't know," he said, his voice even, as if he tried to calm her racing heart.

She turned back to the table. "You didn't touch them, did you?"

He shook his head. "I used a dustpan and broom. I didn't realize how dangerous they might be. I was so creeped out from the dream, I knew I didn't want to touch them."

"We've got to destroy them," Assumpta said.

"How?" said Greg.

She thought about it for a moment.

"Sweep them back into the can," she said. "I've got an idea. I think we need something that's been blessed."

She went to the living room and retrieved her purse. Setting it on the seat of the kitchen chair when she returned, she rummaged through it for the blessed salt and oil.

"What's this?"

"I was going to tell you what I learned at the church today, but we got sidetracked," she said. "I think this might help us get rid of the stone fragments. It might help us get rid of the *hitchhikers* completely."

Greg picked up the salt. "Blessed?" he asked.

"It's a Catholic thing," Assumpta said. "The oil's been blessed, too. First by me, and then by Father Tony."

"*You* blessed the oil?"

Quickly, she told Greg what she did and how she anointed all the entrances in her small apartment.

"I didn't think it had worked at first, since I could still see the little beast this morning, but now I'm not so sure." She gestured toward him with the jar. "Your hitchhiker is large and mine's almost the same size as it was when I first saw it. I'm not sure if it was the anointing or the praying that had some effect.

"I'd planned on doing the same to your house this evening." She unscrewed the lid of the oil jar and laid it on the table. "Lucky for you, you're getting a double-dose of blessing; triple, if we use the salt. And…" she said, her eyes lighting up as another idea gripped her, "we'll protect you the same tonight, by anointing you—your bed, even—with some of the oil."

"And you, too," he said.

"Can't," said Assumpta, her smile deflating. "That's the other thing I was going to tell you about. I can no longer touch blessed things."

"You mean like the devil and vampires?"

She nodded. "Blessed things are my silver bullet."

"I don't understand."

"Watch," she said, pouring the oil over the broken stone in the can.

The oil burst into flame as it touched the shards, sizzling and popping as it ran down over the jagged edges. Smoke roiled up out of the can. Greg and Assumpta stepped back, away from the table. The smoke detector in the living room went off with a blare, making Assumpta jump.

She started laughing. "Thank goodness you don't have sprinklers in here."

Greg grabbed a dishtowel and bolted to the living room, swinging the towel in front of the alarm to dissipate the smoke. It quieted.

By the time he returned to the table, the stones had ceased sizzling in the oil and no more smoke came from the can. They peered into it.

A thin veneer of pristine golden oil covered the bottom. No signs of burning or smoke marred the container. It looked brand new inside. She'd expected the oil to be blackened and to see scorch marks on the can. Instead, the can gleamed like new. The oil looked as pure as that still in the jar.

"You're afraid the oil will do that to you?" Greg asked.

"I'm certain it will." She lifted her stony right hand and turned it palm up for Greg to take a better look. "What do you see?"

"A cross," he said, studying her hand, "And circles. Dots?"

"Beads," Assumpta said. "A rosary."

She told him about the experiments at her altar, and then how she proved to Father Tony that she could no longer touch blessed items.

He swallowed hard. "You're losing your humanity."

"Hardly that."

"Then what would you call it?"

I don't know, she thought. But she knew she wasn't losing her humanity. She'd feel more...*indifferent,* perhaps, if that were the case.

"An infection," she said. "It's like contact dermatitis, only worse. We just need to find the cure."

"Contact dermatitis? Are you nuts?" he asked. Greg turned away from her, running a hand through his longish hair. He let out an angry breath.

"Why are you so angry?" she asked, nearly yelling. "*I'm* the one with the problem here."

He turned back to face her. "Because you're treating it like it's *not* a problem," he said. "Using such soft language, like *hitchhiker* and *infection*, makes it seem like things are not so bad." He raised his voice. "But they really are bad. How can you act like they're not? How do you fix a problem that has no earthly explanation? These things don't exist!"

"But they do exist! Your problem is that you don't believe it. Digging in the dirt all day tells you plenty about how a culture once lived, how its people worshiped, even what they might have believed in. But you've never once come across a civilization that ceased to exist because some evil was visited upon it, have you? How do you know some unnamed evil didn't cause its downfall?" She pushed the can away from her. "How can you not believe evil exists? You've seen these things with your own eyes!"

"How can you ask such a thing? You want to be a trained chemist. There's a logic to science that precludes evil. Good *or* evil, there's no room for either in an analytical mind."

Assumpta laughed, a bitter noise, devoid of humor. "And all my talk about blessed things…?"

Wordless, he faced her, eyes blazing.

"You're scared," she said. "You've never come across anything like this in your life and you don't know how to deal with it."

He shook his head. "No," he said. "That's not it."

"Then what is it?"

"This shouldn't be happening," he said. "Good and evil are what people *do*; they don't exist as entities."

"Do you really believe that, after being attacked by some stoneware succubus?" She lifted her hand. "And this? What explanation do you have for my hand turning to stone in an instant?"

"There must be some sane, *chemical*, explanation."

"Why did you even come to me with your problem if you didn't believe?"

"I didn't," he said, looking away. "Not at first. But I felt like I didn't have any other options."

She felt as though he'd punched her in the gut. She sat down at the table. "I'm your last resort."

At his tight nod, Assumpta asked, "How long did you wait?"

"Weeks," Greg said. "Almost two months."

She frowned. "But the bite you showed me looked fresh."

"It won't heal," he said, pulling the collar away from his neck so she could see the edge of the raw wound. "It's looked the same since the first day."

"And you're seeking help now because you're finally starting to believe?"

He shook his head. "Let's call it pragmatism," Greg said. "I'm still not sure I know what to believe, but I'd rather be safe than sorry at this point."

"Fair enough."

She wasn't going to push her own beliefs on him. He'd have to come around to that all by himself. Lord knew she grappled with her own beliefs on a daily basis.

She took a deep breath. They both had to calm down. Would logic work with him?

"I think the reason my *hitchhiker*," she deliberately stressed the word, "is still small is because of the holy oil," Assumpta said. "Anointing the windows creates a sanctified barrier between your home and the outside world that doesn't let any additional evil in. I'm thinking that means your *new friend*, this *minion*, won't be able to call for backup help if we do this in your house." She wiggled the jar. "I'm not sure what the connection is between the barrier and the size of the creatures, but my guess is that they don't just feed off of you: they gain power from their master."

"*Master?*" He turned away from her, paced to the doorway and turned again. "Just what have we gotten ourselves into?"

Assumpta refrained from telling him she'd been just fine until he'd knocked on her door. She said, "Let me anoint your apartment, like I did my own. Let's try to get your creature under control."

"You think that will work?"

"What have you got to lose?"

"My humanity?" he asked, his eyes deadly serious.

"How?" she asked, feeling her anger start another slow burn.

"What if I can't touch blessed things once you're done?" Greg asked.

"What if you can't? That issue never came up before."

"It could impact my work," he said. "I could come across an ancient church or basilica, or even a simple altar, and not be able to excavate it."

"*Seriously?* That's your job, not your *humanity.*"

"Still–"

She interrupted him. "We don't know for certain it was the anointing that caused the problem with my being able to touch holy things. In fact, it's probably the presence of the hitchhiker itself; look what happened the first time I entered the church after being *infected.*"

Greg crossed his arms on his chest.

"You know," Assumpta said, "if it is the hitchhiker, you're in worse shape than I am. Yours is bigger and more aggressive already. You're probably even more infected than I am. You just haven't seen the effects yet, since there's nothing blessed around here." She spread her arms wide to encompass the entire apartment. "Although I'm sure being dry-humped by a cement succubus isn't any picnic."

She thought of something. "You're apparently so attractive, you've got to beat that thing off with a baseball bat. What if it conjures some friends? Can you take on more than one?"

He shook his head. "One's more than I can handle."

Assumpta gestured with the oil again. "How about we test my theory?" She took a step toward him. "We could even try putting some of this on the bite, too."

She waited several long, tense moments while he considered her plan. Finally, he nodded his agreement.

"Do you have a rag or a paint brush?" Assumpta asked. "With Father Tony's additional blessing, I don't want to chance touching the oil."

Greg nodded. "I'm sure I can find something." A wrinkle creased his brow as he considered the matter. He walked to the kitchen and dug through a drawer. "Will this do?" He pulled a small brush from a drawer in the kitchen.

It looked like a basting brush.

"Perfect," Assumpta said, grabbing it by the wooden handle. She uncapped the jar and dipped the brush into the oil, holding the squat jar in the palm of her hand. "Let's start with securing your apartment first. Then, we can concentrate on you." She lifted the brush. "Where's the door or window farthest from your front door? We'll need to begin there and move forward, closing off the avenues from back to front."

"The only other door is out onto the balcony," Greg said, "but there's a window in my bedroom in the back." He walked toward the room as he spoke. "And a small one in the bathroom."

They passed the bathroom on the right—a galley-style room, both long and narrow—and then came to Greg's bedroom, also on the right. The left side of the hall was a bank of closets, three in all, one after the other.

The room was stark, the bed neatly made, but loose change and receipts littered the top of the wide, low bureau on the far side of the bed. Assumpta tried not to pry as she headed toward the window, but she couldn't avoid making comparisons between his room and her own.

Where her shelves strained under the load of all her books, his were punctuated with woven baskets, clay pottery, and even one large-breasted, full-bellied mother statue, which looked to be carved from stone. She had to keep from smiling and turning toward him when she saw it.

She reached the window, and pulled the brush from its waiting position within the wide-necked jar. She brushed oil up the left side of the window pane, across the top, down the right side, and finally to the left, across the bottom of the sash, creating an unbroken line of blessed oil around the window. She dropped the brush back into the jar.

"Will you pray with me?" she asked.

"Do I have to?"

"I'm not sure," Assumpta said. "But it can't hurt, right? Where's your pragmatism gone?"

"It's a little worse for wear right now," Greg said. "I don't know if I can work up the energy."

"Oh, come on," Assumpta said. "It's *your* hitchhiker. I think we'll have a better chance of…arresting it, if you play an active role in this."

Greg stared for a long moment at the window, then dropped his head, talking at the floor. "I don't know how," he said.

Assumpta hadn't considered that. She'd never met anyone who didn't know how to pray before. Didn't praying come naturally?

She smiled. "It's easy. You simply tell God what's going on and ask for his help. Some people invoke Christ when they ask, or ask for the intercession of Mary—Christ's mother—or even a saint on their own behalf. But we can start with something simple. We'll just talk to the big guy himself."

"But God is omniscient, right? Why doesn't he see what's going on here and just fix it?"

Heavens, she thought. Was he serious, or just being an ass? She'd heard this question a million times before by both unbelievers *and* believers. And every once in a while when she was feeling blue, she'd try it on for size herself. The answer was easy, unless you had no belief in God—*any god*—whatsoever.

Did Greg fall into that camp? How did you convince someone of the existence of any higher power when they lacked the faith to do so?

Now was really not the time to be considering all this, she thought, trying to push that line of thinking away.

She said instead, "God likes to be asked. He's a very polite deity. He won't crash your party without your permission. If you want his help, you've got to let him know."

"So—I'm going to have to beg for it?" Greg asked.

CHAPTER 15

LORD, GIVE ME STRENGTH, SHE THOUGHT. HERE was another conversation she didn't want to have right now. She took a deep breath and squelched a nasty remark that rose to her lips.

"How about if I say the words, and you just repeat them after me?" She looked up at him, eyebrows raised, with what she hoped was an expectant face: a face that said, *you'd better at least try to do it my way, or you're on your own.*

"I think I can manage that," Greg said, looking away.

Assumpta let out the breath she'd been holding and relaxed. "Then let's get this done," she said, turning to the window.

She dipped the brush into the salt this time, letting the grains adhere to the damp bristles, and lifted it to the top left corner of the window.

And then she felt the weight of her *hitchhiker* on her back. She could lift the brush, but not without effort.

"It's here," she said, raising her right shoulder, trying to shrug the creature to a more comfortable location on her back. She found it difficult to lift her arm high enough to reach the top of the window. "I guess it's realized we mean business. Can you see it?" she asked. "I can feel it on my back."

"No," Greg said. He swore. "I thought we could see these things now."

"I think our seeing them or not seeing them is largely a matter of whether they *want* us to or not," Assumpta said. "I guess they don't want us to. It's all part of their plan. You've got to admit, it's pretty unnerving to feel something you know is there, touching you, and yet you can't see it." She shrugged again, throwing her right elbow back swiftly a few times, but still couldn't dislodge the creature. It moved and clung to her right arm and shoulder as if hanging on for dear life.

This isn't going to be easy, she thought, taking a deep breath and stepping closer to the window.

"Ready?" she asked, dipping the brush into the salt again.

"As ready as I'm going to be," Greg said.

"Just repeat after me," Assumpta said. "Lord, with this blessed salt and oil, bind the demon invading this home…"

Quietly, Greg said, "Lord, with this blessed salt and oil, bind the demon invading this home…"

Assumpta wanted to tell him to pray with a little more conviction, but she guessed that asking Greg to do so would clam him up. At least she'd got him repeating the words. It was good for him to be active in the cleansing of his own house.

She thrust her arm toward the top right corner of the window and felt her hitchhiker cling more tightly to her arm.

Good to know they can be surprised, she thought, smiling.

She dipped the brush in the salt again. The creature squeezed her wrist, as if anticipating Assumpta's attempt to shake it off when she reached for top of the jamb again. Assumpta smiled.

"By your word," she said, dragging the brush down to the bottom right sill, "cast it back to Hell where it belongs."

"By your word," Greg intoned, "cast it back to Hell where it—"

The invisible creature tightened its grip even more, digging its sharp claws into the delicate skin of Assumpta's forearm, then raked them backward to her elbow.

She screamed as two sets of four scratches appeared on her arm, then welled with blood. She shook her arm, attempting to dislodge the minion, and felt it scamper to the middle of her back, clinging tightly by a hand draped over each shoulder, its claws rubbing the skin at her collarbone.

It blew its hot breath into her ear and laughed its dry-leaves laugh.

A chill ran up her neck, even as the warm blood ran down her arm. She leaned forward, cooling her forehead on the glass.

"Jesus," Greg said, running from the room. He returned a second later, shaking the folds out of a towel he must have grabbed from the kitchen. He wrapped it around her arm, and wiped at the blood coalescing at her wrist. Nudging her toward a chair, he said, "Come on, sit down. Let's take care of this."

She shook her head and stood firm. "Just wrap it and tie the edges together so I don't bleed all over your hardwood floors," Assumpta said. "We've got to finish."

"What if they hurt you again?"

"They *are* going to hurt me again," Assumpta said. "But consider the alternative if we don't fight for our space. We've only got one each to worry about. If we don't bar the windows, they'll be calling their friends and inviting them to the party. They're just like ladybugs: you let one in your house to stay out of the cold and before you know it, you've got a hundred and fifty congregating in every window, you're crunching them underfoot every time you turn around, and you've got to call an exterminator to get rid of the cute little monsters." She paused for breath. "Who are we going to call if we let these hitchhikers winter over?"

"But you're bleeding," Greg said.

"Women bleed all the time. I can handle this."

"You've got to stop." He fingered the torn T-shirt at her shoulder. "I can't ask this of you, if this is what it's going to take to stop them."

"Prepare for more," Assumpta said. "This was only the beginning."

He looked as if he wanted to argue with her, but she could tell he wavered. He knew she was right; he just didn't enjoy standing around feeling so helpless. *That* she could relate to.

And he didn't realize that it wasn't the blood she was worried about so much as the pain. Pain hurt. A lot. Maybe guys didn't worry about hurt so much. They habitually pounded on each other like two-year-olds, but they didn't deal with blood on a regular basis.

She looked at the window: oiled all the way around, but salted only on three sides. Could she skip anointing the last jamb with salt? Probably; she hadn't used salt on her own windows. But leaving the fourth side bare just didn't sit right with her. What if not connecting it nullified the seal made by the oil? She couldn't take a chance.

Before Greg realized what she was doing, she dipped the brush into the salt, stepped closer to the window, and swiped the salt up the final side of the window, completing the seal.

Her hitchhiker squeezed the flesh at her neck as if in admonishment, then growled. She'd angered it by completing the seal, but why didn't it harm her? Did it need to conserve energy? She'd cut off one more access point for it, after all. Or maybe the growl was for show. The oil had already sealed the window. It didn't matter that she'd taken the time to salt it, too.

"Are you crazy?" he asked.

"Just testing a theory," Assumpta said. "I was trying to predict if they could read my mind. I wanted to see if I could act fast enough to prevent them from hurting me before I could get the deed done."

"And did you prove your point?"

"Not really," she admitted. "I've got too many other questions about—"

It spoke then. "Sorrrrry…you'llllll beeeee sorrrrry."

She froze. Greg stiffened.

"You heard that?"

He nodded. "It's going to get worse, isn't it?"

"Yeah," she said, smiling over her fear to reassure Greg, "But we knew that was going to happen, right?"

"Stop," Greg said. "There's got to be another way."

"We can't give up," said Assumpta. "The fact that they're trying to hurt me proves that we're getting to them. They're worried. They're striking out because we're affecting their abilities."

"They're hurting you."

"The price of every good martyr," she said, feeling flip. She needed to get to the next window before she chickened out, and Greg wasn't helping.

"I won't let you risk your life to help me fix this problem."

"No, just my soul at this point."

Greg didn't look mollified. "You can't do this for me."

"It's no longer just about you," she said, wiggling her stony fingers at him. "Let's just get this done."

He looked grim, but nodded. "So what can I do to help?"

"Lead the way to the next window."

Greg inclined his head to the right. "Bathroom's right next door. There's only a small, round window near the toilet."

Assumpta gathered her tools and followed Greg out the bedroom door and to the bathroom door alongside it. She stopped at the bedroom door and quickly swiped around the frame, including the hardwood floor of the door's threshold.

She stopped at the closets lining the hall, giving them a thoughtful look.

"Closets, too?"

"Not necessary," Assumpta said, "But there are so many doors...it makes me wonder if it wouldn't be worth it to seal those, too."

"I'll pass," Greg said. 'If there's no need, let's not waste our time. He steered her into the narrow bathroom. "I wouldn't want you to run out of oil or salt."

Assumpta lifted the jars to eye the contents. "Good point."

Her shoulder pained her to move it, but not so bad she couldn't get the job done.

The window in the bathroom was small and round, the kind that let in a little light, but you couldn't see out of very well, or at all if you were sitting down.

Assumpta dropped the brush into the jar of oil and pulled it out. She lifted it and placed it on the round frame at the top.

She started to drag the brush in a clockwise motion, when her minion squeezed her rib cage with both hands, digging its claws into her soft flesh, then scratched outward to her sides.

"Ow!" she screamed, her knees buckling. Greg stepped up behind her and put his hands around her waist, lifting her toward him.

"Lean on me," he said. I've got you."

"Just let me catch my breath," said Assumpta, "and we can move on."

She closed her eyes and breathed deeply, leaning her head back against Greg. With his strong arms clasped around her, she wanted nothing more than to sink into him and let him keep her afloat for a while. She'd been on her own for so long, she'd forgotten how good it felt—how comforting—to borrow someone else's strength.

She stood up abruptly.

"Okay." It would be too easy, she thought, to fall into that needful trap. She needed to stand strong. Quickly, she swiped completely around the window, sealing it, once more managing to surprise the demon, and finish the job before it hurt her. "Lead on to the next."

The balcony doors were three panes instead of two: a sliding door made of two panes and a fixed pane to the right of it, which together let a great deal of light into the condo. Assumpta wished her apartment had half as much light coming in.

She wondered, *Should I treat them as three separate doors, anointing around each glass pane, or treat them as one large portal?*

"Can we get it done before they hurt you too much to go on?" Greg asked.

She nodded, continuing to stare at the window. "I think so, but there's no reason we can't be more efficient."

She knelt on one knee at the left-most pane of the door, setting the jar of blessed salt on the floor, then upended the oil into it until the oil covered the salt by an inch. She stuck the brush into the jar and swirled it around, dissolving as much salt as possible into the oil.

"Nice trick," Greg said.

"I thought so," she replied. "I'm sorry I didn't think of it sooner."

She gripped the jar in her left hand, pulled the brush out of the solution with her right, and placed it against the bottom corner of the jamb. She stood, dragging the brush upward, beginning the seal at the bottom of the window this time. She laid a line of salted oil from the bottom left corner all the way to the top.

Her hitchhiker returned, a sudden weight on her back. She closed her eyes and took a deep breath, steeling herself against the pain she knew would come. Then she dipped the brush into the salt-and-oil solution again and lifted her hand to reach the top left corner of the jamb.

The scratches on her rib cage stretched taut, causing a frisson of pain to ring through the torn muscles. Hoping to get through the pain quickly, like ripping off a Band-Aid, she quickly dragged the brush across the top jamb of all three windows, taking two steps sideways so as to not break the line of the seal.

"Bind this demon, Lord," she said in a strong voice, dipping the brush again when she reached the top right corner. "Cast it from this home. Send it back to Hell where it belongs."

She wiped the brush on the lip of the jar so she wouldn't drip oil onto the floor, then reached for the top right corner again.

"Bind this demon, Lord—" Greg started. The rest of his words were lost to her when she felt a presence at her back, an arm wrapped around her waist from the right, and a soft, warm hand glide across her belly.

She gasped. "Greg?"

"What?" he asked.

She looked over her shoulder to Greg, who stood more than a few feet away.

The hand slid up her rib cage, underneath her shirt, and pressed against the wound. She stiffened instinctively against the pain, but instead felt a warming sensation against the ragged scratches. The skin tingled, blood dried against her skin, and all the pain disappeared.

Strange, she thought, feeling the edges of her skin knit together, *but why would it...?*

Then the presence at her back leaned against her. She felt hot, moist breath in her ear, followed by a throaty chuckle. The hand on her rib cage glided higher and cupped the underside of her right breast. Assumpta inhaled sharply, squeezing her eyes closed. "Oh, god."

"What's wrong?" he asked.

"My friend has switched tactics," she said, opening her eyes and looking at Greg. She turned back to the glass doors, determined to focus through the assault.

She touched the brush to the top right corner and pulled it down the frame, bending to reach the bottom corner.

Scratchy fingers undid the clasp of her bra between her shoulder blades, and she felt the hand on her breast slide beneath the scrap of cotton and move higher, palming her nipple, pushing against it, then make tiny circles on her budding flesh. A warm breath blew in her ear.

"No, no, no," she whispered.

"What?" Greg asked, but she couldn't answer. Her breasts grew full and heavy, her nipples peaked, and she heard the quiet, scratching laughter of her hitchhiker.

Smooth flesh turned hard, the aroma of wet cement blossomed in her nose, and cool stone—a mild, sandy grit—grazed against her nipple, sending pleasurable ripples across her flesh. When the creature dragged its gritty palm in a straight line across the soft skin of her breast, Assumpta felt a corresponding twinge between her legs.

"Oh, god," she said, her knees buckling. Greg rushed to catch her before she fell, stepping behind her, grasping her shoulders in his hands. Now it was *his* voice she heard in her ear.

"What's happening?" he asked.

"It's decided to 'make love, not war—'" She gave him a pleading look. "Can you pull it off of me?"

She gasped. A second hand, warm and soft, slid up her left side to cup her other breast. That's when she realized that a single minion could not assault her so extensively. No way could her small hitchhiker hold on to her while clutching both her breasts. Greg's creature had joined it to besiege her in tandem.

"Oh, my god…"

"*What?*"

"Not just my hitchhiker. Yours, too. They're both touching me, Greg."

"I can't see them," he said, patting her back, moving his hand around, as if trying to find the creatures. "I can't find them. I don't feel them," he said. "We could see them before." He sounded frantic. "Why can't we see them now?" he asked.

"That's the key," Assumpta said. "As long as you can't see them, you can't touch them. If you can't touch them, you can't hurt them. You can't swat them off me. Basically, you *can't* help. They've made that impossible."

She took a deep breath, willing the throb between her thighs to subside, but the hands at her breasts were thorough: squeezing and stroking the soft undersides, pressing and plucking her nipples. She wanted to sink to the floor and let the creatures finish what they had started.

"Let's get this done," she said, her voice hoarse. "The sooner we finish here, the sooner they'll stop."

She dipped the brush and ran it along the floor board. "Bind this demon, Lord," she repeated, dragging the brush to the bottom left corner where it had started, creating an unbroken circuit around the window's perimeter. "Cast it out of this home and back into Hell where it belongs."

Greg repeated the prayer, loosening his grip slightly as Assumpta rallied.

The hand fondling her right breast squeezed once more, then released its hold.

Thank god, she thought, dipping the brush. She relaxed, but then the hand swept down her rib cage, over her hip, and down to the juncture between her thighs.

"Oh, god," she said, the muscles in her thighs tensing. She rocked up on her toes, losing her balance. Her left hand flew forward, falling against the glass with a dull thud. She sagged there for a moment, catching her breath, then pushed off, exhaling raggedly.

She heard the laughter in her ear again, almost human, but not quite. The whispered words came, soft and throaty, "You know you like thissss, Assssumpta. You want thissss."

The hand between her thighs pressed on the seam of her jeans, setting off a shock of pleasure. Unseen hips pressed against her ass, rocked against her, starting a slow, hard rhythm.

She cringed. They knew her name? She thought, but how could they not? The creature lived with her. Surely, it knew even more about her than her name. And who was it sharing this information with?

Had Greg heard? She felt her face flame. Certainly he had.

She took a deep breath. She could get through this. She knew she could. Just two more wooden jambs and she and Greg were home free.

She swirled the brush in the salted oil and bent to reach the bottom edge of the first divider. Unseen hips pressed against her ass again.

Pressed.

Released.

She made certain to touch the oiled path from her first sweep around the panes, then dragged the brush upward to the top.

Hips pressed. Released.

The hand on her left breast tweaked her nipple, tugged it gently

"*Lordbindthisdemon.Casthimoutofthishomeandbackinto Hellwhere hebelongs,*" she said.

Greg parroted her rapid words.

Hips pressed. Released.

The hand between her legs retreated a few inches, then delved between her thighs again in a slow glide, curling two fingers upward on its retreat back.

"Lord, bind this demon—" she said.

"Bind this demon," Greg repeated.

The hand slid forward again, edging two fingers along the seam of her jeans, pushing the rough material of her pants and cotton underwear against her own engorged flesh. Assumpta felt herself grow hotter, felt the moisture pooling between her thighs. Her nipples tingled and the ache between her legs grew more insistent.

I'm going to Hell for this, she thought, *for enjoying the feel of it.*

Hips pressed. Released.

She dipped the brush, and she felt the thick, solid tail of her own hitchhiker unwind itself from her waist and snake down to the top edge of her jeans. It slipped beneath the denim, and then beneath the elastic waistband of her cotton bikinis and slid down the crack of her ass, seeking her wetness.

"…cast it out…" Her words were slow to come, thick. Her tongue grew dry as she panted.

"…cast it out…" Greg said.

The hand pushed between her thighs, pressing higher, stroking her core.

The tail inched its way beneath her clothes, finding her center, boldly pressing forward. The hand withdrew and the thick, tapered end of the tail found her slick wetness and eased inside.

"…of this home…" Assumpta groaned, her breath shallow and rapid. She widened her stance, allowing the creature better access.

"…of this home…" Greg echoed.

Hips pressed. Released.

The tail withdrew. The hand pressed forward, stroking. Assumpta's hips bucked. She sank as the shaking muscles in her legs refused to hold her up.

Greg tightened his grip on her shoulders. He pulled her to him and she felt his erection, hard against her ass, as his hands held her up.

Her minion moved, blowing moist, hot air against the side of her neck as it slithered its way to the front of her. She felt one clawed hand at her nape, felt him shift down the front of her chest, then grab her left breast and lift it.

Then a hot, gritty tongue laved her nipple.

The hand between her thighs unbuttoned her jeans and drew down the zipper. It found the edge of her cotton panties, and slid between them and her skin, finally…finally reaching the spot Assumpta yearned for it to touch. Several fingers found her molten center, pressed high, then withdrew. Pressed again, and withdrew.

Please, she thought, knowing it sounded like a plea for mercy, but recognizing in her heart she wanted more.

Hips pressed against her ass, then released.

The hand jammed forward again, thrusting, urgent, then rubbed against the overheated nub of flesh between her thighs.

"…and back to…" Assumpta could barely whisper the words of the prayer.

"…and back to…"

She stretched to reach the top of the last window jamb with the oiled brush, her body taut. Greg was pressed against her, now holding her arm, directing it, as she seemed unable to do. He pushed her forward, bowing her back, stretching her higher. Tighter.

Her minion swiped his gritty tongue across her nipple. Its mouth opened wide to suck at her breast. The nipple extended, the creature's mouth grew hotter, and Assumpta could imagine the flames of Hell licking at her naked skin.

Hips pressed. Released.

The fingers delved between her legs.

Her minion slid his tail down the cleft of her ass, dipped into her core. Then he bit down on her nipple, and rasped his gritty tongue against the turgid, straining flesh.

"Hell!"

She convulsed, all the muscles at her core clenching and unclenching.

Greg still held her around the waist, holding her up. But she could feel herself sliding out of his grasp.

Her knees collapsed. She sank to the floor, Greg lowering her easily, sinking to one knee. He kept his arm around her waist, waiting, while she caught her breath.

A few minutes later, she sat up, brushing the hair out of her eyes. She didn't feel the presence of either hitchhiker, not that she'd be able to tell the difference.

"What the hell just happened?" Greg asked.

"If you don't know, Greg, I'm not going to be the one to tell you."

"Why are they doing all this to you?" he asked. "It's my home we're trying to secure. You're doing this for me." He fingered the torn edge of her blouse. "Even when I try to help you, they ignore me and hurt you. Why?"

"I think I only just realized myself," she said. She stood on shaking legs, dipped the brush once more, and ran a line of oil down the final jamb. Now, all three windows had been anointed as a unit and singly.

"It's not about you at all." She dropped the brush into the jar and set it down on the floor. "Where were you baptized?" she asked, but she already knew the answer.

He looked confused. "I've never been baptized," he said. "But what does that have to do with anything?"

"Everything," Assumpta said. "The creatures have no interest in you, because as far as they're concerned, you're already theirs."

"What?"

"You've never been baptized, Greg. Your soul already belongs to them. If you die tomorrow, you're going straight to Hell."

CHAPTER 16

"YOU CAN'T POSSIBLY BELIEVE I'M GOING TO HELL," Greg said.

Assumpta shifted, pushing her hands against the floor to sit up straighter against the wall. Her stony right hand scratched the floor, and she lifted it away fast, hoping it wasn't a permanent mark.

She couldn't believe Greg wanted to have this conversation right now.

She just got *fucked* by a demon, and he was too busy thinking it mattered if he went to Hell or not. It wasn't like she didn't care, she did, and she was going to help him with that, but *really?* The state of Greg's soul wasn't the elephant in the room.

"It doesn't matter what I think," she said, finally.

"Why not?"

She licked her lips, still dry from the recent ordeal. How could she explain it to him without sounding like a cold-hearted bitch? The fact is, she wasn't really sure if he were going to Hell. Not really. Unbaptized babies who died were sent to Limbo, so it was possible that Greg would go there, too. But he'd had a lifetime to make mistakes, which was why she naturally assumed he'd be going to Hell.

And that bothered her, because she found herself caring about him enough to explore a deeper relationship. He'd make a great boyfriend; was definitely marriage material. He was interesting, and nice, and didn't seem like the usual assholes she met in her neck of the woods, who were charming, but only enough to get their own way or into someone's pants. If she didn't have the evidence of some demonic gargoyles to prove her wrong, she wouldn't have thought he was going to Hell. If anything blossomed out of this business relationship, they'd definitely have to work on that. And, besides, he was intelligent and attractive. She liked him. She could live with that for a while, and ignore the rest, if it turned out permanency wasn't what Greg wanted.

And he's rich, too. Imagine what you could do with access to all that money. The sound of her hitchhiker speaking into her ear startled her. She drew in a quick breath.

"What?" Greg asked.

"You didn't hear it?" Assumpta closed her eyes and willed the little bastard to go away.

Greg shook his head.

Good thing, she thought. "Just my little friend, offering me advice." Her voice was matter-of-fact. Inside, she seethed. If hers was here, then Greg's was, too. How would they ever get rid of them?

Greg smirked. "Telling you how you can send me to Hell even quicker?" he asked.

"Are you kidding me?" Assumpta asked, staring him down. "Now you think *I'm* out to get you?"

"It's not an unreasonable assumption."

"Based on what? You're getting paranoid." She picked at the rip in her shirt. Blood stained both sides of the tear where sharp claws had scraped down her ribs, but only the barest scar remained as proof she'd even been injured.

There was no way she was telling Greg what the demon said. They might have a chance, if she didn't poison it from the beginning by looking like a gold digger. She pulled the edges of the shirt together, suddenly cold.

"What matters is if *you* believe you're going to Hell," Assumpta said, "and you're certain you don't want to go. Make changes in your life so you don't wind up there when you're dead."

"But Hell doesn't exist."

"Obviously, you believe it does," Assumpta said. "Because if you didn't, it wouldn't matter to you what I think, and you wouldn't be so worried about the possibility of burning in the flames of Hell for all eternity."

Greg opened his mouth and shut it again.

"Sit tight," he said, standing. He walked down the hall toward his bedroom.

Assumpta sat up taller against the wall, noticing the waistband of her jeans hung open, the snap clearly popped during her ordeal. She snapped it shut with her stone hand, a click of her fingers against the metal snap she could hardly feel.

Greg returned, shaking out a folded, navy blue T-shirt with one hand. "Put this on," he said, kneeling beside her. She leaned forward and he slipped the shirt over her head. Soft cotton brushed her cheeks and chin, and settled around her neck. Greg placed a hand on her back to steady her as she lifted first her right arm, and then her left to don his shirt.

"My parents were atheists," he said, pulling down the shirt in the back and then pulling away. He sat down beside her as she leaned against the wall again. "They raised me to be the same. I've never considered that they might be wrong—that *I* might be wrong—until now."

He combed shaking fingers through his hair, pushing it off his brow and into a pompadour Elvis would have envied. He licked his lips, then said, "I can tell you how people from all the major religions in the world worship. I'd estimate I know the facts for as many as a hundred or more minor religions, as well. I even know the intimate details of the practiced religions of at least ten dead civilizations: the Aztecs, the Sumarians, the ancient Egyptians..." His voice trailed off. "But I don't know anything about Hell. It's a fairytale, a *Grimm* one, but still just a story. And now I find I need to know as much about it as I do anything else in my field...especially if I want to avoid it. I don't know the first thing about avoiding Hell."

"Have you ever worshiped any false idols?" Assumpta asked.

"No," Greg said.

"Ever stolen anything?"

"No," Greg said.

"Lied about someone's character?"

"No."

He was smiling now. Did he think this was a game? she wondered. Surely he must have heard of the Ten Commandments.

"Ever killed anyone?"

"Jesus, no!"

Assumpta laughed. "Well, you were doing pretty well before you took the Lord's name in vain. But even that can't buy you a place in Hell. You're doing okay for a non-believer, but you do have some ground to make up."

"Like what?"

Where to begin, she wondered…

"You'll need to choose a religion and follow the tenets of its faith—"

"Catholicism?"

"Or any other Christian sect," said Assumpta. "They all believe in the existence of Hell. You could just as easily decide on a non-Christian faith, such as Islam or Zoroastrianism, but probably not Judaism. They don't believe Hell exists."

"I don't want to join some cult. I just want to avoid Hell."

Assumpta let the insult slide past. "Don't you want to go to Heaven?"

"Heaven doesn't exist."

"How can you be certain that it doesn't?"

"No proof."

"I need a drink," she said, standing on shaking legs. The chill of the cold tile had seeped through the seat of her jeans. "Non-alcoholic. Can we continue this discussion elsewhere?"

"Right this way," Greg said, standing and leading her into the kitchen. He pulled a chair away from the table, and motioned for her to sit on his way to the fridge. He grabbed a pitcher of iced tea from the top shelf and snagged two stemmed glasses hanging upside down from a rack above the sink with his free hand.

Greg sat, and Assumpta said, "I don't understand how the demons can prove the existence of Hell, but the other things you've seen—like the crucifix burned into my stony hand—" she held it up for him to see "—*don't* prove the existence of Heaven."

"Not all things have opposites," Greg said. "Maybe demons just don't like what crosses represent. It doesn't mean that a crucifix has godlike power imbuing it."

"And the oil?"

He shrugged.

"You're a hard person to convince," Assumpta said. She took a drink of the tea. "I'm not sure I'm up to the job of teaching what you need to know to avoid Hell."

"You don't have to convince me of anything," Greg said. "Just tell me the things I need to do—or not do—and I'll take it from there."

"According to which religion…and whose interpretation?"

"All of them. That way I can't fail."

Despite herself, Assumpta found herself smiling. "Ever the pragmatist?"

"Ever," Greg said, grinning back at her.

She took a long swallow of the iced tea, then twirled the glass by the stem. "It's not that easy. Besides, I'm not versed in all the religions. You'd be better off mentoring with a priest, or maybe a professor of religion. Hell! You probably know more about other religions than I do, with all your archeological studies." She took another drink. "You know, most religions believe there is only one god in the universe. And there are members of all religions who believe it really doesn't matter what religion you follow, just so long as you declare one and adhere to those rules. That in itself should get you into Heaven."

"Sounds like a bunch of flap to prevent another holy war."

"You want another holy war?"

"Just sayin'," he said. He took a drink of his tea, then set the glass on the table, his fingertips resting on the base of the glass. "You're Catholic?"

Assumpta nodded. "Born, bred, and raised. But I'll be the first to admit I don't always follow the rules."

"Just so long as you know them," Greg said.

"Better than I'd like to," she admitted. "You can't break the rules without knowing them first."

"Then we'll do it your way," Greg said. "Where do we start?"

Assumpta blew out a deep breath. "If you're serious, we need to get you baptized as soon as possible," she said. "If you're baptized, you can't go straight to Hell if you die."

"First thing in the morning?"

"I can't. I've got to look for work."

Greg frowned. "Take the day off. I'll pay you to go with me to the church."

"It's not that easy. I might earn a few dollars going with you in the morning, but I might lose out on getting steady work. Besides, we need to call ahead and set up an appointment with Father Tony."

"Then call him up, tell him we need to see him in the morning."

"Father Tony does confessions on Wednesday; we could probably see him later in the week, or early next week."

"Even if the state of my soul is in peril?" He smiled as though he were joking, but Assumpta got the impression there was steel behind Greg's words.

"I'll try, but just because you are having a crisis doesn't mean they have to treat it like an emergency."

"Then offer him a donation to see us in the morning."

"Bribery will get us nowhere."

"If that's the best you can do," Greg said. "I'll work with it."

Assumpta very gently sat her glass of iced tea down onto the table. If she didn't, she felt like she might slam it down and shatter it to bits. Right now, she couldn't deal with one more mess in her life. But she also couldn't deal with Greg's attempted manipulation, or high-handedness, or whatever it was. Maybe he was just used to paying people to jump. Whatever. She wouldn't jump, and she didn't need his machinations right now.

"Thanks for the loan of the shirt," she said, getting to her feet, "but I've got to be going. There's just one thing…"

She hated asking, but she needed the money to pay the rent. A few minutes ago, she might have felt too embarrassed to ask, but now she had righteous anger burning down her spine. No need to screw up her courage to ask for what he owed her so far.

"About the money…"

"You want it now?"

She nodded. "If you don't mind."

Greg stood, then walked to the oak secretary by the door and pulled his checkbook from the drawer. "What changed your mind?"

"I realized I could use a few extra bucks this month since I haven't found a job yet."

"You mean so maybe you could get yourself a decent meal or two?" He finished signing his name and tore the check off the pad. "Stay a bit longer and I'll make us some eggs, sunny side up."

Assumpta colored, but she took the check he offered. "Can't," she said quietly.

She shoved the check into her pocket without looking at it, then gripped the doorknob, but found she couldn't turn it with her stone hand.

She twisted it awkwardly with her left and opened the door. Then, she felt the same tug on her as in the church, only instead of keeping her from an altar, this pull tried to prevent her from crossing the blessed threshold. She stumbled.

"Assumpta?"

"My minion doesn't want me to leave," she said.

"Why not?" He looked truly puzzled.

"Because he doesn't want me to cross the blessed boundary. I suspect this is going to hurt."

"Then stay."

"I've got to get home," she said. "Thanks for the offer."

As she stepped over the threshold, her minion hissed and dug his claws into her shoulders.

"Shit!" she cried. Even braced for the pain, it hurt.

"I'll walk you to the elevator," Greg said.

"Don't." Assumpta held up her hand. "There's no sense you getting hurt, too. Besides, you'd have to cross back again." She turned her upraised hand into a wave. "Goodnight."

"'Night," Greg said. "Be safe."

She imagined she could feel Greg's eyes on her as she walked away.

If she'd turned around to look, she would have seen them on her, too.

R AIN SPATTERED ON THE SIDEWALK. TINY, RAPID drops hitting the cement with enough force to make a walk home miserable. From the looks of it, it had been raining a while.

Assumpta was damp, her hair limp by the time she'd walked a block and a half to the bus stop, but at least her legs weren't shaking anymore. She hid her stone hand in her pocket, away from inquisitive eyes.

The rain seemed to invigorate her, but she had no desire to arrive home soaked. She could spare a dollar for bus fare if she skipped breakfast in the morning.

She couldn't wait to get home, take a shower, and fall into bed, to rid herself of the faint odor of wet cement and her own sweat. But first, she'd have to bless her own doorway again, because she didn't have any pain when she left this morning. She must have done something wrong.

Slow traffic impeded the bus, and the ride felt longer than usual. But the rain picked up in earnest, and she was glad to be on the bus.

What to do about Greg? He went from needy customer, to willing compatriot, to demanding employer all in the space of a few days. Had she read him wrong? Just when she was thinking it might be nice to explore the possibility of a relationship, he'd gotten all demanding.

Maybe it's the stress, she thought. *Who wouldn't get all weird with a gargoyle hanging around and the promise of eternal Hell if he accidentally tripped down the stairs?*

Her stop was coming up. She stood and pulled the cable on the bus, signaling to the driver she wanted to get off. The bus slowed right in front of her apartment building.

Someone had been evicted earlier in the day. All their stuff was sitting in a huge pile on the side of the road. *Poor bastard.* Now that she had a check from Greg, she wouldn't have to worry about eviction until next month.

She pulled the check out of her pocket and looked at it, stunned to see three zeros in front of the decimal point on the check. With this, she wouldn't have to worry about the rent for a few months.

Crap, no! She couldn't accept it. She hadn't done *this* much work. She'd cash the check in the morning so she could pay off her rent, and then give the money back to Greg when she saw him later tomorrow. She wouldn't feel good holding onto the extra. If only she'd gotten rid of his hitchhiker…

The doors opened.

The bookshelves standing on the lawn looked just like the cheap bookshelves she owned. No surprise there. But the lamp looked familiar, too. And the crate she sat her altar on.

Her heart started pounding in her chest. *Oh, no,* she thought, rushing over to the shelves.

It's my stuff on the curb.

Tears leaked from her eyes, mixing with the rain.

"I'm only a day late," she said. "They've always let me slide a few days. What's going on?"

She heard a chuckle, the sound of withered leaves, and closed her eyes tight. The stiffness went out of her spine and she almost collapsed to the ground. Then anger stiffened her spine again. Could the demons be responsible for this latest train wreck in her life? She looked around.

No crowd. Thank God for the rain. It kept the scavengers away. But it hadn't been raining all day.

Here were her things laid out for everyone to pick through. Her clothes, her books, her dishes. How long had they lain here, exposed to the rain? How many things had already been taken?

She walked to the bookshelves, lying like dominoes on the sidewalk, her books strewn about, half on the sidewalk, half in the grass, muddy and trod on.

Where were her tarot cards? Her favorite ones from Italy, with artwork by Marcelli. She dug them out of the pile. Rain soaked, wrinkles rimmed the edges. If she didn't get them dry soon, they'd stick together and become useless.

At least she kept her dousing items with her at all times. *If she had lost her pendulum...* Well, she could make do with something else, she supposed. But the weight of it was such a comfort in her hand, it would be difficult to locate something similar in a hurry.

But the loss of her books was the most disappointing.

She clutched a first edition of Edward Eager's *Half Magic* to her chest, and looked for Patricia Coffin's Gruesome Green Witch. It was gone. *Fuck!* That had been her favorite.

Now what was she going to do?

CHAPTER 17

S HE RAN TO THE CORNER PAY PHONE AND DUG
Greg's card and a couple of quarters out of her purse.

Ring.

She waited for him to answer.

Ring.

What if he'd gone out after she left? It wasn't that late. Maybe he decided to go have a few beers.

Ring.

He could be in the shower, she thought. "Come on…come on," she said, her fingers drumming on the top of the payphone. "Pick up."

Ring.

She'd try him on his cell phone if he didn't pick up on the next—

"Hello?"

"Greg, I need your help."

There was a pause on the other end of the line.

"Please." Assumpta closed her eyes, wishing for him to help her. If he didn't say yes, she didn't know what she was going to do. Even if she called her father, he wouldn't help. And her mother wouldn't go against her father. And since she and Caroline were on the outs, there was no help from that quarter, either. But Father Tony might be able to do something if Greg said no.

Please don't say no, she thought.

She heard Greg exhale loudly. Then he said, "We're in this together. I'll help in any way I can."

Assumpta exhaled, too, her shoulders slumping. She could feel the tension dissipate, and knew she shouldn't feel this relieved relying on someone else.

"I've been evicted."

"Not a problem," Greg said. He sounded almost cheerful. "You can stay at my house. Come on over."

"My stuff," she said. "I need help with my things. They're all over the place. It's raining."

"Where do you live?" he asked.

She hated telling him. Hated admitting where she lived, but she gave him the address. She had no choice if she wanted to salvage anything here.

There was a pause. "I'll be there in twenty minutes."

He knows the area, she thought, sinking. He knows how bad it is. But he didn't say a word.

When he arrived, she was digging through her books, dumping them into some trash bags she'd found with her kitchen items.

"Thank goodness you're here," she said.

"Least I could do." He brandished two large boxes. "Let's get the most important items out of the rain first." He looked around. "Where's your computer? Your iPod? Any electronics?"

"This is the most important," she said, handing him her father's account book and the box of associated receipts. "Can you get this out of the rain?"

"What's in the box" he asked. "Photos? Scrapbooks?"

"My entire life."

He nodded. "I'll be back for the TV."

She didn't have a TV, a computer, *or* an MP3 player. Very little of her stuff would be of interest to anyone except herself. Most of her things were secondhand, including the books, but she had a few special items she wanted to rescue. The receipt book, of course, and the little bits of jewelry from her grandmother.

The furniture wasn't worth saving. Let the apartment complex worry about getting rid of it. Without the shelves, and most of the books she wouldn't be taking, there was precious little to pack up.

She found the two crates that had been her altar. The bottom one, containing the holy books, decorations, and extra salt and oil, had been spared the brunt of the moisture, thanks to the curtain protecting it.

From the top crate, the statue of Mary had been broken, as had the bowl of sand containing her candles. She left those. The rosary dish had been overturned and stepped on, the beads ground into the rain-soft earth. She tugged the muddy strands from the dirt and pocketed them. They'd need cleansing, but that was easily done. The picture of Christ was missing.

Who steals a cheaply framed magazine cutout of Jesus?

"What next?" *Greg asked, coming up beside her.*

Really, she thought. *What next?*

She pointed to the two crates and tapped the bag of books with her right foot. "These, and some clothes, and we're out of here."

"That's it?" asked Greg.

She nodded, picking up the bag of books and heading to her dresser. "That's it." Assumpta dug through her underthings for the knotted sock she kept her grandmother's earrings and locket in. She pocketed that, then dumped the drawer into a kitchen-sized trash bag. The remainder of the bureau and her closet fit inside it, too. She tossed that into the back of Greg's SUV and made a face. She could have pulled her stuff to his house in her old Radio Flyer wagon.

"Thanks," she said, getting into the car and buckling the seatbelt. "I appreciate this."

Greg focused his attention in the mirror on the driver's side door. He nodded, then pulled away from the curb and made a quick U-turn in the middle of the street.

"I'll be out of your hair just as soon as I find a new place," she said.

"Stay as long as you want." He looked briefly in her direction, then resumed watching the road. "You can stay in the guest room. I store some stuff in the closets, but it goes mostly unused."

Assumpta smiled. Even if she believed he meant it, she couldn't stay. It wouldn't be right. And she had a feeling she could get awfully used to living in luxury, even if it wasn't her own. A girl could grow soft in that environment. She needed to keep on her toes if she was going to get ahead in life.

On the other hand, a hot shower every night instead of lukewarm would be divine. Maybe she and Greg could work out a rental arrangement. *Pipe dream,* she thought, smiling to herself. She couldn't afford even a fraction of what Greg was paying.

IN A SINGLE TRIP, GREG AND ASSUMPTA CARRIED her belongings through the building lobby and into the elevator, and rested them in Greg's foyer until she could decide what to do with them.

"Home, sweet home," Greg said, wincing as he crossed the barrier Assumpta had placed there earlier. He closed the condo door behind them, saying, "We've got to figure a way around that so we can come and go without the little bastards causing us any pain." He walked toward the hall. "Let me get some sheets from the closet."

She nodded, then looked around the room. Where could she set up her altar?

"Why don't you take a shower and warm up?" Greg asked, shrugging out of his jacket. "I'll light a fire and put some sheets on the bed in the guest room. Or, if you're not ready to get some sleep, we can have a drink and chat."

"Sounds wonderful," Assumpta said, grabbing the trash bag she'd dumped all her clothes into. "I won't be long."

"Take as long as you'd like," Greg said. "Would you prefer coffee or something stronger?"

"Maybe some decaf," Assumpta said on her way down the hallway. "I want to have a clear head tonight, and in the morning."

"I'll start the pot after I light the fire."

S HE COULD HEAR THE FIRE CRACKLING AS SOON as she opened the shower door. Once she got past the steam of the bathroom, she could smell the aroma of fresh coffee. It didn't matter if it was decaf, she wanted a big mug, filled to the brim.

Her stomach rumbled.

And a cookie. Maybe Greg had a few peanut butter cookies stashed away somewhere.

She sniffed the coffee again, and smelled...*bacon?*

Turning the corner of the hallway, she could see the fire crackling in the grate. Her things had all been piled neatly in the corner, minus the bag of clothes, of course.

Greg had set her altar crates near the hearth, stacked like a bookshelf. *I can work with that,* she thought, smiling.

She turned into the kitchen to see Greg hard at work, flipping thick slices of bacon sizzling in a cast iron skillet on the back burner of the ceramic range. Onions simmered in a stainless steel frying pan in the front. Chopped mushrooms waited in a small white bowl, as did grated cheese. A carton of eggs sat beside them.

"You've been busy," she said.

"I thought you might be hungry."

"I suppose you guessed *I haven't had time for a meal or two* since I stormed out of here earlier."

Greg colored. "About that—"

"Forget about it," Assumpta said. "You're entitled to your opinions... and as a matter of fact, you wouldn't be wrong this time." She opened the cabinet she knew to hold coffee cups and set two oversize mugs down on the counter. She retrieved creamer from the refrigerator and poured it liberally into Greg's mug, then returned it before pouring hot coffee from the fresh pot into both. "I *am* hungry. I was going to be the worst of guests and shamelessly beg you for a cookie or two."

Greg dumped the mushrooms into the bubbling pan and mixed everything together. He opened a cabinet above the stove and grabbed a stainless steel mixing bowl, into which he cracked six eggs. "I was out of line."

"Apology accepted," she said brusquely. "Stir in the eggs already. Can we make some toast?" She was practically salivating over the smell of the bacon. She couldn't wait…it was one of her favorite foods and she rarely had it, unless she caught a really good sale at the grocery store. Bologna, or peanut butter, was always more affordable.

"Toast would be great," Greg said.

He whipped the eggs with a hand whisk and poured them into the skillet. Steam flashed out of the pan with a loud sizzle, and then everything quieted while the eggs fried. He dumped in the cheese, then used a metal spatula to chop and turn the eggs, making fluffy bite-sized pieces instead of folding the eggs over into a traditional omelet.

"I love breakfast for dinner—or a late night snack," Assumpta said, opening a loaf of bread. She put four slices into the toaster oven, thinking she'd eat three if Greg decided he didn't want more than one. Her stomach growled again. *I could eat a horse,* she thought.

"And it's fairly inexpensive," Greg said.

"If you skip the cheese, and the bacon, and the mushrooms…"

Greg turned and gave her a knowing look. "Which I'm guessing you do most of the time," he said. He turned back and reached for the skillet. Tilting it, he put half the eggs on each plate he'd taken down from the cabinet earlier.

Her face flamed. She could feel the heat rising up her cheekbones. "You read my book," she accused.

"Or maybe I guessed by the lack of pantry items we moved here tonight, or by the fact that you got evicted at all."

She felt like a heel, jumping to conclusions. Hadn't she warned herself of that the first time she saw this place? "I'm sorry," she said, her voice small. How would she make this up to him?

"No apology necessary," Greg said. "I–"

"No, you're right–"

"No," Greg said, turning to her. "*You're right*. I owe you an apology. I read your book." He leaned his hip against the counter, watching her. "I was moving the box and it slid off the top. You said it was 'your entire life.' I thought it was a photo album. That implies sharing. I didn't know it was a private ledger. I'm sorry."

The timer on the toaster oven buzzed. Assumpta piled the thick slices on a plate, grabbed the butter, and walked to the table. Greg followed with the plates, then grabbed their coffee.

"You could have stopped reading once you found out what it was," she said, sitting down. She grabbed the first slice of toast on the pile and started buttering.

"I am all too guilty of finding it extremely interesting," he said, sitting and reaching for the ketchup, salt and pepper. "What kind of father insists a child pay him back for all expenses incurred over the years? I can't imagine living with that personality type. It takes all kinds of psychotic diligence to maintain records like that year after year."

She took a bite of toast, chewed and swallowed. He had a point, but he'd still intruded. "You had no right."

Greg nodded his head. "You're right, I didn't. But I'm glad I did. Now I've got a better idea of why you're working the way you are." He used a piece of dry toast to push a mound of eggs onto his fork.

"You know, legally, your father doesn't have a leg to stand on," he went on. "You really don't have to pay that money back."

"Yes, I do. If I don't pay, he'll throw my mom out. I can support myself, but not both of us. She's never worked a day in her life."

"Admirable, but your mom's a big girl. She can take care of herself."

"I couldn't live with the guilt."

Greg nodded. "I figured as much. That's why I've got a proposal for you."

"I'm not sure I want to hear this," she said.

He looked up from his plate. "Don't worry. It's not anything indecent. It's just that I know you're worried about money, and I have plenty of it. How does fifty dollars an hour sound?"

Assumpta did some quick mental calculating. Fifty dollars an hour equated to...*more than a hundred thousand dollars a year, full-time!* She knew folks in the Roland Park area of Baltimore had tons of money, but not that many tons. Who knew?

Was he insane? She'd be a fool to turn that down, but she'd feel like a prostitute every time she cashed a check. She couldn't do it.

"I don't want your charity."

"It's not charity. Think of it as a full-time gig until we get rid of our hitchhikers."

"But—"

He pointed at her with his toast. "It's not like you're going to milk me dry. And I know you're not going to take advantage of the situation. I know you want them gone as fast as I do." He raised his eyebrows. "Faster, probably. With that motivation, I know you'll work hard. And if you can do it full-time instead of job hunting and worrying about how you're going to pay your bills, it's totally worth it to me."

It made complete sense, but she still found herself waffling. She set her fork down so she could take a drink of coffee. She took a long swallow of the cooling liquid and set the cup back down. After a moment, she decided she really had no choice.

"Okay," she said.

"Okay," Greg said, smiling. He shoved the last bit of toast into his mouth, dusted off his fingertips on his jeans, then held out his right hand for her to shake.

Out of habit, she stretched her right arm over the table to take his hand in hers, then drew it back once she realized she offered him her turned-to-stone hand.

Before she could lower it to her lap, Greg clasped it within his own, giving it a squeeze.

She couldn't feel his hand, but the heat of his palm seeped through the crevices in the pumice-like stone of her own and warmed it. Warmed her.

She hadn't felt this safe in a long time.

DEEP IN SLUMBER, ASSUMPTA TURNED HER FACE away from the warmth of the down quilt and rolled onto her back, slinging one arm over her head and pushing the covers down to her waist with the other. Cool air danced across her skin.

Soft fingers reached for the hem of her shirt, tugged it from beneath the covers, and pushed it upward. A warm hand smoothed across her belly, and higher. The soft, warm pad of a thumb brushed the underside of her breast.

Warm, moist air blew across her nipples, tightening them, making them pucker and ache.

Assumpta, barely awake, thought herself in the throes of an erotic dream.

"These beg for my attention," a voice whispered in her ear while a hand, hot as though warmed from the fire, slid across her breasts.

The bed dipped, and hard flesh slipped across her own. The muscles of her stomach tightened as a hot tongue flicked out and caressed her left breast, gliding from the full underside and over the top. A hot mouth captured her nipple and sucked.

Assumpta felt the pull in her groin, a flash of molten flame from the tip of her breast to her aching core. She felt herself grow hotter. Liquid pooled between her thighs.

Strong arms wrapped around her shoulders and hugged her tight. The hot mouth and tongue moved to her right breast, laved and suckled.

She wrapped herself around him, her arms reaching up to grasp at his shoulders. Her legs twining with his.

His weight slid off to her left side, and she felt bereft, but only for a moment. A hand smoothed down her arm, down her thigh, and nudged two fingers under the edge of her bikini briefs. Clenching it in his fist, he tugged, and they ripped through like paper, tearing off of her with ease.

The fingers smoothed over her mound, dipped two fingers into the crevice between her legs and felt the slickness pooled there.

"You ache for my touch," he whispered, stroking.

Assumpta moaned. She was on fire.

The weight leaned against her again; he laved a budded nipple, then sucked it into his hot mouth. He sucked boldly, flicking her nipple with bold presses of the tip of his molten tongue. Finally, he grasped her nipple between his teeth, biting gently, then abrading the engorged flesh as it slipped from between his teeth and out of his mouth.

He rolled on top of her once more, settling himself heavily between her legs, flesh to flesh, groin to groin.

"You want more of my touch," he whispered in the darkness. "You want me inside you."

Assumpta was beyond speech. She nodded, clutching at him once more.

"You want to come," he whispered again, pressing forward with his hips. She raised her hips to meet his.

"Let me in, Assumpta," the voice whispered, deep and husky. "Yield to me." The tongue slid across her neck and suckled the sensitive spot near her shoulder. Between her legs she felt the weight of a giant erection pressing against her. His hips flexed in rhythm, making promises she wanted him to keep.

The muscles in her groin tightened. Much more of that and she wouldn't need him inside her to climax.

"Say you want me," the voice whispered in her ear.

"I want…" she whispered, her head lolling back into the pillow.

Barely awake, she opened her eyes. He was gorgeous: piercing eyes, patrician nose, full lips. And below that, a body that begged to be touched, the kind that looked equally at home in a T-shirt or a tux. Six-pack abs, strong arms, muscled thighs…

...but he was gray as granite, and glowing in the firelight. She might have mistaken him for a ghost, or an angel, *a fallen angel,* but she smelled the telltale odor of wet cement.

Ripped from the sexual haze as quickly as if she'd been doused with cold water, Assumpta struggled against this new threat, pushing against him, trying to break his grip. The creature was suddenly hard as stone. In fact, it *was* stone. She felt herself rattling against it as she shook in fear. Her heart beat so rapidly, she could hear it in her ears.

It smiled at her: a sex-filled gaze, holding all the promise of a lover.

"I won't hurt you," it said, melting back to flesh and teasing her with a hip thrust. "You'd like it, you know, if we had sex. I could make it so good for you." Its casual voice sounded so matter-of-fact, Assumpta thought she could have been talking to any of the guys she met in the downtown coffee shop.

"No," she said, struggling anew. Its hug was stronger than any of the guys she'd ever felt. And she could tell it wasn't even trying.

It smoothed a warm hand across her right breast, tweaking the nipple. "You liked how it felt. You enjoyed me tasting you." It slid down, grasping her hips and dipping its beautiful face to her mound. It breathed in the scent of her, then placed a moist, open-mouthed kiss in the soft hair curling at the apex of her thighs. "You would love it if I kissed you here. I could make you come five times over before we moved on to anything serious."

"No!" Assumpta said, pushing at its shoulders.

It looked up at her. "Did you know, that when you fuck a creature like me, you're privy to everything it knows? Wouldn't you love to know what we're doing here? At Holy Rosary? With Greg? How about if I tell you how you can get rid of us? How to cure your hand? Or Greg's wound?"

"You're lying," Assumpta said. She pushed up, trying to dislodge it, but it held her hips too tightly in its grip.

She should call for Greg. He would help her—again. *But I am not some helpless waif,* she thought. *I can do this on my own.*

"I can't lie to you," it said, brushing its cheek against her sleek thighs. Its head dipped lower, blowing warm air on her legs, *between* her legs. It bit her gently on her inner thigh, then soothed the abrasion with its heated tongue, moving upward, closer to the place she both needed it to caress and hoped to God it wouldn't touch.

"I can refrain from saying anything, I can tell you only part of the story, but I can't outright lie."

It dipped his tongue into her slit, and she gasped, throwing her head back and squeezing her eyes shut. Its tongue felt better than any sex she'd ever had, thick and solid, slick as marble. Hot. How could a creature of stone be so hot? She pushed against the creature's shoulders, tried to wriggle from its grasp.

"Why can't you lie?" She could barely force the words past her lips. She wanted to give in, relax, let it finish what it started.

Still gripping her thighs, it forced her knees wider with its elbows, opening her wide. It flattened its tongue against the tight bud at her core and pressed, then licked upward in a single strong stroke.

"Power is limited. It's the balance of things." It dipped its head and licked her again.

"So, what's in it for you?" She gasped at its touch. "I've got nothing you could possibly want."

"Pleasure," it said, looking up at her. "How often do you think I get this opportunity?"

She snorted. "And a gold star."

"A gold star?"

She glared at it. "A prize, an accolade, a reward…something for tempting the human, and winning." She found her fear lessening. It wasn't hurting her. It was bringing her pleasure. Could this thing be telling her the truth?

"There is that," it said. "But consider what you'll be gaining in the process. So much knowledge you could put to good use."

"There you go, tempting me again."

"Is it working?" It smiled and dipped its head again to her liquid heat.

Yes. She admitted it to herself. It was very tempting. She had a hard… *male*…in her bed, and it obviously knew its way around women. What would be the harm if she gave in? It wasn't as if she would actually burn in Hell for eternity for having sex, even if it were with a demon.

Was it a demon?

"No," she said for the third time, and the creature disappeared in a puff of smoke and the smell of wet cement, leaving her panting and wet and more unfulfilled than she'd felt in a very long time.

CHAPTER 18

ASSUMPTA WAS AT THE KITCHEN TABLE DRINKING coffee when Greg walked in from the hallway, his large duffle slung low over his shoulder. He dropped it on the floor in the foyer and joined her in the kitchen, stopping first to grab his checkbook and some keys from the secretary, and then for a large mug of coffee.

Butterflies jumped in Assumpta's belly. This didn't bode well. Greg looked grim. "Going somewhere?" she asked. *Or am I?*

Greg took a large drink of his coffee, then nodded. "There's a small dig in South Carolina. One of the college interns uncovered an urn very similar to the one we found in Virginia. The site manager wants me to look at it and see if it's related."

"They can't just e-mail some photos?"

"They did," Greg said. He leaned back in his chair and ran a hand through his shower-damp curls. The action pushed the hair off his forehead. The cut where he'd hit it on the steering wheel was just a pink line now. "And it's because of those that I'm headed out to Devil's Island. But part of the process involves looking at the surrounding area to see if there are other similarities. They could photograph that, too, and they will. But it's not as good as seeing it firsthand."

She took a deep breath. "Will you be gone long?" *Dumb, dumb, dumb,* she thought. Did she sound like some clinging girlfriend? It wasn't as if she had designs on Greg. But she was staying in his house. And being alone had never bothered her before. She'd lived on her own for a lot of years, without so much as the protection of a dog—but then, she'd never been evil-plagued before. Even though Greg was just as much a novice in this arena, he was still a comfort to have around.

"A few days," Greg said. "I'll call you if it's going to be longer than that."

"You're not afraid of *infecting* the crew in Carolina?"

"Sure I am. But I can't *not* do this," he said, taking another drink of his coffee. "I'll be careful not to touch anyone. And I'll do whatever I can to hurry back." He took another swallow of coffee, then set the mug down. "You'll have to postpone our meeting with Father Tony today. Sorry."

"And if you get yourself killed on the way to Carolina?"

He had the grace to flush. "I'll have to take my chances. There's too much at stake."

"Your immortal soul isn't?"

"Is that what we're really talking about here?" He raised his eyebrows and stared her right in the eyes. "Look, I know you're afraid to be here alone. Hell, I'd be, too. But I can't stay. I need to inspect the urn in person to see for myself what it is." He paused. "Do you want to go with me?"

Tempting, she thought, looking into his eyes. Did he want her along, or was he just offering out of kindness? There would be nothing for her to do there. And how would he explain her presence? *This is my friend Assumpta; she was too scared to stay home.*

"I'll be okay," she said. *I can be strong,* she thought.

Greg nodded. He opened the checkbook and wrote, and then pulled out his wallet. He handed her the check, three hundred dollars cash, and the keys. She glanced down at the check. *Two thousand one hundred dollars.* She knew they'd made an agreement, but seeing it come to fruition was another thing altogether. She felt her heart start to pound in her chest. Something good *could* come out of this situation, couldn't it?

"Deposit the check as soon as you can," Greg said. "I'll set up an automatic wire transfer after this. The cash is for groceries and incidentals that might pop up around the condo while I'm gone. The keys are for you, so you can come and go as you like. Feel free to invite someone to stay with you if you want."

She walked him to the foyer so she could lock up behind him. He picked up his duffle. "I'll call you when I get to Devil's Island," he said, opening the door and breaking the salt-and-oil barrier with a mop commandeered for the purpose. Then, he leaned down and kissed her softly on the lips, and walked out the door.

Well, that answers the question about whether he wanted her along or not, she thought.

She felt light-headed as she threw the deadbolt. *What have I gotten myself into?*

ASSUMPTA WAS ASLEEP ON HER BELLY WHEN THE demon materialized under her, soft and warm as a man of flesh. He stroked her back, her flanks. He spread her legs and rocked his hard erection against her, softly, to bring her pleasure.

Her breathing deepened, her mouth parting, each exhale a sigh that dampened her lips.

The demon slid his hands down the small of her back, under her cotton underwear and over the small swell of her buttocks. He arched up, and pulled her toward his erection.

"Wake," he breathed into her ear, and smiled at her as her sleepy gaze took in the perfection of his features. His hands came up, caressing her rib cage and the sides of her breasts, and then traveled down her torso again.

And then she was full awake, pushing against his manly, firm chest, and sitting up, her thighs splayed over him. His erection touched her even more intimately.

Light from the street lamp outside her window streamed into the room. He looked more beautiful than the last time she had seen him, less gray, more fleshly. *Could he control that?*

"I knew you would like it on top," he said, "where you can feel more of me inside you. Give in." He smiled wickedly. "You know you want to."

"No," she said. And then she qualified it. "Not with you."

She struggled away from him, but he put his hands on her thighs and held her down against him. Her heart danced in her chest, but she didn't feel as scared as the last time the demon came to her. Still, she tried to pull free.

"Think of what you could achieve." He loosened the grip on her legs, and stroked them instead, his thumbs pressing intimately into the flesh on the inside her thighs. "Think of what you could know." His hands warmed her skin, their heat much warmer than her own.

She shook her head. But, oh, she wanted to enjoy him. By sleeping with him, could she actually learn what she needed to know?

"Is it my appearance you have an objection to?" He smiled. "I can be whatever you want." His skin pinked, his hair turned darker, curlier, and his full lips became a dusky hue. She smelled chocolate.

He looked more handsome than anyone she'd ever met. A dark Eros.

He laughed, soft and low. "Perhaps you seek something different?" His hair grew out in dreadlocks, his skin darkened. His thighs grew massive, and harder, his chest swelled with muscle, his arms bulged. He reminded her of a football player on the Baltimore Ravens team. He looked—and felt—delicious. She could feel every solid inch of him. This time, she smelled cologne, something tangy and cool. She could swear a breeze blew through the room.

She was tempted, very tempted. For a demon, he had treated her almost fairly. She didn't want to hurt his feelings. He offered her much, if what he said was true. But how could she trust him?

"It's not that what you offer isn't enticing," she said, pushing against his muscles, still trying to break free. "It's that what you offer comes with some serious strings, and I'm not willing to give up my soul for a fleeting moment's pleasure."

"Oh, I assure you," he said, in a voice that sounded like liquid chocolate, "this would be no fleeting moment's pleasure. It's as much for me as it is for you. I will make it last," he thrust his hips against her core, "all," he did it again, "night," and again, "long."

She groaned. He had her so excited, he could almost make her come right there. "No," she said. "You're not my type."

He morphed back to the gray Adonis she had first encountered.

"I can heal your hand," he said, lifting it from his belly and bringing to his mouth. She struggled against the pull, but he was too strong.

His long, gray tongue slid from between his gray lips and delicately touched the tip of her index finger.

The pain was immediate.

"It burns!" she screamed, pulling harder.

"But only for a moment," he said, putting the finger between his lips and sucking it into his mouth.

It didn't hurt so much, but it was warm, tingling everywhere his mouth touched.

She yanked, pulling her finger away, and it was flesh again, pink, as if it had been washed in hot water, but very much her own skin.

He grasped her hand again, much gentler, drew it toward his mouth, and suckled each finger in turn. The pain grew less the more he touched, until finally, the heat of his mouth, the touch of his tongue, felt more like a lover and less like any demon spawn she'd ever imagined.

When his tongue traced the underside of her wrist, she could feel her pulse beat against his hot, moist flesh. She ripped her hand from his grasp, and held it up in the dim window-light to see.

She flexed all her fingers, bent her wrist. *It's a miracle,* she thought, then considered the source, and frowned. Definitely *not* a miracle. *But what do you call an amazing feat performed by an evil creature?*

Was he really evil? She was beginning to wonder.

"I told you I could help you," he said. "Now it is time for you to help me." He reached for the straps of her camisole and pulled them down over her shoulders. The silky material dipped between her breasts.

He reached a hand to one still-clothed breast and swirled his fingers around her nipple.

At the same time, he arched up, pushing his huge erection against her. Making her feel his need. Coaxing a similar response out of her. She felt herself grow wet.

With his other hand, he grasped her behind the neck, and gently pulled her down to meet his kiss. She sealed her lips shut, and he ran his tongue along the seam of them, pressing for an opening. He arched again, pinching her nipple, and Assumpta gasped.

He took advantage, his tongue flowing into her mouth like liquid silk.

She heard the voices then. A cacophony of voices, some screaming, some crying, all trying to be heard at once. She heard her name called half a dozen times, heard it shrieked and moaned and yelled to get her attention.

She broke the kiss and tore her face away from his. "No!" she said for the third time, shaking. *What had she heard?*

He narrowed his eyes at her, staring her down.

"If you're certain," he said, grasping her hand once more and bringing it toward his mouth. This time, he blew across her fingertips, then disappeared.

Alone once more, she turned on her back and slid down onto her pillow. She grasped the covers and pulled them up, her right hand stiff. She turned to look at it, and as she watched, it turned to stone again.

CHAPTER 19

SHE KNEW WHAT SHE HAD TO DO.

She had to go to Holy Rosary and find the relic brought as a gift from the Vatican from one of Cardinal Karol Wojtyla's visits to Baltimore. Saintly artifacts emitted holiness with their very presence. Maybe she and Greg could use it to fight the minions, and use it against the main demon controlling them. Worst case scenario: it could be used to heal Greg or her own stony hand. But demons—even minor minions—wouldn't want to remain for long around a holy artifact, right? She didn't know for certain, but she had to try.

And she hated to go alone, but she hated just sitting and waiting even more. She didn't need to apartment shop or job hunt for the moment, so this was as good a time as any to get it. And when Greg got back, they could use it together.

Sunday morning, she rode the bus to the corner of Bank and Chester and walked to the rectory. Mass had already begun. Even from the street Assumpta could hear the clarion resonance of the pipe organ.

Perfect, she thought. Anyone likely to care about what she was going to do was probably all tied up in church. *No prying eyes.*

She looked up and down the block; no one approached the church. For all intents and purposes, she was alone. She bounded up the steps of the rectory and turned the handle, then stepped cautiously into the foyer.

No pain. Did that mean the rectory wasn't blessed, unlike the church, or that her minion didn't travel with her this morning? She had no way of knowing.

She looked around. It had been a long time since she'd been this far into the rectory. A black-and-white tiled hallway led all the way to the kitchen area in the back. Three rooms veered off on the left, and two on the right. But a wide staircase on the right led up to the second story.

Assumpta pulled her pendulum from her right front pocket and ran her fingers down the string to straighten the kinks. She released the glass and let it dangle, then took a deep breath to center herself. She had limited time before Mass was over and the priests returned.

She started with an easy question to make certain she and the universe were connecting.

"Am I standing in the church rectory?" she whispered.

The pendulum hung slack for a moment, then began a slow clockwise swirl.

Yes.

"Is there a missing church relic in the rectory?"

Yes.

Excellent. She wasn't on a wild goose chase. She would find Holy Rosary's missing relic, use it to rid the church—and her and Greg—of their demons, and then return it. She felt a small pang at the duplicity; she really ought to give it to Father Tony once she found it, but she couldn't be certain he would let her use it before he locked it away again. It had to be done this way.

"Is the relic I seek in a visible location?"

No.

I knew it wouldn't be that easy, she thought. Time to narrow down where it might be hiding.

"Is the Vatican relic in the upstairs rectory?"

The pendulum dropped straight as if someone had pulled it taught. A pause.

The pendulum started a slow swing back and forth.

She knew that meant the answer is not available at this time. Was she asking the wrong question?

Maybe if she rephrased it.

"Am I in the rectory?" she asked.

The glass teardrop stopped its to-and-fro motion and began a slow clockwise movement.

She nodded, bobbing her head up and down. Okay, things were on track again.

"Will I be able to find a relic from Rome from here?"

The circling continued.

She wondered what about her phrasing the first time caused the spirits such problems in answering.

"Will I find the Vatican's relic here?"

The pendulum dropped straight down again. Why was there a problem when she asked about the Vatican?

She had a sudden thought: "Is there more than one relic hiding on Holy Rosary property?"

The pendulum made a clockwise circle.

Assumpta smiled. *Two relics. How would their combined power work against the demons?*

"Will the Vatican relic be found in the rectory?"

The circle slowed and reversed. *No.*

Too bad, she thought. Finding them both here today would have been a massive boon.

She checked her watch. Half past. She had about twenty minutes to find what she was looking for and get out.

"Is the relic on this level of the house?" she asked.

Counterclockwise. The pendulum didn't pause.

"Upstairs?"

Still, it turned counterclockwise.

"Downstairs?"

The pendulum slowed and began a turn clockwise. She needed to find a cellar door. *Where's the likeliest place?* she wondered.

"Are the stairs down in the kitchen?"

Counterclockwise.

She raised her brows and thought.

"Are the stairs down in a hallway?"

Counterclockwise.

"Are they in a mudroom or entryway of some kind?"

Clockwise swirl.

She smiled. *Getting closer.*

She spied a door to her left and opened it. Closet.

She'd walked around the outside of this building a thousand times in her life, but she'd only been inside a few times. The only other entrance to the building existed in the rear. She walked the hallway to the back, passed the kitchen, she noted, to a screened-in porch.

The porch covered an external entrance to the basement, two metal doors she could pull up to reveal a staircase down into the cellar. Her grandparents' old house had had a basement like this. They'd always referred to it as the storm cellar. Very common in Baltimore row homes. When her Mom was a teen, they'd added stairs on the inside of the house so they could reach the basement without going outside. Many folks did. She wondered why the church wouldn't do the same. She guessed the covered porch was their concession to the need.

Well, hell, she thought. If she'd known she needed to get to the storm cellar, she could have skipped the search through the rectory and come right through the tall gate in front, then head to the rear. She'd been entering and exiting this courtyard for years, stopping to fill up her holy water jar from the large blessed urn the priests kept in the back for needy parishioners.

She looked around. Thankfully, no one else was in the walled backyard. Too bad the only exit from the yard was a gate opening on the same side of the street as the front rectory door. It would have been sweet to slip out the back once she completed her task.

"Am I in the right place?" she whispered.

A clockwise swirl confirmed it.

"I hope there's a light down there."

She pulled open the right-side door, and stared at broken concrete steps leading into darkness. *Good thing it was only six or eight steps down.*

She stared down into the hole. She'd seen these storm cellars before, played in her fair share of them as a kid. So why was this one making her feel uneasy?

Because it wasn't as well-maintained as her grandparents', she thought. Where theirs had had overhead lighting and linoleum tile, here a single bulb hung from a wire over a dirt floor.

The cellar must have been used as a root cellar, or cold storage, at one time. Floor-to-ceiling shelves lined each wall and jutted out perpendicularly like a library. Empty glass jars clustered together on the top row of one shelf. An age-blackened barrel rested in one corner. *This place could have held enough foodstuffs to feed a large cadre of men,* she thought.

Maybe with the dearth of young Catholic men joining the priesthood, the church found no need to use this space, and therefore no need to keep it up. *Also stood to reason why you might find a hidden relic here,* she thought. Someone had put it here for safekeeping, and either forgot about it, or forgot to tell someone else about it before he passed away.

But why keep it secret to begin with? Most churches put their relics on display for public veneration…unless they were afraid the artifacts would be stolen. Was that why this one was hidden?

"Is the relic on a shelf?"

Counterclockwise swirl.

"Under a shelf?"

Counterclockwise.

"In the front half of the cellar?"

Counterclockwise.

She looked at the barrel in the back corner of the room.

"Is the relic in the barrel?"

Counterclockwise.

"Under the barrel?"

The pendulum slowed and reversed. Clockwise.

"Bingo," she said, heading to the back of the room.

Assumpta wrapped the cord of her pendulum around her fingers until it was neatly coiled, then shoved it into her right front pocket. She grasped the barrel by the top rim, and tried to pull it away from the wall. It stuck in the dirt, but by rocking it back and forth, she loosened the hold on it, and tilting the barrel on its bottom edge, rolled it away from the corner.

She knelt and clawed at the damp, hard soil once hidden by the barrel, finding it hard to dig with her stony hand, but not impossible. Dirt caked beneath her fingernails, but she'd hardly scratched the surface. Needing a shovel to dig for the artifact hadn't crossed her mind when she started this. Could one of the glass jars be used?

She walked to the shelf and plucked a two-quart, wide-mouthed Mason jar from the nearest shelf and returned to the soil. Facing the top of the jar away from her, she laid the lip of it to the soil and angled it like a shovel, pushing against the base of the jar for leverage.

The first push sheared away about a quarter inch of dirt. The second push, about the same. The third time she tried, the jar sank deeper into the soil at the far edge of the hole she'd planned to dig.

She concentrated there, the jar digging away more soil with each pass.

Even in the coolness of the cellar, sweat beaded on her brow. Her hands ached from clutching and pushing the jar. But ten minutes later, she found something.

Two inches below the surface, a corner of blackened canvas poked out of the dirt. She abandoned the jar and pulled at the soil surrounding the cloth, and after a few minutes of hard work unearthed a canvas-wrapped package.

It weighed about a pound, she guessed, unwrapping the decaying outside layer of canvas to find a second underneath. Within that, she found an ornate, carved box, slightly larger than a pack of cigarettes, made of pink wood, perhaps rosewood or red oak.

There were no markings to indicate what might be inside, nothing to reveal who the box might have belonged to. She ran a finger over the satiny sheen, looking for hinges, and found none. She turned it over to look at the bottom, rattling the contents inside.

When Assumpta turned the box, the lid slid to the right, revealing a slice of the inner cache, some small items trying to escape through the crack. She righted the box so nothing would fall out when she opened it, then slid the top all the way open.

Bones lay jumbled in a heap on a purple satin pillow.

Finger bones?

They were old, brownish in color. Some were pitted.

Without thought, she raised her right hand—her stoned hand—and pushed aside some of the top layer of bones with her index finger.

Her hitchhiker, who'd been silent until this time, screamed and became visible. Its claws bit into her flesh as she felt the pressure of its legs spring and jump away from her. Still yowling, it scampered up the concrete steps and out into the churchyard, fading to invisible the farther away from her it ran.

"Damn," she muttered, reaching up to feel her neck, but was gratified to find her skin remained unbroken. She could do without any more blood or scars from these creatures. *But good riddance,* she thought, smiling. The minion's abrupt departure confirmed one of her ideas: that they couldn't stand to be around the artifact. Too bad it hadn't stuck around longer; she'd have loved to have touched the bastard with these bones. Maybe it would have exploded.

She looked to the box again, once more pushing aside the bones, and noticed that her index finger had turned back to flesh. She could feel the cool, dry smoothness of some bones, the rough texture of the pitted ones, against the pad of her finger. After a few seconds, even her fingers that weren't touching the bones also returned to flesh.

A smile lit up her face again. She had found her cure. She had no idea whose bones these once were, but obviously they were holy. She'd found one of the relics she needed.

She reached for the lid to seal the box, but once she no longer touched the bones, her fingers turned to stone again.

"Well, that's no good." There was no way she was going to hold somebody else's finger bones in her own hand for the rest of her life just to enjoy the benefits of her own flesh. Then she recalled how her other fingers returned to flesh, even though they weren't touching the bones. She had an idea.

She pushed her left hand into the box. It took a minute longer than when she'd touched the bones with her stoned hand, but the fingers on her right hand once again turned to flesh.

I could make a necklace out of one of the bones, she thought, then shook her head. These belonged to the church. She might be able to touch them for a moment, but she couldn't keep them, not even one. There had to be a way for the bones to bestow some holy magic on her to heal her hand once and for all. She'd ask Father Tony when she delivered these later.

First, she wanted to see if they could heal Greg's wounds.

She slid the lid back on the box, wrapped it in both layers of canvas, and shoved it into her purse.

She climbed the steps to the backyard, then closed the cellar doors and headed for the tall gate to exit onto the street. With a sinking heart, she saw the padlock securing the gate. Someone had forgotten to unlock it this morning. She'd have to exit through the rectory after all.

She heard the skirl of the pipe organ and recognized the beginning of the closing hymn. She needed to move fast. People would soon be exiting, if they hadn't started already.

CHAPTER 20

FOUND SOMETHING USEFUL, HAVE YOU?"

Assumpta startled at the sound of Father Hughes's voice. Her stomach plummeted to the tiled floor as the triumphant smile slid off her face.

Had she lost track of time? She couldn't have. All the cars were still parked in front of the church.

That's what she got for not checking the schedule: probably some visiting priest had celebrated Mass this morning, freeing Father Hughes and Father Tony to attend to some other business. And now here they were.

Father Hughes looked pissed, and he approached her with such speed she thought he might do something rash, like take a swing at her. She couldn't run. That would be admitting guilt. But he practically blocked her escape anyway, once he'd gotten close enough to her. He could grab her, if he tried.

"Just getting some holy water," she said, trying to buy some time. If push came to shove, she could pull out the jar in her purse. She tried vainly to remember if it were full.

"If you were after any valuables," he said with a casual flip to his voice, "you should have tried the church. The plates and chalice on the altar could have gotten you at least a hundred dollars at a nearby pawnshop."

"I'm not here for valuables," she said.

"Oh, no?" asked Father Hughes. "Then what are you here for?"

His anger must have blinded his common sense, because Father Hughes stood just far enough away for her to see his aura, brown, with a decaying black around the edges. She knew something wasn't right about him. How could he have risen so far within the church? His soul was rotting from the inside out.

Father Tony stepped closer. He gave her a reassuring smile. Her heart slowed its thumping pace.

"Assumpta and I have an appointment today," he said. "She knew it was possible I'd be running a few minutes late. "

"You had no appointments on your calendar for this morning," said Father Hughes.

"I must have forgotten to update it."

"That's no reason for Ms. O'Conner to be wandering around the rectory."

"I told her it would be okay to go on out back to get some holy water if I hadn't arrived yet."

The older man turned to face him. "You allowed her to roam through these business offices?"

Father Tony nodded. "She's been here many times before. She knows the way."

"You're lying," Father Hughes said.

"Then I'll confess and do penance," said Father Tony. He turned to Assumpta. "Did you get what you needed?"

She almost shook her head *no*, thinking about the little brown bones. Father Hughes' aura flared bright red in anger, covering the sickly brown for only an instant. But she managed a weak, "Yes. Thank you."

"Then let's get going. We've got lots to discuss today."

"I believe we should call the police, Father Tony. This girl has no right going through the rectory. Who knows what she could have taken? At the very least, she needs to empty her purse so that we can make certain she hasn't stolen anything." He reached for her purse, but Assumpta took a step back.

"That won't be necessary," Father Tony said. "I know she'd never do such a thing."

"I insist," said Father Hughes.

"I'll vouch for her," Father Tony said. "If anything's missing, I'll take care of it." He turned to Assumpta again. "Let's get going," he said to her.

Assumpta brushed past Father Hughes and walked beside Father Tony down the long narrow hall to the staircase. They walked up side by side in silence.

When they reached Father Tony's office and stepped inside, Father Tony shut the door behind her with a decisive click. Assumpta let out a noisy exhalation. Then she started shaking.

"Thank you," she squeaked out before collapsing into the nearest chair and dropping her purse at her feet.

Father Tony took the seat beside her. "*Did* you find what you were looking for?" He gave her a pointed look.

"I didn't have much time to look before I got caught."

Forgive me, she thought. She didn't like lying to Father Tony, but she didn't want him to get mad at her again. And she needed to take the bones home for Greg. If Father Tony knew she had them, he'd want her to surrender them. She couldn't do that. Not yet.

Father Tony nodded. "I assume you were looking for the relic. What makes you think it's here in the rectory?"

Assumpta tilted her head and gave him a disbelieving look. "Do you really need to ask that?"

"So, you're going on gut instinct."

"Now you're being deliberately obtuse."

"It's easier to accept that you have some intuition—that you are a student of human nature—than to believe a pendulum speaks to you."

"It's not the pendulum that speaks."

"Is it God?"

"Maybe."

He gave her a dark look. "That's nearly blasphemy."

"Why?" She stood up, glaring at him. "Why is it blasphemy to think that God might be speaking to me through the pendulum? Maybe concentrated prayer doesn't do it for me. Maybe *He* chooses this way to get His point across."

"God doesn't work that way."

"'God works in mysterious ways,'" Assumpta said.

"An over-generalization, boiled down into a trite statement for the masses to latch onto," said Father Tony.

"It's scripture!" she said. "*Oh, the depth of the riches and wisdom and knowledge of God! How unsearchable are his judgments and how inscrutable his ways!*' Romans 3, Chapter 11."

"You would quote the bible to prove a blasphemous point?"

"Isn't that what you do from the pulpit every Sunday?"

Father Tony stood up.

Now I've done it, she thought, backing up a step. *I've gone too far.* "I think I'd better leave."

Father Tony's face was nearly as red as his Christmas cassock, but he didn't say a word as she inched toward the door. Assumpta thought he might be counting to ten to get a grip on his temper. She couldn't blame him. What she'd said was pretty inflammatory.

Finally, he said, "What will you do with the relic if you find it?"

She motioned with her stony hand. "Take care of this, I think."

"Assumpta!" he said, running toward her, staring at her hand with wide eyes. He stopped short, lifted his arms like he might take her hands with his own, but caught himself. He lowered his arms to his sides. "What in Heaven's name is wrong with your hand, child?"

"Not Heaven, Father." She told him what happened.

"I also think the relic will help Greg's bites. I thought I might borrow it to accomplish that and then return it to Holy Rosary." She looked him in the eye and said dully, "I still think it will be a major coup for you if we find it."

Assumpta opened the office door to leave and found Father Hughes waiting in the hallway. "What will be a major coup for Father Tony, Ms. O'Conner?"

164

Assumpta gasped. She hadn't expected anyone to be waiting outside the door.

"If the Pope would visit Holy Rosary on his next visit to the states," Assumpta said, wondering where that lie had come from. "We've already had a visit by one pope—we could be known as the Pope Capital of the U.S."

"That hardly seems a possibility, does it?" Father Hughes said. He turned to Father Tony. "Are the two of you done? I'd like to have a little chat with Ms. O'Conner."

"Assumpta was just leaving," Father Tony said.

"This will only take a minute."

"Another time," said Father Tony. He gestured for Assumpta to precede him out the door and ushered her down the stairs. After a few steps of silence, he leaned close to her and whispered, "I'll look for the relic. I'm still not certain I can let it leave the grounds of Holy Rosary, but if I find it, perhaps we can help you and your friend Greg."

She nodded. It was the best she could hope for, given the circumstances. Maybe he was coming around after all.

They walked the rest of the way down in silence. Assumpta was hyper-aware of Father Hughes watching them as they departed, her heartbeat quickening in her chest.

They stepped out of the rectory into bright sunshine.

"Do not return unless you're here to meet me," Father Tony said, stopping at the threshold. "And if we do have an appointment, wait for me to meet you outside. If you don't see me, don't come in."

"You've realized there's something wrong with Father Hughes, haven't you?" she said. "You can call it gut instinct if you want, but something's warned you about him."

"I know nothing of the sort," he said, sighing heavily. "But I've seen power and blind ambition firsthand in the church, and it pays to stay out of its way. I don't know how simple trespassing has put you in the line of fire, but you're going to have to be careful of Father Hughes from now on. You've made a powerful enemy."

CHAPTER 21

HER DROP-DEAD-GORGEOUS DEMON WAS STANDING at the bus stop when she got there. The end of his red tie lifted and fell in the small breezes caused by passing cars. Wing-tip shoes peeked out from beneath his perfectly creased trouser legs.

"Careful," she said to him as she approached. "Dressed like that in this part of town means one of two things: you're either going to a funeral, or you've stepped out of Little Italy looking to recruit." She stopped just short of touching him. "And no one in this part of town will believe you're going to a funeral on the bus. It's just not done."

She offered it—*him?*—a brief smile. Why wasn't she scared of him? He looked human enough...*hell,* he looked good enough to eat, but that didn't mean he wasn't dangerous. So why was she happy to see him? It wasn't as if he couldn't turn the rest of her to stone in a single breath, right? Still, she couldn't help that happy feeling in the pit of her belly.

He looked down. "What should I have worn?"

"Jeans, steel-toed boots, maybe carried a tool box."

"For a job interview?" He sounded incredulous; a little haughty, even. Like butter wouldn't melt in his mouth, when they both knew it would sizzle away to nothing.

"Even for a job interview." She smiled. "This part of town is blue-collar all the way. But then, you knew that, didn't you?"

He nodded. She didn't doubt for a moment that he knew what she was talking about. He was a demon, after all. He'd lived thousands of years. He had to know everything about everything. And he had offered that knowledge to her. Right? What would it be like to know everything?

"Why are you here?" Assumpta asked.

"I thought neutral territory would be conducive to my convincing you to, ah, take my offer." He shoved his hands in his pockets and looked down. A dark curl fell over his forehead. Anyone looking in their direction probably thought he'd just asked her out. "Perhaps you would not feel so…*pressured.*"

"Isn't that the point?"

Again, he had the audacity to look sheepish. Maybe he wasn't faking that? Yet, she could hardly believe that. He was a demon, right? This was all an act.

"But I have pressured you," he said. "If you're not feeling the stress of it, than perhaps you're coming around to my point of view." He smoothed the tie over his flat abdomen and buttoned the suit to keep it in place. He leaned down to whisper in her ear, "We don't need to take the bus. I can whisk us back to your apartment in *less* than a blink of an eye."

That happy feeling just took a turn south. She grew warm, and knew a blush now crept up her face. "Not now."

"Later?" The look he gave her was pure sex.

"Let's just say I'm keeping an open mind."

"You need additional inducement?" He looked hopeful. "I can offer that as well."

Was he talking about bribery or seduction? Assumpta couldn't tell, but either suggestion had her considering possibilities.

"I need to believe that you're telling me the truth."

"I don't know how I can prove it to you."

"The trouble is," Assumpta said, picking at a thread on her handbag, "that you are untrustworthy by your demonic nature."

He shoved his hands in his pockets and rocked back on his heels. "I'm not—" he started to say, then stopped. "I understand."

"The only way to prove you may be trusted is through deeds at this point. I simply can't trust your word."

"What deeds would you like me to perform?"

Now that's an interesting question, she thought.

He pulled his hands out of his pockets and took a step toward her.

Assumpta felt herself leaning into him, even before he approached. He reached for her arms and pulled her close, wrapping his left arm around her waist and his right over her shoulder. He cupped the back of her head with his hand.

He didn't smell like cement in this human form. He smelled of wood smoke and citrus, and very, very manly. She could imagine him dressed in soft flannel and denim. He radiated warmth, and enveloped her in it.

He leaned his head down and touched his lips to hers, a brief contact, then pulled them away, teasing. Then, he leaned in firmly, pressing lip to lip. His tongue slid out of his mouth and traced the line of her lips, urging them to open.

The arm at her waist slid back, up her rib cage, and she felt warm fingertips brush against her breast.

She opened for him, and his tongue slid into her mouth.

Immediately, she heard the voices again. The sound of a thousand people speaking all at once, all clamoring to be heard. It was like being in a filled-to-capacity concert hall with everyone talking simultaneously, and the band playing on stage at the same time: too many voices, feedback from the speakers, reverberation of the guitar, and the pounding of drums, all an assault on her senses.

She jerked back. The voices stopped.

But he leaned in close, gathering her to him, and kissed her again. At once, she heard the cacophony in her head.

Listen. His voice in her mind rose above the rest.

Assumpta's eyes widened. His eyes danced as he smiled at her. *This is such an easy thing,* he whispered in her mind. I*magine what I can do with a little effort. Imagine what you can do with my help. Concentrate on a single voice—mine.*

She thought, *This is what you hear all the time in your mind?*

Yes, he thought to her. *It's the knowledge of everything. It's always here, I simply have to listen for it…as do you.*

What are all these voices? she thought to him.

They are the voices of those who have gone before.

All of those? Or all of those who have gone to Hell?

These are the voices of everyone who has remained.

"What?" she said, pulling back from him. The voices faded from her mind.

A small crowd had gathered at the stop, waiting for the next bus to arrive. The crowd was ignoring them, but it was clear they were interested.

"What?" he asked, all innocent, taking her cursed hand.

She looked down at their clasped hands. As she watched, the stone of her fingers melted away to flesh again. His hand was warm in hers.

"Let's walk," he said, looking at the others standing around. He tugged her in the direction the bus would have taken them had they gotten on.

"What do you mean by the voices being those who remained behind?" She tried to remember what some of the voices were saying, but she could barely recall hearing them. Their memory continued to fade as they walked.

"The spirits of the dead are all around us," the demon said. "Not everyone chooses to pass beyond the land of the living, once they've 'shuffled off their mortal coil.' So they stick around."

"You can avoid going to Hell?" Assumpta asked.

"Not at all," said the demon. "Once Satan claims you for his own, there's no avoiding it. But not everyone is eager to join Heaven's crowd, either."

They were approaching a sandwich board advertisement for a local café, and the demon steered her around it with a tug on her hand.

She stepped to her right, her hip and shoulder grazing his. "And God doesn't claim you as fast?"

"Uh-uh," the demon said. "Free will and all that, all the way to the last. Why would *He* want you in Heaven if you didn't want to be there?"

"I thought Heaven was a wonderful place to be."

"Not everyone thinks so. The alternative is rather bleak, though, so they spend their time here on this plane, hoping for some conversation. Most of the living can't see or communicate with them, so they are starved for attention."

"And that's why they talk to you."

"Indeed," said the demon. "And what they know is astounding."

They'd arrived at the door to Greg's condominium. She didn't remember walking much beyond the café, or even riding the elevator up to this level. "How did we get here so fast?" she asked.

"I distracted you," said the demon.

She frowned at him.

"I told you I could have you here in the blink of an eye," he said. "Did you really want to walk all this way?"

"I'd intended to take the bus," she said, fumbling in her purse for the keys Greg had given her.

"Here," he said, pulling her key out of thin air and handing it to her. At her angry look, he shrugged. "Just trying to help."

She took the key and unlocked the door.

"May I come in?"

"What, you can't cross the threshold?" She was being snide, and she knew it, but he had annoyed her—on purpose. She hated that.

"Actually, I can," he said. "Anything can. You've sealed the windows and thresholds throughout the house very well, but you've neglected to continue to reseal the door. Every time you go in or out, you weaken the bond. And there's a great big hole in the barrier here—" he rubbed the toe of one wing tip along the bottom of the door from just past center to the hinged edge "where something was dragged or scuffed across it."

Assumpta closed her eyes and leaned her forehead on the door. Well, she knew what she was doing tonight. No rest for the weary.

"I don't want to force my way in. I want you to trust me," he said. "So, may I join you?"

She shook her head, already thinking about what she needed to do to seal the door. *Did she have enough blessed salt?*

"No, you can't come in."

He leaned toward her, lowered his voice. "I can teach you more about the voices. I'll help you learn something you want to know."

"No," she said. "I've got too much to do." *And you'll only be a distraction,* she thought. *A major distraction.* She wouldn't mind seeing him again, though, on her terms. But how to get him to agree? "How about if I let you know when I'm ready?"

He grinned. "'Don't call us, we'll call you?' It doesn't work that way. You can only summon me if you know my name."

"So tell me your name."

He sobered in an instant. "No."

She'd figured he would deny her. Knowing a demon's name gave the ability to command it. It would have to do whatever the summoner required of it. Names were power in the demonic realm. Hell, names were powerful in this realm. She knew that firsthand.

"Then you'll just have to buzz off until another time," Assumpta said. "I'm too tired for any more of this tonight."

He bent to her ear and whispered. Her eyes widened.

"Really?" she said, and he nodded.

"But why would you tell me?"

"Actions speak louder than words," he said.

He was showing her he was trustworthy.

"So, can I come in?"

"Can you help me seal the door?"

A look of horror breezed across his face and was gone. It happened so quickly, Assumpta thought she might have imagined it, if not for the tremor in his voice. "I can't possibly help you in that endeavor," he said. "I can't get that near the holies."

"Then, no, you can't come in tonight, *Jak*." She used a diminutive of the name he'd given her. Something innocuous she could use in public, but not risk anyone else learning his full name.

He grinned once more, and lifted her right hand to his lips and kissed it. Then, he said, "Call me when you're ready." He walked down the hall toward the elevators, and disappeared.

She held her hand up, flexed the fingers, wiggling them, and smiled. He'd given her a second gift. The burn from the rosary and crucifix still marred the skin, but it least it was skin.

She turned the key in the lock and entered.

She shut the door, turned the deadbolt, and was attacked from all directions.

The first blow felt like a hammer to her stomach, knocking the wind out of her and cutting off the scream rising in her throat. She bent, retching, and clawed hands pounded on her back.

The sound of a rising windstorm keened through the condo. Papers blew around the room, books fell off shelves. Did a windstorm rage inside, or was it the inhuman speed of a dozen or more demons careening through the rooms? She wasn't certain.

More claws pulled at her clothing, dragging her prone to the floor. She screamed.

Kicks and punches rained down on her from all angles. Assumpta couldn't count the number of assailants. The pain was unbearable.

The smell of cement, and her own blood, grew thick in the room.

She raised her hands over her head to stop the blows at her face, squeezing her eyes tightly shut. One of the creatures grabbed at her ribs, ripping her shirt and digging four gashes into the delicate skin. She felt a stream of hot blood run down her side. Tears filled her eyes.

"Jak—" she whispered. "Jak—"

Diabolical laughter rang in her ears as the beating continued.

The door opened behind her, and someone stepped into the room. A pair of men's black leather shoes, black slacks, walked beside her. Her blood pooled around her, nearly touching the hard soles of his shoes.

"Enough," he commanded, and the beating stopped. "It won't be long now."

Silence fell. She could hear the slow thud of her heart ringing in her ears.

The man bent to Assumpta's purse and removed the relic, pocketing it in his greatcoat, then walked out the door, pulling it shut behind him.

Her eyes drifted shut. With effort, she forced her heavy lids open, but her eyes wouldn't focus. Was it dim, or was there a problem with her vision? She coughed, spewing more blood onto the floor. The cold of the tile floor seeped into her bones.

She couldn't move, couldn't summon the energy to cry out for help. She wasn't certain if she could.

Assumpta closed her eyes. Before she blacked out, she thought one word: Jak's full name.

JAK APPEARED, SMILING, THE INSTANT THE SOUND of the last letter of his name cleared her thoughts.

"God Almighty," he whispered, morphing from the dark Eros form back to his cement Adonis so he could save his energy.

He stuck his finger in Assumpta's blood and drew a perfect circle around her on the floor. With a snap of his fingers, four black candles appeared on the circle, one at each compass point: north, south, east and west.

He whispered a word of *command*, and the candles lit simultaneously.

On his knees outside the circle, he cried out to the archangel Michael for protection, then sank forward until his forehead touched Assumpta's blood, and recited prayer after fervent prayer to the Lord in Heaven, begging for her life.

CHAPTER 22

ASSUMPTA CAME TO WHEN THE DOOR BUMPED HER in the head.

She groaned, rolling onto her back. Every bone in her body hurt. There was something sticky on her face. She put two fingers to her brow and came away with congealing blood.

"What the hell?" Greg asked, poking his head through the door. Through slitted eyes, she saw his face drain of color. He squeezed through the opening, let his duffle fall to the floor, and dropped to his knees beside her, smoothing her hair away from her forehead with his left hand.

"Don't move," he said, pulling his phone from his hip and flipping it open. "You need an ambulance."

"Don't—" she croaked, her throat burning and dry. She tasted the sharp, metallic tang of blood on her tongue.

"Assumpta, there's blood everywhere. We need to make sure you're not bleeding internally. You could die."

"No ambulance." Her voice was stronger this time. She struggled to sit up, and Greg put a hand on her back, pushing her up. "If you take me to the hospital, they're going to book you for assault and battery."

"They wouldn't."

"Of all women who are assaulted and beaten, eighty percent of the

175

time it's a spouse or boyfriend." She hoped that wasn't true. But she needed a convincing statistic to keep Greg from dragging her to the emergency room.

"You shouldn't be moving," he said.

"I won't die. I remember—"

She remembered the pain, the stabbing cuts, the slice of nails and claws on her skin. She turned her arms over, looking at her wrists, the soft undersides of her forearms. She rubbed her right thumb across her left wrist, noting the absence of wounds, the absence of marks of any kind. Even the gravel scars she'd gotten as a child when she fell off her new bike were gone.

Yet, her hand was stone again.

Then she remembered *Jak*, kneeling beside her, candles flickering, talking softly. *Had he been praying?* She looked around for the candles, seeing none.

"Do you remember who did this?" Greg motioned with his hand to encompass the strewn papers, the paintings fallen to the floor, and ashes from the fireplace smearing the walls in a long trail from firebox to kitchen.

"You know who did this."

He nodded. "Our hitchhikers." Quiet tension laced his voice. Anger tightened his face. "We have got to find a way to get rid of them." His voice gentled. "But first, we've got to take care of you."

She pushed herself to her feet, feeling surprisingly steady, and walked toward the kitchen. "I need a rag."

Gently, Greg swung her up in his arms, and carried her toward the bathroom instead. "You need a shower." He sat her on the toilet lid. Then he opened the glass door of the shower stall and started the water. He leaned against the wall, arms folded on his chest. "You get cleaned up, and I'll clean the foyer." He paused. "And the rest of this place. Hard to believe two creatures could do such damage."

"Not just ours. They brought some guests. And their leader."

"A leader? He's the one who did all this damage?"

"He didn't touch me. He merely directed. Didn't even arrive until they were nearly done. Then he came through the door and told them to stop." She tested the water and adjusted the hot valve to warmer. "He took the artifact, and left me to die. Greg…" She brushed the hair out of her eyes so she could see him more clearly. "Their leader is human. I didn't see his face, but I know who it is. Father Hughes."

"Father Hughes?

"Another priest at Holy Rosary. He's the pastor—in charge of the church."

"Sonofabitch!" Greg's aura flared red around him. She didn't even have to squint her eyes to see it.

"I thought something was off about him," Assumpta said. "The last time I saw him, I got a look at his aura. Greg, his soul is foul. Tainted. He messed up when he let me see it, because in the past, I could never get a read on him. It's as if he knew just the way to keep out of my line of vision. I think he knows I have some…talents, though I can't imagine how he could have guessed. Father Tony wouldn't have told him."

"Why not?"

"He's my confessor."

Greg raised an eyebrow.

"Catholic thing. Confessing sins. Father Tony's not allowed to talk about them with other priests."

"Your abilities are sins?"

"In the eyes of the church, yes. Although Father Tony's not convinced I even have talents." She looked up at him and smiled. "Though I do believe I'm slowly bringing him around."

"He knows about the minions, though?"

She nodded. "Of course. And my hand." She lifted it for an inspection. Blood covered her palm, but it didn't look any different than its usual stony form. "It's going to cause him some problems."

"Why?"

"Well, he's known me since childhood, and knows the kind of person I am. But my talents have been associated with the devil, at least according to the Church. So he's conflicted. *How can such a kindhearted girl be in league with the devil?* Wait until he finds out about Father Hughes. Father Tony believes he's just trying to climb higher in the church. He has no idea."

Steam began forming in the bathroom.

"You take your shower," Greg said, moving to the door. "I'll clean the mess. Then we're going to talk about what to do next."

Once he left, Assumpta shed her blood-covered clothes and stepped into the shower. She turned her back to the stream of hot water, letting it massage the top of her head and run down her shoulders. Steam filled her nostrils, cloying, almost suffocating, but the heat penetrated her bones, warming her.

She soaped and scrubbed, going over every inch of her body as she did so. Though the drain ran red with blood, she couldn't find a single cut or bruise to prove she'd been beaten or stabbed near to death this afternoon.

It was Jak, she knew it. He'd heard her call, and he'd come to her rescue somehow. But what had he done? Whom had he called?

She imagined him on his hands and knees, licking every wound closed with that miracle tongue of his, closing the rips and tears, smoothing out the bumps and bruises. The thought made her weak at the knees, as she imagined him licking other places, too.

Was she sick? Daydreaming about sex in the same thought as being rescued by a demon?

He hadn't licked her, she thought, though she couldn't know for certain what he did. But she would have remembered that—at least, she hoped she would.

He hadn't touched her. He had lit candles and prayed. If his prayers didn't heal her, than the higher power to whom he called must have done so.

Not Satan. Satan wouldn't have healed her wounds. Did Jak not answer to the devil? Could a demon pray to God? She didn't think so.

Who was Jak? *What* was he? She couldn't work it out in her mind.

He can't be all bad, she thought. Anyone who came to her when she called, and helped her in her hour of need, was not self-serving.

Maybe he only saved you so he could fuck you later.

Where had that thought come from? Mortified, she could feel the blush rise up her face even in the warmth of the shower.

No, she thought. There's more to him than he presents. He's not entirely evil, though he certainly walks a dark path.

Could she help him? If she tried, what risks would she be taking?

The odor of cement rose out of the drain and her heart started thundering in her chest. Assumpta slammed the taps down, turning the water off, and reached for her towel. She wrapped her hair in it, pulled her terrycloth robe off the hook on the back of the bathroom door, and donned it as fast as she could.

She avoided looking into the mirror.

She hurried to the living room, the raucous laughter of her minion at her back. A fire burned behind the blackened screen. Vacuum tracks marked the bit of carpet around the tile floor. Greg's plaster-of-paris handprint sat as if undisturbed on its special plinth, but one of Greg's mother-goddess statues was missing, probably a casualty of the attack. No blood remained in the foyer, but pink and brown streaked the walls as if Greg had sponged them. Only paint would erase those tracks.

Across the room, Greg poured amber liquid into two brandy snifters.

"In a hurry?" he asked, walking over.

"Minion," she said, as if that said it all. "In the shower with me."

"You're okay?"

"Fine." She sat on the sofa, pulling her feet up under her, and grabbed a throw from the back of the sofa to cover her knees. Greg handed her a snifter of brandy. She took a tiny sip, letting the bitter alcohol roll around on her tongue before swallowing it. A tiny warmth suffused her chest, and she took a larger sip.

Greg smiled. "You look a whole lot better. Before—"

She told him what happened, glossing over the injuries she'd suffered, and telling him nothing about Jak.

"But you're okay now?"

"Yes, but we no longer have the artifact."

"That's the least of my worries. What's important is that you're okay." He looked down into his drink.

"We needed that artifact," Assumpta said. She told him where she'd found it. "I opened the small box and put my hand inside, and my minion ran off as if its tail were on fire. We could have used it to fight them off. Maybe even heal you." She raised her stony hand. "When my fingers came in contact with the bones—"

"Bones?"

"Finger bones, I think. But there were no markings. I don't know which saint they belong to, either. When I touched them, my fingers turned to flesh again."

"Isn't that, well, gross?"

"Better than the Miracle of Lanciano, Italy, where they keep 1300-year-old flesh and blood in a sanctified crystal chalice on a high altar so you can stare at its decomposing mass during Mass. At least bones are dry."

"But it's *bones.*"

"I would not have pegged an archeologist as squeamish."

"I'm not squeamish. It just seems to me that the body of a purported holy figure in the religion ought to be laid to rest with a bit more pomp and reverence."

"It's just a body," Assumpta said. "Although the Catholics would agree with you on principle. That's why they don't allow cremation. When the trumpet blows at the end of time and we all rise up, we need a body to rise up in and all that. But relics like these were big business in the Middle Ages. All kinds of people got chopped up."

"But—"

"It doesn't matter," Assumpta said. "What matters is that when I touched the bones, my fingers turned to flesh again. Even when I touched them with my left hand, my fingers became flesh. It took longer, as though the holiness seeped into my bloodstream and had to find its way over to the *infection*, but it worked. If those bones can do that for my hand, what do you think it will do for your bites?"

"But it's gone," Greg said.

"We could steal it back."

"No way." Greg stood and started pacing. "It's one thing to take something from an empty rectory. I'm not letting you attempt to steal anything from Father Hughes. He nearly killed you." He paused. "Would any relic do?"

She thought for a moment. "I suppose if it were as holy as this one, it could work. Do you know of another relic?"

"I have several contacts in the archeological community. Someone might have something. I could probably arrange a loan."

"Father Tony mentioned another artifact at Holy Rosary, but it's been lost for decades. No one knows where it is, but rumor suggests it might be in the church somewhere." She let out a heavy sigh. "It might take some work to find, but we could look for it."

"No. Not just yet. We don't even know where to begin to look for that. It could be a wild goose chase." He sat again, turned toward her, face earnest. "There's got to be a way for me to put this right."

"It's not your fault, Greg."

"Of course it's my fault," he said, standing again and pacing to the fireplace. "If I hadn't asked you to help me with this, you wouldn't be plagued with your own hitchhiker. You wouldn't have been alone in my apartment, and you wouldn't have been attacked."

She couldn't argue with his logic, but it made no sense for him to take the blame.

"You couldn't have predicted this," she said. "It's okay. I'm not angry with you."

He sat down beside her. "Assumpta…" He put a hand on her knee.

She'd known this was coming. Had dreaded it since the day he kissed her. He was going to make her choose between him and Jak. He didn't even know about Jak. As if she did.

Greg leaned in to kiss her, and she pulled away.

"I'm sorry," he said, moving inches away from her. "It's too sudden, I know, after what happened tonight."

"It's not that, Greg."

He looked at her. "There's someone else." It was a statement, not a question.

"No," she said, then took a drink of the brandy. "Not a person."

He gave her a questioning look.

"A few hours ago, if you had walked in on me, we probably would have needed that ambulance, but…" She took a drink of the brandy, then forged on. "They came out of nowhere, as soon as I opened the door. More than I could count." She paused, felt the blush on her face, embarrassed, because she wasn't stronger. "There was nothing I could do."

Greg's face grew grimmer as he listened. She told him about the speed of their attack, about not knowing whether it was that or the number of them, or whether there had been an actual windstorm in the apartment.

"And this non-person?"

"I'm getting to that." She took another drink of brandy. "He's come to me before, though not with any intended malice. He wants me to do something for him. He—"

She didn't know what to say. How do you explain that he was not a bad demon—she wasn't sure he was a demon at all now—who wanted to have sex with her? And that by doing so, she would be helping him? Why would she want to do it? Was she getting anything out of that deal? Well…great sex, apparently. Probably, if the lead up had anything to do with it.

But it was *sex*, for heaven's sake. She wasn't one of those Catholic prudes who was saving herself for marriage, but she also didn't run around having sex at the slightest provocation. She liked to know someone for a while first. Make sure she wasn't going to get AIDS. Can you catch an STD from stone? What if he had some weird demon disease? Wasn't turning to stone bad enough?

She looked down at her stone hand, wondering if it would ever turn to normal.

"What does he want you to do?" Greg asked.

She took a deep breath. "I'll get back to that. First, let me tell you what he did *for* me. I was dying—lying there in my own pooling blood, with the rest of it draining out of me from the cuts and slashes of the demon claws. There were several, including at least one stab wound just under my ribs." She leaned back into the sofa cushion and rubbed the area.

"I knew there had to be more to the story. There was just too much blood on the floor for there to be nothing wrong with you," Greg said. "It looked like the aftermath of a massacre."

Assumpta nodded. "I was as good as dead, and there was no one here to hold my hand while it happened. But I knew if I called *him*, he would come, and he did. I had no expectations of anything but to have someone here while I died. Greg, I have no idea what connections he had but I remember him praying, some candles, and not much else. I woke up when you bumped the door against my head."

"Why didn't you tell me this earlier?" he asked.

"I wasn't sure you'd believe me if I told you what happened."

"After all we've been though?"

"What have *we* been through?" she asked, feeling a touch of anger. She'd been trying not to feel resentment, but it just seemed to bubble up out of her. "You came to me looking for help, and I was infected. I've been beset by minions. I've been the target of a seduction. I've nearly been killed. I've gone looking for something to help us—and found it." No need to mention that she no longer had it. "What have you done?"

CHAPTER 23

I'VE SUPPORTED YOU," SAID GREG, JUMPING OFF the sofa and pacing angrily to the liquor cabinet. He turned back to face her. "I've given you food, a place to stay, and money besides."

He set his glass down, then retrieved the brandy and poured himself another two fingers of the amber liquid.

"But—"

"And, I turned all your paperwork over to my accountant to see if he could get you out of that goddamned mess your father's blackmailing you into." He slumped back onto the sofa. "Not that he's really got a leg to stand on."

"You had no ri—"

"And," Greg said, cutting off her objection once more, "I rushed down to South Carolina to see if that urn had anything to do with ours. I'm contributing as much to this endeavor as you are."

Well, that told her, she thought, teeth clenched. Very quietly, she asked, "Have you considered how easy it is for you to give those things and how very hard it is for me to accept them?" She pulled her knees to her chest and wrapped her arms around them, suddenly chilled.

Not easy, she thought. With a father like hers, she'd had to learn to stand on her own, early on, even before he hit her up for almost two hundred thousand dollars. And she was proud of what she'd done so far. She didn't need Greg's help. She didn't *want* to need his help.

The mantle clock ticked, marking off the silence between them.

"What did you learn in Carolina?" she asked, wanting to put the argument behind them.

Greg took a drink of his brandy. He took so long, she wasn't sure he was going to answer. Finally, he said, "The urn could be a duplicate of the one we found in Virginia, though it's in much better condition. It's almost like it's been housed in a warehouse. You'd think it had been crafted just last week."

"Could it have been kept safe somewhere?" Assumpta sat back against the sofa. "Could there be more demons inside of it?"

"You know, I hadn't given its condition much thought until now. But maybe it *has* been kept safe somewhere…although where, I've no idea. I suppose it could have been kept in a private collection, but that wouldn't explain how it was found buried in Carolina." He looked into his brandy glass. "We are talking demons here…could it have been held somewhere…*otherworldly* until now?" He shook his head. "Even that doesn't sound plausible to me. As for other demons… I had a good look at it. On the surface, it doesn't look like the seal's been broken, but I found a very slender hole drilled into it, almost needle-thin. I thought at first that something had tried carefully to get into it, but in retrospect, I suspect that something very carefully bored its way out— so that it wouldn't be caught. Whatever was in there was long gone."

"The archeologists in Carolina hadn't seen the hole?"

"They had. But it's so small, they didn't realize its importance. I didn't enlighten them—"

"They would have called you crazy," Assumpta said, looking up.

He nodded. "I thought as much, too, so I kept my mouth shut. They got permission to open it up and let me observe. Of course they found it empty—but I have to admit I was holding my breath the entire time. What I know about demons tells me that it didn't matter how small that hole was, they were getting out. But the pragmatist in me believed we might find something; nothing could get out of a hole that tiny."

"Of course. Were you able to examine the inside?"

"Yes, and I found tiny scratch marks on the inside near the hole. The other archeologists agree that something bored out, but their theory is some kind of bug, perhaps imprisoned with grain. It ate the grain then bored its way out. I didn't disagree." He flashed her a quick smile and took a drink of brandy. "But it's what's on the outside of the urn that was so compelling."

She took a drink of her own brandy, and raised an eyebrow to show her interest.

"Our urn had been so banged up, we couldn't see all the markings on it. This one is nearly pristine. The markings are Roman. Our minions probably date back to Cicero."

"How do you know it's the same type of urn? What accounts for finding two different urns of the same kind, in two different locations?"

Greg gave her a pointed look. "When I think of the same thing in two different locations, I think—"

"Decoy," said Assumpta. "Do you think the one in Carolina was the decoy?"

"That's what I was thinking."

"What about the hole drilled in the bottom? That doesn't make sense."

"I have thought of another reason, but I find it unlikely, unless—"

"Tell me."

Greg licked his lips. "What if, instead of a decoy, it was a matched set. One urn, holding all the minions, was sent to one location, and a second urn, holding the leader—"

"Father Hughes."

"Or whoever is possessing Father Hughes. The urns are separated by a great distance so that even if one were to break open—"

"The entities inside couldn't be reunited," said Assumpta, "at least, not very easily."

"Right," Greg said. "It seems plausible, but it makes a lot of assumptions. For one, it presumes that even if both jars broke, there would be no means of the master contacting his minions. I can't believe that."

"It's not like they had a cell plan and could phone each other."

"Right again, but we're not talking about mere mortals. We're talking about godlike beings."

Assumpta stretched her legs out on the couch. "But I'm not sure that they actually have some special communication powers. If they did, why do the minions need to leave us every so often? Couldn't they communicate with their master from here, otherwise? Let's assume they can communicate. What's another reason that they'd have to leave here?"

Greg shrugged. "More questions to ponder."

"And here's another thing: if the two urns were meant to keep the things inside separated, why were they found so close together? Why weren't they at least on different continents?"

"I've been giving that some thought, and I don't really like what I've come up with."

She gave him an inquiring look.

He answered her with a question. "What if the urns had been half a world apart from each other...but something brought them closer together?"

"Like what? A spell?"

He looked down into his brandy. "What if someone—some *thing*—carried one of the urns here, meaning to find the second and join them?"

"It seems like that thing was already here...and done just that."

"I know, so does that mean we have to deal with something else? Something orchestrating this entire affair?"

Assumpta dropped her head back on the sofa and closed her eyes. "I certainly hope not. I don't know how much more of this I can take."

"Me either." He sipped from his drink. "So, what do we do next?"

"We?" she asked. "*We* don't do anything. *I*, on the other hand—" she looked up from her cup and looked Greg in the eyes "—am going to sleep with the enemy."

CHAPTER 24

GREG COULDN'T HAVE LOOKED MORE STRICKEN if she'd poleaxed him. "You're going to have sex with a demon?"

He looked down into his lap and she couldn't see his eyes. What was he thinking? It was hard to tell from the tone of his voice, and that bothered her. Greg was acting as though he had a claim on her. *Did he?*

She responded softly, trying to get him to see her point of view. "His name is *Jak,* Greg. And I'm not certain he's a demon. I'm not quite sure what he is, but I think he might provide some of the answers we need."

"He's cement, right?"

"He first appeared to me that way, yes. But he's manifested in flesh, too."

He looked up. "Listen to yourself, he's *manifested*. He's not human. Why would you want to sleep with anything that isn't human? He's got to be a demon—cement and all—just trying to fool you by appearing to be something else sometimes. Look what the little ones did to your hand. What do you think a life-sized one is going to do to you, especially if he doesn't use a condom?"

She flushed. "There's no need to get crude."

Obviously, Greg wasn't as cool about all this as she'd thought. Then again, he hadn't had so long to think about it, either.

"I could have been much worse, trust me." He tilted his head back and finished his drink, then stood and walked to the mantle, placing his glass on the black metal beam. "You've got no reason to believe this thing isn't going to harm you like the others. He's trying to make you trust him, so that he can do more evil to you before all this is over. How do you know he isn't in league with the others?"

"I don't," she said shrugging. "But, he saved my life. I can't believe anything evil would keep me alive on a whim."

"So this is guilt sex? You wouldn't fuck him if he hadn't saved your life?"

She hadn't really considered it until now. Is that why she was leaning toward sleeping with him? People had tried to guilt her into doing things before, and she'd not given in –well, except for her father, but only because he threatened to kick her Mom out of the house. But saving a life is the ultimate thing you can do for someone…just powerful enough to make you consider doing pretty much anything in return.

Is that a better reason than because it feels good? Because she had a feeling that was going to happen, too. She just didn't know which was more compelling at this point.

"Something evil *would* save your life, Assumpta," Greg said. "You told me so yourself when we were anointing the windows here. The minions were hurting you, but not killing you, because if you die, you're going straight to Heaven and out of their reach. I'm the one they'll kill at the slightest provocation." He swiped his right hand through his hair, pushing his long bangs out of his eyes. "There's your proof that he's evil."

"I don't think he's evil."

"So it's okay to sleep with him? He's still not human. What if he changes you? What if you become less human?"

She hadn't considered that. Could that be what Jak referred to when he said he omitted something from the conversation?

CHAPTER 25

ASSUMPTA GOT OFF THE BUS AND WALKED TO HER parent's house, heavy of heart. She'd see if her mom was doing all right, hand her father the check, and then leave. With this debt hanging over her, she didn't feel welcome. She didn't even feel she could enter without knocking. Her greedy father had messed everything up.

Next time, she'd meet her mother for lunch and give the check to her. Her father couldn't find fault with that, right?

Assumpta skipped up the three front steps and knocked on the storm door.

Her father answered the knock almost immediately, opening it wide and letting her in.

"You got my money?"

She stifled an urge to scream at her father. Her words were clipped. "Wouldn't be here if I didn't. Where's Mom?"

"Kitchen, making dinner," He took a swig of beer from the can he held. "You staying?"

"Not if I have to pay for it." She walked through the living and dining rooms to the galley kitchen in the back of the house. Her mom was wiping her hands on a towel. The aroma of fresh chicken soup came off the steam rising from the stove. Carrot and celery scraps lay on the cutting board near the sink.

She gave her mom a blinding smile and a long hug. "How are you doing, Mom? Everything okay?"

"Just fine. Though this thing between you and your dad—" She shook her head. "I knew no good would come of it."

"He's not hitting you or anything, is he, Mom? How about mental abuse? Is he treating you like he treats me?"

Her mom looked astonished at such a question, and shook her head. "Not at all!"

Assumpta nodded. She could believe her mother. "If things get bad around here, call me."

Her father came to the kitchen doorway, leaning one shoulder against it. "Your mom's fine. You think I'm some kind of monster?"

"If the shoe fits," Assumpta said, approaching the door. "Excuse me." Her dad glared at her, but let her by.

"Hey! You leaving? Where's my check?" He followed after her. She stopped at the door and held out the monthly payment. "Here's your check. See you next month." She opened the door and walked back down the steps to the sidewalk.

"Hey! What's your hurry? Don't you want to visit with your dad?"

She turned back. *Of all the nerve.* Was he feeling guilty?

"You want to visit?" She was certain the look on her face showed all kinds of confusion.

He shrugged, looking away. "Why not? You're my only kid."

"A kid you weren't eager to have! Why do you want a relationship with me?" She shook her head. "No. Not until we settle this debt between us. It's unnatural. You're not a dad."

"I'm your father! I fed you and clothed you. I took you to the movies."

"And you want me to pay every penny of that back. You didn't do those things out of love for me. You did it out of duty." She crossed her arms across her chest. "Are you willing to forgive the loan?"

"Not a chance."

"Then we've got nothing to say to each other." She walked toward the bus stop.

"You're cold, unloving!" her father yelled after her. A half-empty beer can sailed by her right ear and landed on the sidewalk, spilling foamy beer on the concrete. *"You're* the unnatural bitch."

She paused, wanting to hurl back an insult of her own, but knew it wouldn't do any good, so she continued on her way. The door of the row home slammed shut behind her, echoing through the tiny street.

Jak appeared by her side.

First, he wasn't there, and then he was. He said, "You've got to hate that."

"You heard all that?"

He nodded. "Just one of my tricks. I can watch, but not interfere."

"Do you ever get to interfere, Jak?"

"I did once," he said, smiling thoughtfully. "And one of these days I might get to again, if things go right."

"And what would those things be?"

"I couldn't say," he said.

She nodded. His words were vague, but she got the feeling they were meant to be. He implied that he didn't know, but he really meant that he was forbidden to do so.

"What happens if you do say, Jak?"

His cheerful smile disappeared. "Oh, I could tell you, but then I'd have to go, for good. Telling you this much is not quite crossing the line."

"I'm dying of curiosity," she said, smiling at him. It was so easy to be with him, to banter. *Why couldn't he be human?* She chuckled. Would it matter if he were human? He'd probably be some Mafia guy. She'd be no better off.

"Well, there is one way you could find out…" He wiggled his eyebrows and gave her an over-the-top leer.

"We're back to that, are we?"

"We're never far from it," Jak said.

They walked a few moments in silence. "Is your dad always such an asshole?"

She stopped and turned to face him. "What are you playing at?"

"Just trying to get to know you better," Jak said. "Taking an interest in your life. Maybe offer some advice."

"You're a demon!" she yelled, and then realized they were drawing attention to themselves, and started walking uptown again. She spoke between clenched teeth. "All you've wanted from me so far is sex, Jak. We're not friends. I can't even write you off as some poor excuse of a toxic relationship. We have no relationship." She stopped. "What makes you think you're qualified to even give advice?"

He was fading from her side. He'd never done that before. Torment blanketed his face. "I was human once," he said, then faded away.

She felt terrible, and that didn't bode well. Why did she feel bad for a demon?

CHAPTER 26

ASSUMPTA LAY IN HER BED IN GREG'S GUEST ROOM, knowing what had to be done. Dreading and anticipating the situation, though she wasn't certain which she felt more: dread or anticipation. She just knew that she *had* to sleep with Jak.

She'd nearly been killed by the demons. The game couldn't go on any longer. Though she had no way of proving it, she didn't think Jak had lied to her about anything. Though he was leaving something out, she was certain. Why else would he tell her he could omit, but he couldn't straight-up lie?

Still, she had to take the chance. Kill or be killed, and Jak was the key. By sleeping with him, she would find all the answers to her dilemma: how to heal Greg, how to banish the demons, and how to find the missing relic from Holy Rosary.

And, maybe, once she was healed, she could walk into any church without fear of pain. Then again, maybe she wouldn't want to walk into any church anymore. If the church couldn't accept her for who she was, why did she have to accept it? She could find her own peace elsewhere.

She closed her eyes and summoned Jak.

No sooner did the last syllable of his name fly past her lips then he appeared on the bed beside her. Shirtless, bronzed skin appearing sun-kissed, wide-shouldered and slim-hipped, he looked good enough to eat.

"It's time," he said.

She nodded. "But not here. I couldn't be so low to do this in Greg's home."

"Say no more," Jak said, placing a hand on her thigh and running it up to her waist. The warmth of his hands left a fiery trail on her skin.

In the blink of an eye, they were gone, whisked away to an ocean paradise. They lay in a hammock on the deck of an old-fashioned clipper, anchored in a secluded bay where the salt tang of the water tangled with the smell of bougainvillea from the nearby shore.

The hammock swung gently on the swells and dips of the waves washing on to the beach. Water lapped gently at the hull and thundered onto the sandy coast. A fresh breeze caressed them.

"Here?" Assumpta asked, her shoulders, hips and thighs pressed tightly against him. She'd never done it in a hammock, though she was game to try, but it didn't feel right for the first time with Jak. She looked around, searching for other people—*other beings*—saw none, and let out a quiet breath, thankful. She wasn't into exhibitionism.

"No," he said, rolling her on top of him. "This is just for relaxing. There's no need to rush."

He put his hand behind her neck and pulled her down to meet his kiss. His other hand rubbed her back, squeezed her shoulder, and caressed the side of her breast. They kissed for a while, hands exploring each other, until she said, "I'm ready."

Jak lifted Assumpta out of the hammock, then set her lightly on her feet. Still holding her hand, he tugged her down a short staircase into the captain's cabin, a surprisingly bright area belowdecks with several windows opening off the rear of the ship. The huge platform bed, large enough to play on, and covered over with dozens of pillows and a hunter green satin spread, dominated the left side of the room.

Jak looked at her and smiled. With a saucy wink, he snapped his fingers, and the pillows were gone—except for those at the head—and the covers were turned down.

He put his hands on her shoulders and pulled her close. "Who do you want me to be?" he asked.

She smiled, but she wasn't up for fantasy tonight. "Just be yourself."

"Ah, but which *self* do you want me to be? The self I was when I walked the Earth? The self I am when I beg you for your attentions? Or, the self I am in the other world when I'm not here begging for you?"

He had a trinity of selves, she thought.

She hadn't known she would have a choice. She thought she would see his stone self, gray and beautiful like Eros, and smelling slightly of cement. Beautiful, but dark. She was afraid his otherworldly figure might be too frightening a visage for her to enjoy the act. So she chose the third option. "When you were human, like me," she said.

He smiled. In an instant, he looked like his former Roman self. Dark, curly hair, a patrician nose beneath laughing green eyes, and a warrior's chest Assumpta itched to run her hands over. Heavy muscles covered his thighs and his arms looked strong enough to lift her over his head.

She reached out to grab his biceps and found her hands hardly touched their circumference.

He winked again, and they were naked on the bed. She lay on her back. Jak rolled on top of her, kissing her neck, her chest, and slowly working his way down her body. His warm hands stroked her, heated her, and, coupled with his other attentions, excited her beyond all measure. Her blood grew hot for him, grew hotter as she returned each caress with her own.

His tongue delved into her belly button, a quick tickle, and then it was gone.

He inched lower, his warm hands sliding on her thighs, pushing them apart, making room for his broad shoulders—the only part of him she could now touch.

Assumpta tried to tug him higher. She burned for him already. "Let's just get to—"

He ignored her, running his tongue up the inside of her right thigh from knee to the crease between her legs. He blew hot air on her slit, then ran his hot, thick tongue up the seam of her. She convulsed, her hips bucking in reflex.

"Jak—"

Ignoring her, he inched forward, delving his tongue inside her. He pressed it against her bud, flicking it to life, sucking on it while Assumpta crooned with pleasure. She felt the heat pool between her legs, felt her own slickness begin to run. Jak wasn't *only* his former self. His tongue, though warm and soft, had the sandpapery feel of a cat's. Or a demon's. Each delicious stroke of it brought her closer to her own culmination.

His strokes became deeper and deeper, rhythmic and penetrating, until she exploded in his mouth.

But he refused to let her rest.

His tongue was long and thick, and gave such divine pleasure, she came again almost immediately. The third time she came, she begged him to come into her.

"I want to hear the voices," she said. "I want to know what I need to know." And she knew if he were this good with his tongue, his sex would be even better. She wanted to feel him inside her, moving between her thighs.

"Pleasure before business, my sweet," he said, plundering her depths with the slow slide of his index finger, then two fingers, then three. He continued to tongue her clit, keeping a steady rhythm with his fingers.

With his left hand, Jak grabbed Assumpta's right knee and squeezed it, then slid his hand down to her ankle. He lifted it, putting it over his shoulder, then moved closer, naturally pushing her knee outward, opening her wider to his attentions.

Assumpta lifted her left leg to Jak's shoulder, too, felt him smile against her thigh as he kissed it, then nudged that knee outward. She'd never felt so exposed before. She'd never felt anything so good before.

Jak reached for her right leg again, running a strong hand from knee to thigh, then slid his hand beneath her. He withdrew his right hand—

"Oh, don't stop what you're doing," she said, wondering briefly where this hussy had come from. She'd never begged for more during sex. Maybe that's why sex had been so lackluster before.

Jak laughed, low and deep, "Just wait," he said, sliding his right hand beneath her. He lifted her, changing the angle of his touch, and licked her, running his tongue beneath her folds before penetrating her fully with his tongue.

"Oh, my god," she whispered, barely able to articulate the words. What was he doing?

Jak laughed again and she came in his mouth, arching her back, belly clenching, and pulling him closer still by her ankles locked around his neck.

He continued to stroke her deeply with his tongue, slower and slower, while her clit still throbbed, causing orgasm aftershocks while she caught her breath.

A short time later, he crawled up her sated, relaxed body, and smiled into her slumberous eyes.

"Feel good?" he asked.

She could only nod.

"I wanted you to enjoy it," he said.

"We can enjoy it anytime you like," she said, thinking she could make a habit of this very easily.

"No," he said sadly. "Only once, but we'll make it a *very good* once. Ready?"

She nodded, and he flexed his back, nudging her open with the tip of his cock. When she smiled, he pushed his thick, rock-solid cock into her, filling and stretching her, completing her, like she'd never been complete before. Her nipples peaked, bathed in the heat of his breath. She could weep with the pleasure of it.

At once, she heard the cacophony of voices. The roar of a thousand, simultaneous speakers, all vying for her attention, shattered the quiescence of the secluded bay.

She dragged her hands up to her ears and pushed against them, as if she could keep out the voices in her head.

Jak withdrew, the slow friction driving her crazy, the voices growing quieter. "Focus," he whispered in her ear. "Ask a question, and listen for a single voice to have the answer."

He thrust forward again, and bent his head to her breast, laving one nipple with his sandpaper tongue.

Assumpta was torn between listening for the voices and concentrating on the sensations his hot tongue wrought on her breast. More heat than she ever felt possible pooled in her loins. Jak withdrew again, the slow drag of his cock feeling delicious between her legs.

He held her tight, and she clutched at him, feeling the hard muscles tensing and relaxing with each flex of his hips. For the moment, he was hers.

He thrust forward again, turning his head to take her other nipple in his mouth and draw upon it. He nipped with his teeth, sending sharp jolts of sensation down between her legs.

Ask, he said in her mind.

"I find that I don't want to," she said, and he laughed, gripping her harder. His sex seemed to grow inside her, filling her more. He withdrew again, and the voices quieted.

"How many things can I know?" she asked, wondering if she shouldn't have thought about this more before she'd called him to her.

"You can keep asking," he said, and licked the underside of one breast, then laved a raspy tongue over her nipple and blew hot air across it to make it bud, "for as long as we make love. Once we're done, you can't ask anymore." He nipped her other breast, then soothed the hurt by suckling it in his mouth.

He thrust in slowly, and pulled out just as slow.

Then in and out again, in a deliberate, primal rhythm.

Assumpta felt another orgasm building. She didn't think it would happen this soon.

"How long can you keep this up?" she asked, breathless.

He chuckled again, filled her with his length, then rained a dozen slow kisses on her neck. "For an eternity, if you want," he whispered in her ear.

"Tempting," she said, smiling. Assumpta raised her knees so Jak could come into her further. "More," she said, then lifted her hips to meet his thrusts.

When he was as deep into her as he could go, when the voices were loudest, she thought, *I need to know how to banish the demons.*

Jak withdrew, and the voices quieted, but one or two seemed louder than the rest, and Assumpta concentrated on these. As Jak filled her again, the cacophony filled the void, but Assumpta found she could focus on only the voices providing her answers. They talked, sometimes in a discordant unison, and she listened, while Jak continued his dance.

He slid his arms under hers and cradled her head in his hands. He kissed her, thrusting his tongue in and out of her mouth in the same rhythm he thrust his body in and out of hers.

She felt the tensing of her thigh muscles as she exploded into orgasm.

Jak waited for the aftershocks to cease, the voices in her head to quiet, as she concentrated on the fullness between her thighs. He still hadn't come. They were going to do this some more.

Assumpta smiled.

"You liked that," he said.

"Of course."

"Then let's do it again, this way," he said. He slid from her, then helped to roll her over until she was kneeling on the bed. He propped several pillows under her belly to support her, then entered her from behind. He tucked one arm around her waist to hold himself snug against her while he pistoned in and out. He snaked his other hand forward and slid it around her breast, rolling the nipple between two fingers and gave it a little tug.

Ask, he thought to her.

Oh, god, she didn't want to. She wanted this to go on and on for as long as it could. The slow, powerful slide of his cock filled her with such pleasure, she thought she could die of it.

In, he thrust, pushing to the hilt and, in this position, filling her more than she'd ever felt before.

Out, he withdrew, the sweet friction making her breathless.

In, he thrust, pushing against her. She melted against the pillow, barely able to keep upright on her knees.

Out, he withdrew.

In. The voices, the noise, the cacophony were all bearable now. She'd learned to tune it out, maintaining a bit of static in the back of her mind. She concentrated on Jak's lovemaking.

Ask.

"Okay, okay," she said. She closed her eyes, concentrated, then asked. *How can Greg and I be healed? Where will I find the relic brought from Rome by the cardinal? How can I retrieve the first relic from the demons' leader?*

Jak thrust into her, and pulled out.

In and out.

His speed steady and unwavering, his pace fast enough to keep the voices loud enough in her head that their dimming was hardly noticeable. Several voices spoke up from the din, and she concentrated on the answers, still aware of the pleasure between her thighs, the warm arm wrapped around her waist, the insistent fingers at her breast.

Jak increased his pace.

He pounded into her. The bed's platform rattled with his exertions. The pillows shook beneath her. He grabbed her shoulders, pulling her to him, and hammered into her with more force.

She spread her knees a little wider, tilted her pelvis so he could come into her deeper, reveling in the hard-pounding rhythm, the heat of him slamming into her, and the sliding friction. She was getting close. She was going to come again. She squeezed her eyes shut, anticipating it.

He thought, *Did you get all the answers you need?*

Yes, she answered, beginning to like this form of communication. *I know what I need to do.*

He pistoned into her, his warm, solid flesh banging solidly against hers. His hands caressed her bottom, massaged her flanks, kneaded her shoulders as he kept the cadence.

In. Out.

In. Out.

Her nipples were tight beads of desire, her breasts heavy with arousal, swaying with each thrust and pull of his sex. She pushed back against him, meeting each lunging motion, lamenting each retreat, tightening her muscles in a feeble effort to keep him inside.

Suddenly, her thigh muscles clenched, then her belly, and the fiercest orgasm she ever knew rocked her as Jak continued to pound into her.

He seemed to swell inside her, then he, too, shattered, clutching her shoulders and pulling her tight against him as he spent himself.

Jak withdrew for the final time, and rolled onto his back on the bed. He pulled her down to him, encouraging one leg to scissor between his and wrapped one arm around her, pulling her close, almost chest to chest.

Assumpta floated on a pleasant euphoria, while Jak stroked her back.

When her breathing quieted, she finally felt able to think about what she needed to do next. She knew—

She stiffened against him.

"I'm sorry, Assumpta," he said, his voice soft and low in her ear.

"I can't remember what the voices told me!"

"I know," he said sadly. "That's the part I wasn't permitted to tell you when we discussed this."

CHAPTER 27

ASSUMPTA AWOKE IN THE MORNING IN HER BED in Greg's guest room, remembering the sex with Jak. Every kiss, every lick, every suck. Her body still felt warm and sated.

But she was angry, because it was all for naught. She gave herself to *the demon*—no, not a demon, a—*a what?* in exchange for knowledge—*and pleasure*—if she was going to be honest with herself, but she was right back to where she'd been before they'd fucked.

She didn't know anything, she thought, as she dressed. So, what was she going to do now?

"Here," Greg said when she stepped into the kitchen in the morning. He pushed a thick, three-ring binder across the table. He grinned, clearly excited by the contents. Then took a huge swallow from the mug of coffee by his hand.

"What's this?" She took the binder, but proceeded to the coffeepot for her first cup of the day, the aroma of freshly brewed coffee a stronger lure than whatever he had to share.

"Open it."

She poured coffee, dropped an ice cube into the mug, then took a huge gulp of the cooling brew before topping it off and heading to the table. She sat, then opened the binder, careful to avoid a stack of fresh toast and a bowl of fruit already there.

"You're awfully excited," she said.

He just smiled at her.

The first page was a computerized and annotated ledger account, beginning July 8, 1988—the day she was born—and ending December 31, 1988. The receipts from her box had been arranged in date order, oldest to newest behind it. Behind a tabbed page after those receipts was the ledger for 1989 as well as those receipts, followed by the tabbed divider for 1990, and so on up to the present.

These documents represented a computerized version of her father's expense book, she realized: her life, really, in greater detail than she cared to examine. The ledgers recorded each expenditure, the category of expense, and the amount spent, along with a running total, an off-set column, and a notes column. The page was a standard width, so the notes column contained a series of codes referring to explanations rather than any actual notes. Entries with notations usually had the expense offset.

Her Christmas lists and birthday wish lists were filed, along with a few notes in her mother's handwriting about what Assumpta had asked for over the years.

Assumpta looked up at Greg, stunned.

"I told you I had my accountant looking into it," he said, his smile growing larger.

"This must have taken days," Assumpta said, amazed that anyone would go through the trouble for her.

"He's been doing this kind of work—"

Assumpta raised an eyebrow at him.

"Well, not exactly this kind of work," Greg qualified, "but ledgers and receipts and financial investigation stuff, for years. It took him less time than you think."

Assumpta continued to flip pages.

"The best part is in the back," Greg said.

She turned to the last tab.

Greg couldn't contain himself. "It's a complete account, from start to finish, in reverse. Alec tallied up all the receipts and then started deleting out the ones that didn't match up on your wish lists. He also took out anything that could be even broadly interpreted as not counting according to the terms of your contract with your dad. The best part is, he found several accounting errors introduced by your dad into the handwritten ledger. His total was off from the beginning. So, you owe even less than you'd thought."

She turned to the last page to find the total. Alec had shaved off more than thirty-five thousand dollars.

She whistled long and slow. "My dad is not going to like this."

"That doesn't matter. The facts are written in the receipts. He could dispute the interpretation, but I think he won't bother."

"You don't know my dad." She closed the ledger and took another drink of her coffee.

"But I know human nature. And Alec has an excellent idea I think your dad will agree to. You won't even need to show him this ledger. It's brilliant, and I'm sorry I didn't think of it first. But going to Alec was brilliant. I pay him to come up with strong money ideas, and I think he really came through on this one."

"I'm listening."

"You're paying your father off a few bucks at a time, right?"

She nodded. "It's all I can afford. Although, with what you're paying me, I'll be able to do more."

"Well, he doesn't need to know how much I'm paying you. Just do this: offer him a smaller lump sum payment right now if he agrees to payment in full."

"How much?"

"I don't know. How greedy is your father? Offer him a third."

"Where am I going to get forty thousand dollars?"

"From an advance on the salary I'm paying you."

"*What?*" She couldn't believe that he'd offer it. What kind of person gives a virtual stranger a loan of that magnitude?

"I can't take your money, Greg." *Tempting as it is,* she thought.

His smile dimmed. "You have to," he said. "It's the only way you'll get your father off your back." He picked up a piece of toast and buttered it. "Not that I want you beholden to me. Wouldn't it be better to have it over and done with instead of hanging over your head for years, causing all this stress?"

"You know, I really don't like the idea of switching one debt for another. I know I'm not legally responsible for paying off my dad, but I'd be responsible for paying you back."

"But the loan you'll owe me will be half, or even a third, of what you supposedly owe your dad. And I'm also paying you enough to cover it."

She smiled at his last point. He really wanted her to do this. And what he said made a lot of sense. But, she also knew her father. If she offered him a third, he'd be asking for half...even if he didn't know what half was. She'd have to lowball him even further.

She nodded her head. "Okay. I'll do this, but I want a contract between us, just so you know I'm not going to run out on you."

"I trust—"

"We'll have a contract or I'm not taking the advance."

"Okay, if you insist." He got up and grabbed the coffeepot, then refilled their mugs before sitting again. "I'll have my attorney draw it up today."

"I'll give my dad a call."

CHAPTER 28

H ER DAD HAD HIS PERPETUAL BEER IN HIS HAND when he opened the door.

"So, are you going to tell me what brings you here more than once in the same month?" He was drunk already, at four in the afternoon, and surly.

"What? A daughter can't visit her family when she wants to?" She stepped into the living room and sat in the chair across from the sofa.

"My daughter usually doesn't want to." He pushed the door shut with more force than was necessary, rattling the glass squares in their frames.

"You're right. And that's because we always argue about money. But I think I know a way to put an end to all that."

"You do, do you? Well, I'm all ears." Her dad set his can down on the worn coffee table, sat, and propped his feet up next to the can.

"Where's Mom?"

"I sent her out for more beer when I heard you were coming. You were so secretive on the phone, I knew this couldn't be good."

Assumpta silently counted to ten. Her dad was such a rat bastard. "Why?"

"Because I had a feeling when you said you were dropping by that there would be another argument, and I didn't want your mother caught in the middle of that."

She didn't know whether to cry or applaud. Was her father finally concerned about her mother's feelings, or did he have a sixth sense about a payoff and didn't want her mother to know? It wouldn't matter. She'd tell her mom afterward. She couldn't keep her mother in the dark about the money when she deserved a share of it. Knowing her father, he'd find a way to conceal it and keep all the money for himself. On the other hand, that might be a good thing: maybe he'd spend it all on booze and drink himself to death. It would save Assumpta and her mother a ton of grief.

She took a deep breath and blew it out, making a mental note of her last thought. Did that qualify as wishing someone dead? She might be making a trip to confession sooner than she realized.

"I would like to offer you a deal," Assumpta said, dropping her purse to the floor. "In return for a lump sum payment right now, you'll forgive the rest of the loan."

"How much are we talking?"

"Twenty-five thousand dollars."

"Why would I want to give up more than a hundred thousand dollars for a measly twenty-five K right now? No deal." He reached for the beer can and took a deep swallow. "You must think me a fool."

"I'll think you're a fool if you don't take the money," Assumpta said. "Consider this: you're forty-six years old. Let's assume you'll live another twenty years—that's longer than Grandpa did. That means you'll be able to collect two-hundred-and-forty more payments from me." She took a pad of paper out of her purse and did the math for him. "If I can only pay you fifty bucks a pop, you only stand to collect twelve thousand dollars. I'm offering you twenty-five."

"I plan to live longer than that."

"But do you know for sure you will? Even if you don't drink yourself to death in twenty years, you could be hit by a bus tomorrow."

"Don't backtalk me, little girl," her father said. "You're still my daughter."

"And we're still talking business, Father. When we're done with business, we can try to find that father/daughter relationship you seem to want so bad."

Red climbed from his cheekbones to the roots of his hair.

"Even if I don't live more than twenty years, I expect you to be able to pay me more than fifty dollars a month. Everyone earns more the older they get. You should be able to find a better paying job than you have now."

"Since you've taken away any chance I have at college, I don't see how that's going to happen," Assumpta said. "But you'd still be better off taking the deal." She scribbled again on the paper. "If I could pay you a hundred dollars a month for twenty years—and that's starting right now, which I absolutely can't—then you'd still only get twenty-four thousand dollars from me. But as it goes, you won't get even that."

"You could luck into a really good job."

"What are the chances?"

There was a brief silence.

He asked, "Where are you going to get twenty-five thousand dollars anyway?"

Did she have him? Assumpta could almost smile, but she didn't want to show her joy too soon. Lord knew her father wouldn't allow her to have that little bit of happiness in her life. Still, this might work.

"Let's assume I won the lottery," she said.

Her father smiled and sat back in the sofa. "Well, darling, if you won the lottery, you have an obligation to help out your family. Was it the megazillions? How much did you get?"

"I never said I won the lottery."

"You as good as said it."

"Even if I did win the lottery, why should I share it with you? You've never shared any of your lottery winnings with me."

"I've never won that much, a couple hundred here and there with the pick-three."

"So if you'd won a million, you would have shared?"

He had the grace to look red-faced.

"Look, Father, I'm offering you a really good deal right now. Why are you trying to spoil it? This could be good for both of us." She brushed the hair out of her eyes with her good left hand. "When's the last time you had more than a couple thousand dollars in your pocket other than a paycheck?"

She doubted his checks even amounted to that much, but he didn't need to know she thought that. A subtle bit of flattery on her part couldn't hurt.

He crossed his arms over his chest, sat back into the sofa and stared at her. He was thinking so hard, she could hear the gears turning in his mind. *Greedy bastard.* She just knew he was trying to figure out a way to get more money out of her. But the deal was sound. And he knew it. He just didn't want to give up the thought of getting all the money he thought she owed him. Maybe if he'd been smart enough to invest in her to begin with, he might have. Then they'd all be better off.

"Forty thousand," he said.

She knew this would happen, and she'd planned for it. She hoped she could be convincing with the next part. She looked at her dad with what she thought was a sad face.

"I didn't get that much," she said.

"Well how much did you get?"

"About twenty-five thousand," she said, hating to have to lie outright. Now she really would have to go to confession.

"Okay," said her father, learning forward to grab his beer again. "I'll take twenty-five now and you can pay off the other fifteen on the same monthly schedule we've established."

"That's not the deal I'm offering you."

"Well, it's the deal I'm wanting."

She'd planned to haggle with him to keep the figure closer to thirty thousand, but dammit, he was being such a jerk about this. She wondered, *Was it about the money, or about the power?* He seemed to be having such a good time lording it over her head that she owed him, she was beginning to think it was about having the upper hand.

With the salary Greg was paying her, she had the upper hand. But her dad didn't know that, and he was being an ass. She'd had enough.

She made a split-second decision, and stood.

"You know what, Father? I find that I'm not in the dealing mood right now. You can take your forty grand request and shove it. I'll bring you fifty dollars when I swing by next month." She walked to the door. "Tell Mom I'll call her."

Her father was on his feet in an instant. "Now see here," he just about yelled. "If you won the lottery, you can afford to pay me much more than fifty dollars a month. In fact, you might as well just turn it all over now. You owe me."

She turned back to him. "Lottery winnings are not mentioned in our contract."

"Then we'll amend the contract."

"Not without my consent, you can't. Besides, I didn't win the lottery, Father."

"That's hardly believable, considering the conversation we just had."

"I never said I won the lottery. I said, let's *assume* I won it. And you did." She'd planned for this, too. She pulled a Maryland State Lottery pamphlet out of her purse and handed it to him. "Lottery winners' names are public knowledge. You can call and ask if I won. You'll see that I didn't."

"Then what was all this about? You just wanted to play a game of *what if?* Do you enjoy pissing me off?"

"Actually, a friend was planning on loaning me the money. But I find that I don't want to borrow it now. Pissing you off hadn't crossed my mind, but I find myself enjoying it."

She walked out the door.

"Assumpta!"

She ignored him and continued walking down the steps. After a moment, she heard the door slam behind her.

When she got to the bus station, she let out a deep breath. It hadn't gone a lick like she'd planned it. She'd have rather paid her father off with the advance on her salary, as much as it would have burned her to accept it, and not had the threat of it hanging over her head for years to come. On the other hand, knowing that her father probably wouldn't get more than twenty or thirty percent of what he figured she owed him over the next twenty years was poetic justice.

And her dad didn't have to know she was making a decent income. It was against the terms of the contract, but as far as she was concerned, the entire thing was illegal, and one big mess of emotional blackmail. She didn't feel the slightest bit bad about keeping the terms of her deal with Greg mum.

CHAPTER 29

"HOW CAN WE HEAL GREG'S WOUNDS?"

Assumpta sat on the floor in her bedroom in Greg's house, legs crossed, holding her pendulum over a paper alphabet chart on the floor at her feet. The alphabet ranged in a semi-circle, *A* on the left and *Z* on the right, with lines like spokes radiating from the bottom center to each letter.

Jak's curse might have made her forget what she'd learned from him as soon as he had left her, but she had known it, albeit briefly. So she should be able to retrieve that information. Unless the curse, or whatever it was, actively schemed against her, she didn't see a reason for this not to work.

The pendulum swung back and forth to the left side, an inch or so at first, then wider out to the edge of the graph where Assumpta had written the letters in large, box script.

"C?" she questioned aloud, and the pendulum continued to swing. "B?"

The pendulum ceased its wide swing and settled back to center. Assumpta wrote *B* on a piece of paper, and the pendulum began the wide swing again, in the same pattern as before.

"A," she said, certain the next letter was a vowel. A was the closest vowel on that portion of the chart and an easy guess. The pendulum settled. Then, it began to swing again, due north toward the top of the chart.

"N?"

It continued to swing.

She sighed. Message charts drove her crazy with frustration. Getting the information was slow and tedious. The twenty-questions method gave quicker results, but only when you knew the questions to ask.

"P?"

The glass teardrop fell and began its next wide swing, further to the right.

"Bap," she said. "Bap. Baptize?"

The string slackened, then started a clockwise turn Assumpta knew to mean *yes*. Why hadn't she considered that, especially when things seemed to conspire to keep Greg away from the church?

"Thank you," she said. "What will banish the demons?"

She fought with the pendulum and the chart for several minutes, until it signaled, *relic*.

"The gift from the Polish Cardinal?"

The pendulum circled clockwise.

"Thank you," she said again. "Will that help with Father Hughes as well?"

The pendulum continued to circle clockwise.

"How does the relic work?"

The pendulum swung north-northeast on the chart.

"R?"

It continued to swing.

"S?"

It continued to swing.

"T?"

It dropped, then began to swing nearly due north.

"O?" she guessed.

The pendulum slackened, and she dropped it to the floor and rubbed her arm, which ached from the strain of holding the crystal teardrop over the paper. After a moment, she lifted her arm and let the teardrop glass dangle on its braided string once more.

"T-o-" she said. "What's next?"

The painted glass swung short swings at first, then widened outward to the right, not quite reaching northeast from due north.

"T?

It continued to swing.

"S?"

It continued to swing.

"R," she said, certain, but the glass continued its focused momentum.

"V," she tried, and "W," but it continued to move to and fro. She ran her free hand through her hair. Q was too high for the angle the pendulum made, yet X was too low.

Still, she tried it. "X?" and then "toxic," speaking the first word she could think of with those letters. But she knew that whatever she needed to banish the demons would be *toxic* to them. It would be no help for her to receive that answer.

The pendulum continued to swing.

The only letter left at that trajectory was a vowel, U, but it seemed so unlikely.

"U," she said, and the pendulum dropped.

"T-o-u," she whispered even while the crystal started on its next path, swinging left. "Toud, toub, touc," she said, then paused. "Touch."

The swinging stopped, and the pendulum hung slack.

She had to touch the demons to banish them. *Every one of them?* It seemed an impossible task. And she had to get close to them, too. Close enough for them to touch *her*. Close enough for them to slice and dice her with their claws.

I don't know if I can do it, she thought. She said aloud, "I don't even know where the relic is."

As soon as she finished speaking, the glass began moving left and back along the flat bottom line of the semi-circle.

"A," she said, and the pendulum swung north, bisecting the semi-circle.

"M?" she said, then, "L," when the pendulum continued to swing. Once she guessed L, it changed to a northeast trajectory.

"Altar?" she guessed, and the string slackened and the glass came to a stop.

"On the altar?"

The pendulum spun counter-clockwise.

"Under it?"

The pendulum slowed and began a clockwise motion.

"Under it," she affirmed. The teardrop glass hung still.

She took a deep breath. She'd saved the most troubling question for last. She asked, "How can I return my stoned flesh to normal?"

The pendulum hung slack, revealing nothing.

CHAPTER 30

GREG MANEUVERED THE CAR THROUGH THE snarled morning traffic, accelerating into openings with a grace Assumpta hadn't expected. The drive had taken less time than it would have by bus, but they were still late for their appointment. She hated being late, but didn't want to bring it up. Greg had been silent the entire drive. No sense starting an argument over something they couldn't help now.

Luckily, Chester Street was deserted. Early Mass had let out twenty minutes ago, and they pulled into one of the many open parking spaces in front of the church. She slung her purse over her shoulder, exited the car, and jogged up the granite steps to the heavy church doors.

Before she reached the top, Father Tony pushed open the door on the far left and smiled broadly.

"Good morning! Good morning! I've been waiting for you," he said.

Morning sun bathed his ankle-length white robes in a rosy-golden hue, but his purple and gold surplice—the waist-length robe worn on top of the other—seemed to gleam in the sharp light. A large crucifix dangled almost to his waist. "I love baptisms," he said. "Bringing a new lamb into the fold, renewing the vows of the attendants… It's a beautiful rite."

Assumpta nodded, barely listening. She was more interested in getting past the pain she knew she'd encounter passing into the church. They could swap pleasantries later, *much later*, like after the baptism was done. Ever since Greg had made the decision to go through with it, she felt as though they couldn't get it done soon enough.

She stepped over the threshold, wincing in anticipation of the pain as she stepped into the church, and—

Nothing.

No pain.

Where's my hitchhiker? she thought, looking around. Had it left in order to tell the others what she and Greg were doing? No matter, she thought, feeling suddenly lighter. She could almost skip. Its absence meant she hadn't had to suffer the consequences of its claws as they'd passed over the threshold. *Thank heaven for small favors. With a little luck, maybe that's the last we'll see of any of them today.*

Out of the corner of her eye, she saw the marble bas relief of the saints over the basement door writhe and turn, and one of the minions—not hers—climb up the wall. Was it leaving to tell Father Hughes they'd arrived?

Fucker, she thought. *How many more were hiding in the sanctuary? So much for luck.*

"It's highly unusual," Father Tony said as he turned to the left instead of heading straight forward into the main sanctuary, "to have an adult baptism without a coinciding confirmation into the Church." He paused in front of a rack of prayer cards and weekly missals. "Actually, we would just do a confirmation and have it all done at once. But since your soul is in mortal danger, Greg, we'll do this now, and you can continue your journey into the Church at another time." He walked across the narthex into a small chapel and motioned for Greg and Assumpta to follow. "There are classes starting next week," he said, with a hopeful lilt in his voice.

Greg looked in Assumpta's direction with an expression she read as, *Really?*

She shrugged and entered the tiny chamber. "You don't want to do this at the front of the church?" she asked.

"It's not often I get to use the small chapel for rites," said Father Tony. "Since it's only the three of us, I thought we'd use it."

The small chapel couldn't have been larger than ten feet by ten feet, with just enough room for the three of them to stand together around the marble baptismal font, a freestanding basin that looked like a very large birdbath with a domed, marble lid on top.

A statue of Saint Joseph stood on a pedestal in the front left corner of the room, his chipped brown robes and sandaled feet at eye level. A bas relief of the crucifixion hung on the same wall in the center, and a statue of Mary, on a pedestal matching Saint Joseph's, filled the right corner. Two banks of pillar candles, many of their flames already lit and flickering, stood in front of Mary and the crucifix, and a bank of votive candles stood in front of Joseph. Every votive candle was lit, the brass offering box wired to the front of the stand jammed full with dollar bills. Two prie-dieux, kneelers for those wishing to light a candle and pray, stood in front of the candles, leaving only about three feet of open floor space around the baptismal font in the back left corner.

Twin chandeliers hung down on either side of the bas relief, old-fashioned fixtures that had been installed when the church was first wired for electricity. Someone had twined blue ribbons in the three chains holding the lamp next to Mary, and brown ones in the chains of the lamp near Saint Joseph.

Father Tony squeezed behind the font and pushed the hinged lid open, then pulled a small container of oil out of his pocket and set it on the marble edge. He turned to Assumpta. "I assume you're standing as Greg's sponsor. Do you have the baptismal garment?"

She nodded and pulled a thin, white scarf out of her purse.

"What's a sponsor?" Greg asked. He stood to Assumpta's left, hands in his pockets, but looking all around the room.

He's studying the chapel with an archeologist's eye, Assumpta thought. *Rather clinical.* She'd have to ask him later how it compared to some of his digs.

She said, "A sponsor is someone who stands up for you at the baptism; kind of like a best man at a wedding." She smiled at him. "Technically, it makes me your godmother. I'll be assuming the role of *raising* you into the Catholic faith. Your parents should be here, too, but—"

"They're dead," said Greg.

"I'm sorry, Greg," Father Tony said.

Greg nodded. "They've been gone a long time."

"But they're missed nonetheless, I'm sure," Father Tony said, reaching for the scarf. He squeezed Greg on the shoulder, then laid the scarf on the edge of the font next to the oil.

"More than you know, Father," Greg said. "More than you know."

Father Tony smiled and clasped his hands together in front of him. "Are we ready to begin?"

Greg and Assumpta nodded.

"Come closer to the font, Greg. I'll need to touch you during certain times of the ceremony."

Greg stepped forward, and Father Tony smiled. He said to Assumpta, "What name has this child of God been given?"

She said, "Gregory Claude."

Greg turned and stared at her. She gave a little shrug. She'd deliberately omitted telling Greg he'd have to share his given name during the ceremony. She hadn't wanted an argument. And since he hadn't asked, she'd found concealing it from him very easy.

He turned back to Father Tony. "Can I take a different name?"

Father Tony smiled. "That's not the way it works for baptism," he said. "But you can take a new name at confirmation if you want." He turned to Assumpta. "What do you ask for in God's name for Gregory Claude?"

She ticked them off on her fingers: "Baptism, faith, the grace of Christ, and eternal life."

Father Tony cocked an eyebrow. Only one of the four responses was required, but Assumpta wasn't taking any chances. In the eyes of the Church, they all equated to the same thing, but Greg didn't realize the difference. Perhaps the demons didn't, either.

Father Tony said, "You have asked to have this man baptized. In doing so you are accepting the responsibility of training him in the practice of the faith. It will be your duty to bring him up to keep God's commandments as Christ taught us, by loving God and our neighbor. Do you understand what you are undertaking?"

"I do," said Assumpta, suddenly feeling the weight of her minion on her back. She smelled the odor of wet cement. The creature put its claws into her hair and yanked, and she felt her head pulled back. Tears wet the corners of her eyes.

"My minion is here," she said, struggling against the continued tug at her hair.

"Mine, too." Greg's face had gone white. His posture was stiff, as if he were in pain and trying not to show it.

"You're aware of the presence of another?" Father Tony asked. He looked confused.

"The demons, Father," Assumpta said. "As I've been telling you."

Father Tony looked around the room, his brow creased. "I see no one. Nothing."

"We don't have to see them to know they're here," Greg said.

"You can feel them?"

Assumpta nodded, feeling the creature tug again.

Father Tony said, "And they don't want Greg to be baptized." His tone flat, he looked worried, thought Assumpta, or maybe just confused.

"No," she confirmed. "They don't want Greg to be baptized. And they'll try to stop us, I'm afraid. Are you still willing to do this for us?"

"Of course."

"Then, whatever might happen, whatever you might see, don't stop. Greg needs to be baptized. Just do it now."

He looked at her sternly. "There's done, and then there's done *right*. We can skip a lot of the pomp and ritual of the ceremony, but Greg is a man, not an infant. He is not without sin. We can't skip the lot of it, and I'm certain your demons know it."

Assumpta sighed. "Very well, but get on with it."

Father Tony nodded. He turned to Greg. "Gregory Claude, the Christian community welcomes you with great joy. In its name I claim you for Christ our Savior by the sign of His cross. I now trace the cross on your forehead, and invite your godparent to do the same." He leaned over the baptismal font and traced a cross on Greg's forehead.

"Ah!" Greg's knees buckled and he collapsed to the tiled floor, nearly hitting his forehead on the edge of the font.

Confusion plain on Father Tony's face, he moved around to the front of the font to help Assumpta pull Greg to his feet. Four streaks of blood appeared on Greg's right shoulder, seeping through the thin cotton of his shirt. They stretched nearly shoulder to elbow.

"What's happening here?" Father Tony asked.

"The demons, Father," Assumpta said. "I've tried to tell you."

"I didn't believe they would manifest like this," he said. "I thought perhaps you heard voices, or saw some shadows." He crossed himself. "I understand now what they're capable of. Are you okay, son?"

Greg nodded. "Let's get this done as fast as we can."

"Of course," said Father Tony.

Assumpta reached to make the sign of the cross on Greg's forehead and her arms were grasped from behind. She looked over her shoulder and saw nothing, but whatever it was increased the pressure, squeezing her elbows together painfully. "I can't make the sign on Greg. Something is holding my arms."

"What can we do?" asked Father Tony.

"Keep going," Assumpta said.

Honestly, she didn't know if she *should* make the sign on Greg's forehead. Would doing so constitute being *holy* in the midst of the rite? What if her fingers started to burn while she did it? Would she have burned Greg, too? That was just what he needed right now: a cross burned into his forehead. The world would see him as a religious nut.

"It's all right," Father Tony said. "It's tradition, but not required for the rite." He set his prayer book on the edge of the font. "Normally, we would have a reading here, but I'll just paraphrase from the Gospel of Mark: People were bringing children to Jesus for him to place his hands on them, but the disciples rebuked them. When Jesus saw this, he was indignant, and said to them, 'Let the little children come to me, and do not hinder them, for the kingdom of God belongs to them. Truly,' he said, 'anyone who will not receive the kingdom of God like a little child will never enter it.' Then Jesus took the children in his arms and blessed them."

A breeze blew through the chapel, fluttering the prayer cards and missiles in the nearby stand. Father Tony looked up and around, his eyes scanning the small room.

He spoke quickly, "We would normally say the Prayer of the Faithful here, but I know Assumpta to be faithful and if you seek Baptism, Gregory, you must have some faith, too. We'll skip that as well."

He reached for his prayer book and opened to a page marked with a purple ribbon. He spoke quickly, pausing only long enough for Assumpta to make the responses, "My dear brothers and sisters, let us ask our Lord Jesus Christ to look lovingly on this man who is to be baptized."

It sounded to Assumpta that he was paraphrasing much of this, too, toning the ceremonial language down into brief statements that encompassed the needs of the rite, if not the pomp of it.

Father Tony said, "By the mystery of your death and resurrection, bathe this man in light, give him the new life of baptism and welcome him into your Church."

Assumpta said, "Lord, hear our prayer."

Greg had his eyes closed and his hands clasped tightly together at his waist. A bead of sweat rolled down his forehead. She couldn't see what his demon was doing, but it certainly caused him pain.

Father Tony said, "Through baptism make Gregory your faithful follower and a witness to your gospel."

"Lord, hear our prayer," Assumpta said.

Greg grunted and he dipped again, going down on one knee. A second set of scratches appeared on his left shoulder. Eyes open, he lifted a hand to the baptismal font and pulled himself up. He steadied himself with a second hand on the font.

Greg's eyes met Father Tony's.

"Lead Gregory by a holy life to the joys of God's kingdom."

"Lord, hear our prayer."

"Make the life of his godparent an example of faith to inspire him."

"Lord, hear our prayer."

Father Tony wiped a hand across his sweaty brow. "Is it getting warm in here?" he asked. All the exuberance he'd had at the beginning of the rite seemed to be gone.

"Are you feeling all right?" Assumpta asked.

Father Tony shook his head as if to clear it. "Tired all of a sudden," he said. He looked up with a curious expression on his face, as though he were trying to understand something. "I feel like a great weight is sitting on my shoulders." He shrugged, doing a little jig step at the same time, as if trying to dislodge something. "Dear God," he whispered, and the blood drained out of his face.

Assumpta felt her eyes widen, seeing the moment Father Tony understood. He literally had a demon on his back. Then, the confusion cleared from his eyes, and he stood up taller, pulling his shoulders back. He said, "We'll skip the rest of the requests as they don't matter to the act of baptism. However, I will invoke the prayers of the saints—all at once, Assumpta—instead of one by one."

She nodded.

Father Tony said, "Holy Mary, Mother of God, Saint John the Baptist, Saint Joseph, Saint Peter and Saint Paul, Saint Gregory for whom this child was surely named and all holy men and women…"

Assumpta said, "Please, pray for us."

"And now, we will have the exorcism," Father Tony said.

Greg looked at Assumpta with shock in his eyes.

"I'd forgotten," she said to him, "that there's a rite of exorcism before baptism. Father," she turned to Father Tony, "could I be included in this rite?"

"It's unusual," he said, "But nothing about this has been usual." He thought for a moment. "You realize this rite of exorcism is largely symbolic—meant figuratively to cast out Satan so that the newly baptized can be raised without his evil influence."

She hadn't. She'd just heard the word *exorcism* and thought she could wrap up two problems with this rite in a nice, neat bow. "It's a start, Father." And she meant that, too. If she could begin with casting out the lead devil's influence, it might make getting rid of the other buggers easier.

Father Tony nodded. "All right then. As you say, it can't hurt. I think you should be included."

Out of the corner of her right eye, Assumpta saw the figure of Christ on the bas relief begin to writhe on his cross. A second later, a minion peeled itself away from Christ and crawled up the wall and over the ceiling to above the baptismal font. The water began to steam, and the surface roiled like a pot simmering on a stove.

"You'd better make this quick," Assumpta said, following the creature with her eyes. "I think they are calling out reinforcements."

Father Tony said, "Almighty and ever-living God, you sent your only Son into the world to cast out the power of Satan, spirit of evil, to rescue man from the kingdom of darkness, and bring him into the splendor of your kingdom of light. We pray for Greg and Assumpta: set them free from original sin, make them a temple of your glory, and send your Holy Spirit to dwell with them."

He looked at Assumpta, and she was certain he took liberties with the baptism rite with his next plea. She hadn't heard such a strong prayer—no, demand—at any baptismal service she'd attended. He spoke the words in a rush, as if worried he wouldn't be able to get them all out: "I command you, unclean spirit, whoever you are, along with all your minions now attacking these servants of God, by the mysteries of His virgin birth, the passion, resurrection, and ascension of our Lord Jesus Christ, by the descent of the Holy Spirit, by the coming of our Lord for judgment, that you tell me by some sign you will depart this instant."

A sudden wind blew in through the open chapel door, making the candle flames dance. Many were extinguished. Father Tony looked up to the ceiling, following Assumpta's eyes, but continued, "I command you, moreover, to obey me to the letter, I who am a minister of God despite my unworthiness; nor shall you be emboldened to harm in any way these creatures of God, or the bystanders, or any of their possessions."

Assumpta wondered, was Greg "a creature of God" yet? Did he have to be baptized first, or was he one simply by being born? She wondered vaguely if the demons had to obey Father Tony if Greg wasn't yet "a creature of God."

Father Tony leaned forward and put the heel of his left hand on Assumpta's brow and the heel of his right on Greg's. He said, "And they shall lay their hands upon the sick and all will be well with them. May Jesus, Son of Mary, Lord and Savior of the world, through the merits and intercession of His holy apostles Peter and Paul and all His saints, show you favor and mercy—"

Fire exploded on Assumpta's forehead. She cried out, squeezing her eyes shut. The hands that held her captive released her so suddenly, she felt pushed toward the font, breaking contact with Father Tony. She lifted her free hands to her head, rubbing her left palm across her forehead, smoothing away the pain. The wind blew harder, and Father Tony had to speak louder to be heard above it. "We ask this through Christ our Lord."

"Amen," Assumpta said, grabbing at Greg's elbow with her left hand. "Say it," she croaked, her voice tight with pain.

"Amen," he repeated.

Then the pain stopped, and she could stand upright again. She blinked the tears from her eyes and stepped closer to Greg, who seemed oblivious to all that was going on around him, though his own hair whipped around, and the collar of his shirt lashed against his neck, turning more red as it swept through the bloody scratches over and over again.

The wind whipped her hair into her eyes. It gained speed, swirling around the small chapel. The old chandeliers swung from their chains and went out. Candles flickered, casting hellish shadows on the bas relief of Christ.

"Keep going, Father," Assumpta said.

Father Tony stuck a finger into the mouth of the oil bottle and pulled it out, then leaned forward and made a cross on Greg's chest. He shouted to make himself heard over the wind. "We anoint you with the oil of salvation in the name of Christ our Savior; may he strengthen you with his power, who lives and reigns forever and ever."

"Amen," Assumpta said, and nudged Greg again.

"Amen," he said.

Father Tony turned his gaze upward and looked to the ceiling, saying, "We now ask God to give this child new life in abundance through water and the Holy Spirit."

The wind shrieked into the little chapel. The old ribbons in the chandelier chains shredded, dropped onto the candles and caught fire. The lamps circled on their chains, pushed by the fierce wind into ever-widening circles.

Father Tony raised both hands over the water in the baptismal font, frowning slightly. "Steam?" he murmured to himself, and lowered his right hand to touch the water. "Ow!" He drew his hands back swiftly.

Assumpta nudged Greg and looked up, pointing with her chin at the minion perched on the ceiling like a spider.

"I see it," he said.

"See what?" asked Father Tony, now shouting over the wind.

"One of the demons, Father," Assumpta said, just as loudly.

Father Tony looked up, just as he'd done a few minutes ago. "I see nothing."

"It's because they don't want you to see them," Assumpta said. "The demon over the font is boiling the water."

"Well," said Father Tony, looking back to Greg, "There's nothing wrong with a little boiled water at a baptism. It's probably sterile now," he said, smiling, though the smile looked strained.

Father Tony clutched his prayer book to his chest and raised his eyes to the ceiling. He prayed, "Father, you give us grace through sacramental signs, which tell us of the wonders of your unseen power. In baptism we use your gift of water—"

The wind buffeted past him, blowing in the doorway and whipping around the small chamber. The statue of Saint Joseph tottered on its pedestal. Father Tony's cassock whipped in the onslaught.

"Faster, please, Father," Assumpta said.

Father Tony nodded. He placed his right hand over the font and lowered it toward the steaming water. The wind circled the room, gaining speed. Stacks of prayer cards and missals blew in off the racks near the doors, flapping noisily. Sharp as razors they circled in the wind, cutting by them with each pass. One flew by Assumpta, slicing the bridge of her nose.

"Ow!" she cried, reaching up with a hand and pulling it back with blood on her fingers. Father Tony turned to her. "Keep going, Father, please," she said, digging into her purse for a tissue.

He nodded, turning back to the water. "We ask you, Father, with your Son to send the Holy Spirit upon the water of this font. May all who are buried with Christ in the death of baptism rise also with him to newness of life. We ask this through Christ our Lord."

"Amen," Assumpta said.

He turned to her. "Assumpta, you have come here to present this man for baptism. By water and the Holy Spirit he is to receive the gift of new life from God, who is love. On your part, you must make it your constant care to bring him up in the practice of the faith. See that the divine life which God gives him is kept safe from the poison of sin, to grow always stronger in his heart.

"If your faith makes you ready to accept this responsibility, renew now the vows of your own baptism. Reject sin; profess your faith in

Christ Jesus. This is the faith of the Church. This is the faith in which this man is about to be baptized."

Father Tony gave her a grave look, "Assumpta, do you reject Satan?"

"I do," she said, using the traditional response. The wind whipped faster through the small chapel. The edge of the white scarf dangling down the side of the baptismal font rose up and snapped in the wind. With a sudden gust, it flew from the font and circled the room, coming to rest across the tops of the votive candles. It burst into flames.

Assumpta reached for the scarf, but Greg pulled her back from the fire. "Keep going, Father," he said.

Father Tony nodded.

"Do you reject Satan's works?"

"I do!" Assumpta cried out, straining to be heard over the wind.

Father Tony was yelling, too. He said, "Do you reject sin, the glamour of evil, and refuse to be mastered by sin?"

"I do," said Assumpta.

"Do you reject Satan, father of sin and prince of darkness?"

"You know I do, Father," she said. She knew what came next, the threefold profession of faith. She hoped to forestall him and said, "I also believe in God, the Father almighty, creator of heaven and earth. Now, let's get on with the baptism before we can't."

Again, Father Tony nodded. He said, "This is our faith. This is the faith of the Church. We are proud to profess it, in Christ Jesus our Lord."

"Amen!" Assumpta shouted. "Get to the baptism, *please*."

Father Tony turned to Greg and said, "Is it your will that you wish to be baptized in the faith of the Church, which we have all professed with you?"

Greg nodded.

"Say it aloud," Assumpta said.

"I do," Greg said.

The wind increased. The rocking statue of Saint Joseph toppled forward off its perch, striking Father Tony in the shoulder and knocking him forward. He struck his head on the edge of the marble font and collapsed.

The wind stopped, but the scarf and several prayer cards and pamphlets still burned on top of the candles.

Greg looked horrified. He bent to help the priest the same time Assumpta did, then both backed away without touching him.

"Now what?" Greg asked.

"Call 911." Assumpta wished she could feel for Father Tony's pulse. "Tell them I think he's breathing. I can't tell, but he's not blue."

Greg stepped into the narthex to make the call.

"Assumpta?" Father Tony awakened.

"You're okay?" At his nod, she shouted, "Wait, Greg!" He stepped back into the chapel. "Hang up. If we can do without paramedics, all the better. How would we explain all this?"

She stood. Time to get this over with. Before she could think of the consequences, Assumpta dipped her hand into the boiling baptismal font. Immediately, her stony fingers turned to flesh, then reddened from the hot water. She cried out in pain, but heard the shriek of her minion as it released her and disappeared.

She didn't see it go, but felt the immediate relief of its weight from her back. She could only assume where it went. She looked up, thinking it might have joined the one still clinging to the ceiling above the font, but she couldn't locate it.

Hand dripping, she took a step toward Greg and raised her hand to his forehead and drew a cross. In a strong, clear voice, she said, "I baptize you in the name of the Father, and of the Son, and of the Holy Spirit."

She dipped her hand again into the font, blanched with pain from the hot water, and again made the sign of the cross on Greg's forehead, repeating, "I baptize you in the name of the Father, and of the Son, and of the Holy Spirit."

Father Tony stirred. "Help me up, child," he said to Assumpta.

"Should you be standing?"

"Saint Joseph delivers a terrible blow," he said, "and my head aches like the dickens, but I'm well enough to finish this. Now give me your hand." He grabbed it before she could step away, and pulled himself to his feet. "You made a good start, but Greg's not safe yet."

Father Tony dipped his finger into the small bottle of holy oil still sitting on the edge of the baptismal font, then made the sign of the cross on Greg's forehead and said, "God the Father of our Lord Jesus Christ has freed you from sin, given you a new birth by water and the Holy Spirit, and welcomed you into his holy people. He now anoints you with the chrism of salvation. As Christ was anointed Priest, Prophet, and King, so may you live always as a member of his body, sharing everlasting life."

"Amen," Assumpta said.

Father Tony reached for his prayer book. He sorted through the colored ribbons marking places in the book, then slid the white one from between the pages. With a yank, he pulled it free.

He laid the book back on the edge of the font.

The minion who'd been hanging on the ceiling above the font, crept down the wall toward them.

"No," Assumpta said, moving around Greg and putting herself between him and the demons.

"It's all right," Father Tony said, tying the white ribbon to the button on Greg's shirt nearest his heart. "Greg has been baptized. His soul is safe."

"You can see them?"

He nodded, giving her a rueful look. "My eyes have been opened."

He looked around the room, as if surveying the damage. "The scarf was only a symbol, only a reminder for Greg, really. This ribbon will do just as nicely." Father Tony looked at Greg, smiling. "But you really don't need it."

"But the baptism—"

"Is complete," Father Tony said, "though I don't know if that makes it better or worse for you. Better for you in terms of saving your soul, but not so good for now, I think, since we've angered the demons even more."

CHAPTER 31

ASSUMPTA SAT IN GREG'S KITCHEN, DRINKING HER fourth cup of coffee and making a list of things she needed to do once her job with Greg ended. The end couldn't be that far off, now that she knew what must to be done to get rid of the minions. She just needed to talk it over with Greg and decide the best course of action. After that, she'd be home free to get done everything in life she'd wanted to do, and couldn't, thanks to her dad. And so far, her list contained the only three things she hadn't yet been successful in doing:

- find a job
- get an apartment
- go back to school

Would she accomplish helping Greg and still be no better off than she was? Pity. If she were a smart girl, she'd find a way to make things work between them. All her troubles would be over: she'd have her meal ticket, a place to stay, and probably the funds for college.

And her Dad could go suck rocks, because she'd have Alec the Accountant in her back pocket. And probably a lawyer or two.

But she was a *good* girl—and smart—she was just good first. And that made a world of difference as far as her finances were concerned. Good girls finish last. But at least they make it into Heaven. She had that going for her.

Too bad she only *liked* Greg.

She heard footsteps in the hall, and then Greg walked into the kitchen, smiling. He grabbed a cup of coffee from the pot, then sat down across the table from her. He looked like a kid on Christmas morning. And so cute. She wished, not for the first time, that she liked him in *that* way.

Greg pulled the shirt away from his neck and showed Assumpta the bite marks.

"Scabs!" she said, smiling, genuinely happy for him. Greg nodded, his face turning slightly pink. "You didn't think the baptism was going to work," she accused.

"You're right." He fiddled with a few paperclips she'd piled on the table. "Honestly, I was playing the pragmatist angle. It was my last resort."

"And now?"

"And now I think there might actually be some power out there watching over us. I just find it hard to believe *It* would have let me be demon-fodder."

"*It* couldn't help you if you didn't belong to *It*. You had to commit," Assumpta said. "And all those dead civilizations you dig up? How do you feel about them now?"

"Like they knew more than I did," Greg said. "I admit it."

She paused. "Have you seen your hitchhiker lately?"

"Not since the baptism."

"Me, either." She frowned. "Yet, I don't feel like it's gone for good."

"The baptism wouldn't keep them away?"

Assumpta shook her head. "There's that brief prayer of exorcism before the baptism rites—but it's basically a renunciation of Satan. It's not a true expelling of demons. I know Father Tony added more to your rite than is customary, but my guess is that any effects he managed were purely temporary. Technically, I'd say Father Tony had no power over the minions. Either they were scared off and will return soon, or their master has better things for them to do now that you're baptized."

Greg leaned back into the chair and took a long, thoughtful swallow of his coffee. "You don't think it's possible they were scared away by the rite?"

"Well, anything's possible. I just think it's more likely that Father Hughes is planning his next move."

"What's our next move?"

She told him what she'd found out about the location of the relic.

"So all we need to do is ask Father Tony to let us borrow it for a while?"

"He can't authorize that. I'm not certain he would, even if he could. I've brought it up theoretically, and he was categorically opposed, even when he had no idea if the relic even existed anymore."

"You don't think he would change his mind, even after seeing the demons for himself?"

She remembered the conversation in the church, where he accused her of tempting him to relent and allow her to use the relic.

She shook her head. "I think he'll stand on principle."

"So, you're talking about a stealth mission."

"Not exactly." She hadn't really given it much thought. But some ideas occurred to her as she spoke. "I don't want to break into the church. There are moral implications there that don't bear thinking about, let alone the legal consequences if we get caught. Father Hughes will certainly press charges if we're found there after hours." She put down her pencil. "We need to enter the church while the doors are open—"

"—and stay until everything is locked up. Then we'll grab the artifact and scram."

Assumpta laughed and threw her balled-up napkin at him. *Why couldn't she like him?* "You watch too many movies," she said. "Holy Rosary holds confession before Mass on Saturday night. We can examine the altar then, while Father Tony is stuck in the back of the church behind closed doors with parishioners seeking penance."

"And if we find something?"

"I guess we scram."

CHAPTER 32

GREG PARKED IN FRONT OF HOLY ROSARY AND Assumpta felt a strange sensation of déjà vu as she got out and opened her umbrella.

"You go to confession every Saturday night before Mass?" Greg asked.

"Hardly," Assumpta said, hurrying up the granite stairs. "Let's just say I have a real problem confessing my sins to a priest. Why do I need an intermediary between me and God?"

"Because the church says so?" Greg pulled the door open and raised an eyebrow at her.

Assumpta gave him a stunned look, though she shouldn't have been surprised. There was nothing like a fresh convert to regurgitate the catechism.

"The church also says only men can become priests, forces the nuns to take a vow of poverty, and tells me it's wrong to use birth control. I've got issues with those, too."

"Then why do you feel a need to confess tonight?"

She opened the church door, and stepped over the threshold, wincing in pain as she crossed into the holy. There'd been no way to avoid that—if her minion were still with her.

Apparently, it was.

She sighed, stopping in the narthex until she was ready to enter the sanctuary. She certainly didn't want to have this conversation inside where anyone could hear. But, how could she explain it to him without feeling like a hypocrite—or looking like one? Especially when she wasn't certain she'd even sinned.

The church taught that premarital sex was a sin, but was it a sin in the eyes of God? Why would He frown upon such a natural act between two consenting adults? She and Jak had both wanted to do it, and so they had.

But having sex with a demon? That probably ranked right up there with fornicating with the devil himself. But, she didn't think Jak *was* a demon. She just didn't know *what* he was. He wasn't human. Was he a ghost? That made the problem marginally better, because at least ghosts *used* to be human, right?

Was he an alien? That sounded far-fetched even to her. But if he were, her problems were solved, at least from the demon standpoint, not the unmarried standpoint.

She had a strong suspicion that the problem wasn't a matter of theology, but a matter of upbringing, habit, and good old-fashioned Catholic guilt.

"Let's just say that I'm feeling the need for a little guidance that only a man of the cloth can provide in these situations," she said. "If Father Tony thinks I'm off base, he'll let me know in the confessional. I'll only be a few minutes. Then we can check out the altar."

In the narthex, a minion crawled over inner doors leading into the sanctuary. Two statues of angels flanked either door, their hands clasping bowls of holy water. By rote, she reached out her hand to touch the water and cross herself, but pulled back just in time. The fonts boiled as she walked past them, sending up a cloud of steam toward the guarding minions.

She crossed herself with her right hand—forehead, heart, left shoulder, right—then pushed through the wooden door into the church.

Greg followed. The confessionals were here in the back of the church, so they didn't need to walk far. She chose the face-to-face booth because it felt more natural to her than talking to Father Tony's side, especially with the screen between them to shield her identity. But after all these years, she knew Father Tony knew it was her. He knew her voice, her speech, even if he couldn't see her in the dim confines of the confessional.

She knelt and pulled the door closed, then made the sign of the cross again.

"Bless me, Father, for I have sinned. It's been eighteen months since my last confession.

"Father Tony, in that time I have been disrespectful to my father, sworn on many occasions—probably daily, to be honest—and taken extra sugar packets from McDonald's when I buy iced tea, so I can save a few dollars at the grocery store." She took a deep breath. "And I have also had sex with a very caring someone who I am sure is not human."

A chuckle sounded from the other side of the screen.

A mortifying blush rose up Assumpta's face. She knew no one could see her, but she felt the heat of it just the same. Father Tony had never laughed in the confessional before. In fact, he had always been professional, not revealing that he knew it was her.

"Father!" she hissed. "This is not a laughing matter."

"It is from where I'm sitting," he said, the voice thin and raspy.

A chill swept through her. *Oh, god,* she thought.

"Did you find it more exciting than fucking your boyfriend, Greg?" He leaned forward and touched the screen, so Assumpta could see the outline of his lips moving against it, the form of his body looming toward her.

Instinctively, Assumpta leaned back. She reached for the doorknob.

"Women become addicted to fornicating with the devil's minions. Was its dick huge? Could it fuck you all night? Did it satisfy your every need?"

"You're not Father Tony," she said. *Oh, god. Where is Father Tony?*

His laughter filled the confessional again. "Right in one, Assumpta. But then, you have a knack for always knowing what's going on."

"I know you're not Father Hughes, either—" Assumpta said, desperately clawing at the doorknob. It refused to budge.

"But of course I am," he said.

"You're not fooling me. You may possess his body, but he's still in there somewhere. Father Hughes—"

"He can't hear you," the demon said curtly. "I hear him screaming to come out every once in a while, but soon, he won't exist at all." The laugh came again, an inhuman sound, ratcheting down her spine.

Assumpta moved her hands to her purse. What could she do? She had her holy salt, the holy oil, but those could hardly get her out of here. Even if she tossed the salt through the screen to land on Father Hughes, it wouldn't guarantee her freedom. In fact, it might hinder it. If she assaulted him, he might get angry enough to kill her. But he was going to kill her anyway, of that she was certain. Maybe she could get Greg's attention. She took a deep breath, intending to…

"Don't yell, my dear," the creature said. "It will only go worse for you."

Assumpta reached into her purse for her holy water and salt. She found the salt first, opened it, then dumped some into her palm. "It can't possibly get any worse," she said, punching through the thin metal screen between her face and Father Hughes'. She threw the salt at his face.

The creature screamed and put his hands to his eyes. Even in the dim light of the confessional, she could see the skin pulling away from his face where he wiped his hands against it. Blood welled in the ruts. A horrible odor filled the confessional. *Burning flesh?*

Assumpta threw her shoulder into the door and tried to force it open.

"Greg!" she yelled. She threw herself against the door again and again.

CHAPTER 33

A SSUMPTA!" GREG YELLED.
    She heard him grappling with the door, saw the door shake as he yanked on the doorknob.

"Get back!" he yelled. No sooner did she lean back into the farthest corner than Greg kicked through the door, splintering the old, dried wood in one blow. He clawed at the opening, breaking away slivers and widening the hole. Then he reached through and pulled Assumpta from the confessional.

Beside them, Father Hughes tumbled out the door to his knees, screaming in rage, or pain, clawed hands still scrubbing his face. Then he put his palms to the floor and pushed himself to his feet, leaving bloody handprints on the black-and-white tile. Blood droplets welled on his face where each grain of salt had struck him. His face looked buckshot, with rivulets of blood and flesh seeping down from his eyes like melted candle wax. A twisted grin marred his disfigured face.

He raised a bloodied hand toward Assumpta.

Shaking all over, she fumbled for the opened jar of salt and, keeping hold of the glass, flung the salt at him in a sweeping motion. Most of the grains bounced harmlessly off his surplice and dropped to the floor, but some struck his face. He screamed, a hand swiping at his eyes. Blindly, he lunged for her.

243

"Run!" she cried, grabbing Greg's elbow and hustling him up the center aisle of the church toward the altar.

Her pendulum had revealed that the relic lay beneath it, one of the most holy places in the church, hiding in plain sight. She just needed to get the relic before the demons got to her.

She ran faster than she'd ever run before.

"What if it's not there?" Greg asked, running beside her.

"It will be there," Assumpta said. The pendulum had never failed her.

She leapt onto the marble dais—a thirty-foot wide raised platform that touched three walls in the front of the church—and ran behind the free-standing altar in the center. She'd never been on this side of it. Glimpsing the hundred or so empty pews from this angle, she could only imagine what it felt like during a mass when all of them were full. *Father Tony must feel like a rock star.*

She skirted the altar to the right, around the double prie-dieu where the altar boy always knelt and rang the Sanctus bells at mass.

She looked up. The ceiling crawled with dozens of minions, one for each saint depicted in the mosaic. One for each angel guarding the saints. One sitting on the larger-than-life-sized statue of Mary—a bastardization of The Pietà—on the platform fifteen feet above the altar on the back wall of the church. It played with the golden crown on the Christ Child's head, and chittered at her like a squirrel might. Assumpta took a step toward the altar, and the minions started to crawl across the ceiling and down the walls toward her.

She slung her purse at Greg. "Get the oil."

Greg looked around and whistled.

"You'd better find it quickly."

He rummaged through her bag and found the jar, then dropped the purse to the ground and uncapped the oil.

God, she hoped she had the strength to go through with this. Jak couldn't help her. Greg could only do so much without a relic to fight them on his own. How long would the oil last before they overtook him? And how do you fight a demon when you don't have the right weapons?

She was going to have to fight them to get the weapon she needed to fight them. *The circular paradox would send her thoughts reeling, if she let it.*

She fell to her knees behind the altar, pushing aside a rubber mat Father Tony stood on during Mass. Nothing.

"I've got an idea," Greg said. She spared a glance behind her to see him drizzle some oil on the ground, then smear a large circle around them and the altar, nearly reaching to the marble wall behind it. "That should hold them back for a while."

Assumpta fervently hoped so.

She pushed aside the altar cloths, looking for a chamber under the broad structure, but there was none. Two marble blocks comprised the sides of the altar, and a third lay across them to form the top. She looked to the floor beneath it.

There it was: she could just see the lines cut into the marble, a groove on one side which might be a hinge, and a ring to lift the marble slab door, roughly eighteen inches long.

"Hurry up," said Greg. "I'm not liking what I'm seeing."

She glanced up and saw at least a half-dozen minions converging on the ceiling over the altar.

"I'm moving as fast as I can." She grasped the ring with her left hand, and pulled. She stood, clenching the ring, and yanked, putting her back into it. It didn't budge. "I'm not strong enough to lift this. I'm not sure if it's just the marble that's too heavy, or if it's just stuck."

"Maybe it's gummed up with spilled wine and the accumulated dust of over a century of saying Mass at Holy Rosary."

Assumpta wondered if it were blasphemy or sacrilege to speak so disrespectfully? At least he'd learned his lessons about the parish.

She reached for the last of her salt, moving away from the altar, but conscious to remain within the circle Greg had drawn. "See if you can get it open. I'll keep the minions at bay."

"The one in Mary's lap is too close for comfort," Greg said, keeping his eye on it as he moved to the altar.

"I see it," she said, realizing it was her personal minion. She'd recognize that ugly fucker anywhere. It leered at her, then slid off Mary's lap to stand upright, clutching the marble pillar for balance. Its free hand grasped its erect penis with a clawed fist and jerked up and down the length of it while it laughed at her.

Then it fell to all fours and climbed downward, moving closer.

A movement from the corner of her left eye caught her attention. She turned to look.

Another minion, much larger than her own, crept across the ceiling toward her. A third joined it, then a fourth. If they all rushed her at once, she didn't think she could survive—just like in Greg's condo. Jak wasn't here to save her this time.

And just like that, she was shaking from head to toe, and freezing, as though an arctic wind had blasted through the sanctuary. Her hands felt almost too numb to grip her jar of salt.

What kept the minions from attacking her now? Greg's circle? The altar? The tabernacle, which held the blessed Eucharists—the unleavened wafers of bread? She could only guess. If it were the wafers keeping the minions at bay, then maybe she should have some in hand. But obtaining them meant she had to step out of the circle Greg had made to reach the tabernacle on the back wall. It wasn't far out of the circle, but out was out.

She heard the scrape of stone on stone, then a clink.

"Greg?"

"I've got it," he said. "The box is beautiful, but locked."

"Break it."

He sighed, and she wondered if he worried about damaging a beautiful—possibly sacred—church object. Did it go against his archeological ethics?

He's a pragmatist, she reminded herself. *He knows the necessity.* She heard something hard smash against the marble floor, then the squeak of hinges.

"You should do this," Greg said.

She nodded, not certain if he could see her or not. "You keep watch," said Assumpta, turning back toward the altar and kneeling.

The box *had* been beautiful, elaborately carved and stained, inlaid with glass beads—she couldn't believe they might be gemstones—and quite probably gold. Cotton batting covered whatever lay in the small chest. She flipped it up, and a chorus of hisses echoed all around her.

"They don't like whatever you did," Greg said. "They all backed away from us."

"All I did was uncover it," Assumpta said, staring at *it*.

A cylindrically shaped, eighteen-inch length of wood rested in more cotton batting. One end looked as though it had been sawed from another length. The opposite end was splintered to a jagged point. Three or four inches from the sawed-off end, a shallow groove encircled the staff.

If this was what she thought it was, it was worth millions—more, even. *No*. If this was what she thought it was, no amount of money could express its worth.

She shivered. Her heart raced. She could feel it beating in her throat. Heat infused her face. *This was bigger than life.*

"Oh, my god…" she said, filled with such reverence she hadn't the words to speak.

"What?"

"Look," she said.

"It can't be…"

Assumpta touched the wood with her left hand, running her palm down the length of the silkily smooth wood until she reached the splintered, jagged end.

A bead of sweat rolled down her back.

Then, hands shaking, she grabbed the grooved end with her right hand, and her stone fingers immediately turned back to flesh. She lifted it from the box, hefting the weight of it, feeling how it balanced in her hand. Immediately, she felt calm. She could do this.

"They're coming closer again," Greg said, the fear evident in his voice.

She stood, tightly grasping the end of the broken-off spear, pointing it toward the minions, several of whom were close enough to throw salt on. She pointed the weapon at them, and a woman's scream broke the silence in the church.

Assumpta whirled to face the rear of the sanctuary.

A woman who had been kneeling in a pew about midway from the back of the church stood and backed away from the center aisle. She clutched her rosary beads to her chest, and recited the Hail Mary aloud.

The wreck of Father Hughes shambled up the aisle toward her, arms raised, hands tangled in his white hair. The woman screamed again and shrank against the pews, her legs collapsing beneath her. Her weeping echoed through the sanctuary, and Assumpta heard the dry-bones laughter of her minion echo across the vaulted ceilings.

Father Hughes trudged toward the altar, passed the hysterical woman, and, as if as an afterthought, dropped a hand in her direction and made a shooing motion. She flew out the far side of the pew into the right aisle and struck the wall, collapsing under the third Station of the Cross, depicting where Jesus stumbled for the first time.

Father Hughes continued to approach the front, walking up the center aisle. As he got closer, Assumpta watched him—*no, she watched the demon that possessed Father Hughes*—raise both arms to and yank at his hair. Father Hughes' face split down the middle and peeled away from the demon skull, revealing its hideous visage.

Glistening purple skin broke through the old priest's body. It ran wet with...*what?* The blood of Father Hughes?

"Oh, my god," Assumpta said, crossing herself. "Oh..." She looked away, her stomach churning. Then she turned back. She couldn't let it sneak up on her. She had to watch what it did, where it went, and look for her chance to kill it. She gripped the broken spear shaft tightly, and waited.

No longer able to speak through a human mouth, the demon hissed and made guttural noises that might have been speech. Did it taunt them? Assumpta nearly laughed. Insults didn't hurt if you didn't know the language they were made in.

It continued to press forward, coming nearer to the altar.

The arms continued to tug, splitting the old priest's body even further, until muscled shoulders, then hips, appeared and the human body peeled backwards to drag along the tiled floor, bumping the fractured skull along, weeping a mass of blood and brain on the tile.

Finally shedding the human skin, the entire creature emerged: a lumpy face with a distended jawbone where top and bottom teeth were never destined to meet; predominantly bipedal with cloven hooves and clawed hands at the end of muscular thighs and arms.

With the sound of a flag snapping in the wind, a pair of large purple wings, bat-like and leathery, slick with blood, veined in black, whipped out from behind it. They flapped—testing—and it rose a few inches off the floor and dropped down again, unable to remain airborne.

It walked slowly, dragging one leg, obviously injured.

Assumpta wondered if she'd done that with the salt. And why couldn't it fly? She hadn't done anything to its wings, hadn't even known it had wings until now.

She moved around the altar, stepping out of Greg's circle, toward the center aisle, hefting the weapon in front of her.

"You realize there's only one weapon that spear haft could have come from, right?" Greg whispered, finally getting a long look at the relic.

She whispered back, "Since we found it in a jewel-encrusted box beneath an altar of a church, I know what you're thinking. And I can only agree."

She stepped off the dais toward the newly hatched demon. It was still about thirty feet away, plodding slowly toward her. Every few steps it tested its wings, like a fledgling bird, anticipating flight.

"The spear of Longinus. The weapon that pierced Christ's side as he hung dead on the cross." She felt, more than saw, his nod. "It's hard to believe that so large a piece of it exists. It would have been chopped into splinters and sold to the highest bidder in the Middle Ages."

"So, you're not sure."

She shook her head. How could she be? She couldn't believe she could remain this calm. Was it a property of the relic?

A minion screeched from its perch on the ceiling above them, and dropped down on Assumpta's shoulders, claws outstretched.

She screamed in pain. Greg thrust the uncapped jar of oil toward it, sending a stream of the sanctified chrism across its shoulders. It howled and lost its grip on Assumpta, sliding down her back, claws tearing at her clothes. Pain bit her.

She whirled around, slamming the ragged end of the spear into the demon. Greg covered his eyes.

Assumpta heard a sizzle, then a small pop, and the demon exploded with the smell of sulfur and wet cement. Rock-hard shards flew in all directions.

"I'm sure now," she said, wiping blood from the corner of her eye.

"One down..." Greg said.

"And a gazillion to go."

"They're moving closer again," Greg said. He was out of the protective circle of the oil now, too.

"Right. The big demon first." She turned back to face the aisle and hefted the broken weapon. The demon had gained ten feet on her while she'd battled the minion.

Clackety.Clackety.Clackety.

A minion hurtled across the floor toward them from the right, claws scratching the tile with each bound.

It leaped at Greg, knocking him from the dais. The oil bottle fell from his hands and shattered, spilling oil and glass all over the tiled floor.

The minion somersaulted over Greg and hit the dais on its back. It slid across the floor for a few feet, struck the altar, then burst into flames and exploded.

Greg scrambled to his feet and stepped back on the dais.

"Get back up here," Greg said, backing up. "I've just realized, they can't come to us up here. It's like the whole area is a demon-free zone—" he wiped the gore from his cheek "—more or less."

"But we can't get them either if we stay there."

She strode toward the big demon, determined to confront it before its wings grew strong enough to keep it aloft.

Greg looked conflicted, but followed her, the Gospel clutched tightly in his hands. He could beat the demon with it, she supposed, but it made a better shield than a weapon. With luck, it was blessed, too.

"Stay back," she said. "Keep the minions at bay while I fight it. I hope it'll be too busy to direct them."

"I can do that," he said, and Assumpta thought she heard a note of relief in his voice.

She nodded. The demon seemed to have sensed her intention. It stopped a few paces beyond the first pew into the open area before the dais and waited. Ten feet stretched between them like a canyon.

She had to bridge that gap.

Taking a deep breath, she raised the weapon and ran toward the beast. Heat blazed off the creature, drying her skin. It felt like standing next to a roaring fire.

It raised an arm to strike her, but she'd anticipated that.

She thrust the spear haft at the demon just under its outstretched arm. It sank into its leathery skin, and the demon roared. She twisted the haft—not an easy feat—and leaned her weight into it, pushing the broken spear another inch or so into its molten flesh.

The demon raised a meaty fist and struck her hard against her ribs. She lost her grip on the spear—her hand immediately turned to stone again—and she tumbled away from the creature, striking her chin on the marble edge of the dais.

Good, she thought, as she fell. She wouldn't be close enough to the demon when it exploded to receive any more damage.

She closed her eyes and counted silently: one, two, three. Nothing happened.

She opened them again. She watched, sickened, as the demon grasped the end of the spear shaft with both clawed hands and ripped it from its body. It tossed the spear aside.

The hole in its flesh closed. It tested its wings again, lifted about ten inches above the floor this time, then fell swiftly, unable to keep aloft. Then it hissed and walked closer to the altar, and her.

CHAPTER 34

HANDS GRABBED HER, AND SHE WAS PULLED BACK onto the dais, the marble edge scraping painfully against her back. Her head hurt, too. She was almost too tired to move.

"Why didn't it work?" Greg asked her, dragging her closer to the altar.

She shook her head slowly. "I don't know. The touch of the relic should have banished the demon." She thought back to how she'd asked the questions of her pendulum. She'd asked how to banish the minions, and the pendulum told her to touch them with the relic.

"Oh, no," she said.

"What?"

"I didn't ask the right question!" She scrambled to her knees, suddenly full of energy. "I asked if the relic *would help with Father Hughes, too.*"

"So why didn't it?"

"Because the demon wasn't possessing Father Hughes when I struck it. If it had been, it would have probably separated the two, maybe banished the demon, but now I'm not so sure."

He knelt beside her on one knee. "What do we do now?"

"I don't know." Despair filled her, weighing her down. Her shoulders slumped.

She had held in her hands a weapon that had touched the blood of Christ. It had destroyed the smaller demons. Why had it had no effect at all on the larger? Surely the demon was not stronger than Christ?

She tightened her resolve. "We have to kill it."

"How?"

"It's still vulnerable to holy objects," Assumpta said. "We just need to find something holier than that relic."

Greg looked dubious. "Holier than the Lance of Longinus?" He looked up. "And these things are getting closer again."

She wondered, *What's holier than a relic?*

Assumpta smiled. "What's the holiest of holies?" she asked Greg. It should have been an easy question for someone currently studying the faith.

"Bread and wine."

"*Transubstantiated* bread and wine," she corrected. "The actual body and blood of Christ." She stood and hurried behind the altar to the small cabinet on the back wall. "Let's see if there's some in the tabernacle."

Assumpta pushed aside the gold curtain with the chalice embroidered on it, then opened a small gold door, her stone hand making a tinking noise as it struck the metal cabinet. Inside, the ciborium, a gold-plated bowl with a lid, was veiled with a scarf.

"We're in luck," she said, relief flooding her. "We have transubstantiated hosts."

"How do you know?" Greg asked.

"A priest wouldn't cover unconsecrated hosts."

Assumpta pushed off the scarf, pulled the bowl from its niche and lifted the lid.

Her heart sank.

Half full. With so few precious wafers, she was going to have to aim instead of just slinging the bowl at the demon.

"I'll do it," Greg said, reaching for the wafers.

"No," Assumpta said. "I have to do this." She walked toward the edge of the dais, toward the demon. It stretched its wings, able to keep aloft for more than a second or two now.

If she didn't get this over with soon, it would be able to fly over the altar and carry her and Greg off. She wouldn't be able to fight it. Yet she knew if they left the safety of the dais again, she wouldn't survive.

She stepped to the edge of the platform, her toes hanging over the step.

"Don't stand so close," Greg said.

"I can't help it. I need to be as near as I can in order to hit my target. I can't afford to miss." She looked down at the wafers in the bowl. She had how many? Fifteen? Twenty?

Hastily, she made the sign of the cross and said, "Forgive me, Lord, I know that more than one piece of you is going to land on the floor."

"What?" Greg asked.

She didn't have time to tell him how bad it was if a transubstantiated host fell to the floor. It would need to be dissolved in water and poured onto consecrated ground. Or eaten by a priest immediately afterward—if he didn't mind eating the host off the floor. But would it lose its power over the demon? She didn't know. And she hoped she didn't have to find out. If she could hit her target the first few times, maybe she wouldn't have to worry about that.

She picked up one of the hosts, a flat disc of bread slightly larger than a quarter, and held it between her thumb and forefinger as if she were going to toss the ace of spades. She needed the edge to cut through the air and fly fast, rather than being slowed by the flat side.

The demon had backed up a few paces. Had it sensed the power of the Eucharist? She didn't know. Could she make that distance with the host?

She flicked.

The white disc flew about ten feet, then veered sharply upward and lost momentum. It dropped to the floor.

"Damn," she muttered, and reached for a second one.

The demon raised its arm and gestured with its wrist.

"Watch out!" Greg said. She looked up. One of the demons on the ceiling abruptly let go and dropped. Assumpta covered the bowl with one hand and stepped backward.

The minion fell on her right shoulder and slid down her arm. The jarring weight brought her down on one knee, and the demon fell off onto the dais. It screamed, and Assumpta briefly smelled wet cement before the overpowering scent of burned flesh pierced her nostrils. She gagged, squeezing her eyes shut, and the creature exploded, more flesh than stone.

Charred bits of flesh and blood splattered her right arm and the right side of her face. She forced her gorge down, and stood.

Gore covered Greg, standing beside her. "Keep them off me," she said. He nodded and looked around, then stepped to the altar and exchanged the Gospel for one of the tall candlesticks there.

She stepped forward again. The creature took two steps forward and ground the dropped host beneath its heel.

It roared, lifting its foot, wisps of smoke curled from the bottom. Despite the pain, it stomped the host again, grinding its heel into the tile. With a scrape of its foot, it took another step forward. Behind it, a small circle of tile smoldered, black and smoky. It flapped its wings, and the pungent odor of burning linseed oil filled the air.

Well, that answered her question: any consecrated hosts that fell to the floor would be useless.

She flicked another host toward the demon. It struck on the chest, sticking, burning. The demon roared, flapping its wings, and raising itself a few more inches off the ground, propelling itself forward several feet.

Oh, Lord, she thought, taking a step backward.

"Incoming!" Greg yelled. She heard the whine of the candlestick whipping through the air and the thud of something hard hitting concrete. Greg grunted. Something small slapped the marble of the dais to her left and sizzled. A small pop later, and nothing remained.

She flicked another host at the demon, but the disc veered to the side, landing on a pew to the right. She tossed another, striking it on the shoulder. Again its wings flared.

Could she hit its wings?

Quickly, Assumpta threw another host in its direction. She'd aimed too high and it sliced over the demon's right wing and fell behind the creature.

She flipped another host at its chest. It hit on the arm, smoking and burning. The demon roared again, wings whipping out, and Assumpta quickly flung another host, aiming for the demon's wing.

It struck, quickly burning a hole through the thin membrane.

The demon screamed, flapping his wings. It moved closer.

One of the larger minions ran up the aisle, passed the winged demon, and barreled toward the altar. It leaped, striking Greg in the chest and knocking him over. Out of the corner of her eye, Assumpta saw him lose his grip on the candlestick when his head struck the marble floor. His legs tumbled over the edge of the dais. Faster than she could blink, a horde of minions attacked Greg's legs, jumping and pummeling them, then started dragging him from the altar.

God save him, Assumpta thought, knowing she couldn't. Not now. In an instant, she knew she had to make a choice, and make it quick: attempt a rescue and hope she could fight all of them off, and then kill the demon leader. Or, kill it first, and hope the others would find their way back to Hell once they lost their leadership.

There was no more time.

She reached into the bowl and grabbed several hosts with her right hand. Immediately, her hand turned back to flesh, and she was able to grip the hosts more easily. She set the bowl on the altar and grabbed the remaining hosts in her left hand.

Jumping off the dais, she ran toward the demon, arms outstretched, intending to press the wafers against him: she would take no chance of winging the hosts at the demon and have them drop to the floor where they would do no good.

She'd nearly reached it when it sidestepped her.

257

When she saw the minions pulling Greg off the dais and toward the demon, she understood.

She wasn't the target.

The demon spread its wings and took flight, moving around Assumpta and toward Greg. With almost angelic grace, it landed at Greg's feet and stepped closer, its clawed toes touching the bottom of Greg's feet and then sinking into them.

It was taking over Greg, like it had taken over Father Hughes.

"No!" Assumpta yelled, and ran toward the coupled pair.

The demon leaned at an awkward angle, sinking slowly into Greg's prone form.

Assumpta clenched her fists around the sacramental hosts and, spreading her arms wide, leapt at the demon.

With a rock-solid thud she crashed against it, scraping her face against the rough skin of its wings, and clutched it with all her strength. The two of them disconnected from Greg and tumbled to the floor.

The demon howled, trying to shake her off, then stopped abruptly.

This is even better.

Assumpta heard the voice in her mind, felt the hard body of the demon go soft, like warm cement, felt herself sinking into it, filling her nostrils with the scent of it, cloying, suffocating.

The demon laughed, and it was her own voice. Then she realized she hadn't been sinking into the demon's flesh…*it* had been sinking into *hers.*

CHAPTER 35

ASSUMPTA BURNED. SHE FELT THE HEAT OF HELL emanating from the demon spirit within her. Energy—*life*—coursed through her veins, more than she had ever known before. She could do anything.

She could fly. Even with the demon's wings sunk beneath her own skin, she knew she could fly if she simply willed it.

I could grow to like this, she thought, *to have all this power.*

"Yes," she whispered, then realized it wasn't her own voice.

"No!" she shouted, understanding where this conversation went.

Drop the flesh of Christ; it burns, the demon commanded.

She looked down at her hands, smoldering. Her poor, abused right hand, stone for so long, now flesh and burning. She hadn't felt the heat of it with all the power emanating through her. But seeing the flesh turn black, the smoke rise from her clenched fists…she nearly did drop the hosts.

Instead, she did the only thing she could think of to bring the demon down. She brought her hands to her chest, opening the palms wide to spread as many of the wafers from her throat to her belly as she could, clustering several in the location of her heart.

Then it really did burn, her shirt catching fire, and the hosts—still whole—submerging into her skin.

She fell to her knees, the pain so intense that she could no longer hold her hands to her chest. She let them fall to her sides, burned fingers bent like shriveled claws.

"No! No, no, no!" she screamed, but it was the demon yelling with her own hoarse voice. Acrid smoke filled her throat, choking her. She coughed, barely able to breathe.

It's not over, the demon thought, its mind—*its body*—still connected with hers. And she knew without being told what it would do next.

Vaguely, as if in the distance, she heard the screams of the demon's minions, their protests, a brief second before each exploded in turn, those closest to them detonating first and then the others, farther out toward the rear of the church.

Power surged into the demon.

"Yes!" it roared. And she could feel it, too. He had killed off all his minions, taking back their power for his own. He was healing himself.

She brought her hands to her chest again, feeling for the hosts. She located several, and one at a time, peeled them from her body, the pain excruciating.

Yes, the demon whispered in her mind.

No, she thought. There was one more thing she could try.

"*Oh, my God, I am heartily sorry...*" she whispered the words of the Act of Contrition, the prayer said after confession to show regret for having sinned. It was the only one to come to her mind for this situation.

There were specific prayers to be said for the dying, but could you say them for yourself? Especially if what you planned to do was virtual suicide? Probably not.

I'm definitely going to Hell for this one, she thought.

Assumpta raised the wafers to her lips and ate them. Her mouth burned. Her teeth heated, feeling like hot, ceramic stones in her mouth. She swallowed, then gagged, but forced herself to consume the wafers, her lips and tongue blistering from the heat. The discs burned like molten lava all the way down her throat and into her belly.

She curled into a fetal position, eyes squeezed shut, pulling her knees to her forehead, writhing against the pain.

"Let me die," she prayed. "Let me die."

"No, no, no!" the demon bellowed.

Assumpta felt a tug at her back and a cooling sensation.

And then the demon exploded around her.

CHAPTER 36

GREG SHOOK ASSUMPTA AWAKE.

It must have been hours later. Darkness lay behind the stained glass windows, draping the church in gloom. Candles still flickered on the altar. Eerie quiet pervaded the sanctuary.

"Are you okay?" he asked, his words echoing in the stillness.

She sat up, free of pain, rubbing a hand across her eyes. It came away dry, when she had expected blood. "Yeah, I'm okay. Really tired."

She stood and assessed the damage to her clothing. Burned shirt, torn pants. *When had that happened?* And thankfully free of demon gore. All the scratches and scrapes she'd gotten in battle: *gone.*

Mouth still dry, she stumbled on the next words. "How about you?" She looked him up and down, taking in the lack of damage. "I thought they had you."

"Me, too. I feel like I've been run over by a steamroller." He shoved his hands into the front pockets of his jeans, looking down. "I didn't expect to walk away from this. Literally. When they pulled me off the dais, they crushed my legs. I was certain they were broken. I couldn't fight the minions off. Yet, here I am. Alive. Unbroken."

Greg nodded at the altar. "Come see what I found."

"You didn't wait?"

"It's only been a minute or two. But it's extraordinary. You won't believe it." He stepped up on the dais, and she followed, then stopped. Father Hughes's bloodied form lay a few feet away in the center aisle.

His body whole, he lay on his back, hands stretched out to the side as if he'd lost his balance and fallen. A large pool of blood fanned out from his head, touching the pews on both sides of the aisle, just turning the collar of his cassock red.

"Is he—?"

"Yeah," Greg said. "I checked."

"We need to call the police."

"He'll keep," Greg said. "Here, look."

She followed him to the altar.

The box lay on top of the unsullied white altar cloths. Pristine. Bejeweled. Beautiful. As though Greg had not shattered it apart. The lock hung from the hasp, open.

"It looks exactly like it did when we found it," Assumpta said, pulling the lock from the box and opening it. She pushed aside the cotton and ran her hand—her now unblemished right hand—down the length of the satiny wood.

"The spear was in the box when I found it on the floor behind the altar," Greg said. "And look—" He stepped to the tabernacle and opened the door. Pulling away the veil, he showed her the ciborium, half-filled with hosts. He put it back and veiled it, then shut the door with an audible click. "Look around. It's like nothing ever happened here."

She looked. Except for Father Hughes, the church looked as it always had. Nothing remained to prove a demon battle had just been fought—except for perhaps the silence, and the emptiness. No one was there but the two of them. Even the parishioner the demon had pushed aside was gone.

"Father Tony?"

"I haven't seen him," Greg replied.

She nodded. "We'll find him. Let's put the spear back in its hiding place first."

She tugged her pendulum out of her pocket, wrapped the end of the string around her second and third fingers, and let it fall. "Then we'll call the authorities about Father Hughes."

Greg nodded, and replaced the spear—box and all—back in its niche beneath the altar.

"Is Father Tony in the church?" Assumpta asked. He could be, she knew. Tied up somewhere. Dead. Who knew what the possessed Father Hughes would have done to him?

The pendulum started a narrow swing to and fro, then widened and turned counter-clockwise.

"He's not," she said to Greg.

"Is he in the rectory?" she asked.

The pendulum continued on its counter-clockwise path.

"Still *no*," Greg said.

She nodded. "Is Father Tony in his office?"

The pendulum dropped abruptly, then turned clockwise.

"Bingo," she said, dropping her arm. "Let's go."

"Wait," Greg said. "Do you really think this is over?"

"I do."

"Use your pendulum. Ask the universe."

That hurt, and she didn't know why. He didn't trust her? And since when did he believe so much in the pendulum? On the other hand, maybe he was just as rattled as she over the situation. Maybe it was his pragmatism.

She raised her arm again, letting the crystal dangle, and asked, "Is it over? Are we free of this demon and its minions?"

The pendulum started swinging, back and forth, then dropped suddenly to its starting position.

"Too many questions," Greg said.

"Not if the answer is the same for all of them."

It started to swing again—

"You can't be certain."

"I am."

The pendulum swung clockwise and Greg relaxed.

"Okay," he said, letting out a deep breath and starting for the door.

"Wait." She coiled up the pendulum and shoved it into her pocket, then knelt beside Father Hughes's body.

"What are you doing?" Greg asked.

"Father Hughes—the demon—took the other relic from me when he attacked me at your house. Maybe it's here."

"You're going to rob a corpse?"

She gave him a dirty look, but moved closer anyway. She felt a strange warmth in her chest, almost the sensation of being hugged, but not quite. "The relic belongs to the church. I'm just getting it before the authorities take the body away. What do you think they'll make of a pocket full of ancient bones?"

Her hand tingled when it got close to the body, then she felt a quick burst of heat, and a series of finger bones tumbled out of the dead priest's pocket and wormed across the floor into her hand. She squeezed them tightly, comforted, despite their roughness in her palm.

Greg stumbled back. "I don't believe what I just saw."

She turned to look him in the face. "You accept that a church has been returned to normalcy after a demon battle has been fought inside it, but you can't accept a few bones falling out of the pocket of a body once possessed by a demon?"

He shook his head.

"Well," she conceded. "they might have had a little divine help."

"Point taken," he said, still looking a little pale. "Can we get out of here now?"

"I'm ready," she said, standing, and walked toward the door.

CHAPTER 37

FATHER TONY STOOD BACKED AGAINST HIS REAR office wall, a look of terror on his face, a pentagram the size of a communion paten chalked on the floor in front of him. A short, black candle burned in the center of the pentagram, white curls of smoke eddying up from its green flame.

"Father Tony." Greg approached the terrified priest.

"Don't touch me!" he screamed, sinking down against the wall. "Christ protect me," he muttered, bowing his head. "Our Father, who art in Heaven…"

Greg stopped, and Father Tony looked up again, in the direction of the candle. "Don't come any nearer! Beast!"

The priest continued to pray, trying to take his eyes off the candle but unable to do so, even with his head facing the floor.

"I thought he was talking to us," Greg said. "But I don't think he's aware of us."

Assumpta approached the candle. "He's trapped in a personal hell." She bent and blew out the flame, then she lifted a foot to kick the candle aside.

"Wait." Greg grabbed her elbow. "What do you know about pentagrams and demon spells?"

"Not much." She stared at the encircled, five-pointed star, the points and angles so precise it could have been stenciled. "But I think it's too small to have trapped a demon or even to call one. This looks like spell-casting to me. Blowing out the candle didn't do any good. Maybe if we smudged out the pentagram, it would help."

"What if it makes things worse?"

She looked at Father Tony. "Can it get any worse?"

Father Tony bobbed his head down, turning it away from the candle, yet not able to turn away completely. His hand fumbled against his chest, reaching for his large, metal cross but unable to grasp it.

"No," Greg said.

Assumpta kicked the candle out the pentagram, half-expecting it to explode. When nothing happened, she ran her right shoe across the chalk, smudging the lines together, over and over until she obliterated the image.

"Now what?" Greg asked.

"We have to bring him around."

"Do you want me to shake him out of it?"

"Don't be absurd," Assumpta said. "Just talk to him. Touch him gently."

Greg looked dubious, but approached the cowering priest. "Father Tony," he said, laying a soft hand on the priest's shoulder.

"Don't touch me!" Father Tony lifted his arm and struck Greg's hand from his shoulder. His hard-soled shoes sliding against the polished hardwood floor, he tried to push himself further away from Greg. Finally, his right hand finding the metal crucifix on his chest, he lifted the cross between himself and Greg as if to ward Greg away.

Greg rubbed his wrist and backed up.

"Let me try," Assumpta whispered.

"Be careful. He might find the courage to hit you."

She nodded and stepped around Greg. "Father Tony," she said, her voice soft and cajoling. "It's Assumpta. I need you to help me with something, Father."

The priest shook his head. "No, no. I won't fall for any more of your tricks, demon." He raised the crucifix again. "Begone from this place."

He looked at her, seeing her, but not seeing her. *Seeing something.* "Foul beast. Go back to Hell where you belong." Father Tony stopped struggling, stopped trying to avoid the evil he'd cowered from for so long.

It was as if Assumpta's words, her presence, were giving him courage.

"Keep going," said Greg, a hopeful expression on his face.

"I'm not a demon." Assumpta took a step closer to Father Tony.

"*Trickster.*"

She took a step closer. "It's me, Father. Assumpta."

"Stand back," Father Tony said, "or I will burn you with this cross." He pushed it toward her as far as the heavy chain around his neck would allow.

"It's me, Father," she said again, reaching out to him. She wrapped her hand around his, gently squeezing it around the crucifix. "Assumpta."

She felt a jolt of heat from Father Tony's hand beneath hers, exactly like she had felt when she retrieved the finger bones from Father Hughes, and then it was gone.

Father Tony's vision cleared. "Assumpta?"

She released his hand. "Welcome back," she said, bending to help him up. Greg stepped forward and lifted him by the elbow.

"Feeling better?" asked Assumpta.

"It didn't happen, did it?" he asked, looking down at his clothes and brushing a hand across his chest.

"What didn't happen?" Greg asked.

"A demon came and took me to Hell," Father Tony said. "Chained me to the wall of a stone cell. I don't know how long I was there—"

"You never left your office, Father," Assumpta said, "though I've no doubt the demon was here."

"It was—it—"

"Forget about it." Assumpta put her hand on his shoulder, gently patting him. Again, heat sparked in her palm, each time she touched him.

"Did you feel that?" he asked, looking at her.

She nodded. "Am I hurting you?"

He shook his head. "You calmed me. Your touch is like—this is going to sound blasphemous, but I mean it with all sincerity. It's like being touched by the hand of God. Soothing. Light. I could almost feel His presence."

She looked at Greg.

"What?" Father Tony asked, seeing the look pass between them.

"A lot has happened while you were trapped in your office, Father," Greg said.

"We need to get back to the church," Assumpta added.

"It's late," Father Tony said. "Can it wait until morning? Let's get a good night's sleep and we'll talk then."

"You're not worried about nightmares?" Assumpta asked, knowing that they couldn't wait until morning. She just wanted to know. Did she really help him? What was the heat that had sparked between them?

"I—" He stopped to think about it. "I remember Father Hughes coming in to visit. He brought a candle." He paused. "I was so scared. I remember being deathly afraid. I told you I'd been to Hell…but I can't remember it now." He looked at her. "Your touch…"

"We can talk about that," she said, "but not now. We've got to go to the church. Father Hughes is dead, I'm afraid. We need to call the authorities."

His eyes widened. Shocked, he nodded, and walked to his desk. "How did it happen?" He picked up his prayer book and stole, putting the one in his suit-jacket pocket and draping the other around his neck.

"We'll fill you in as we walk," Greg said, then started from the beginning, when he and Assumpta had arrived for confession, and concluding with Assumpta's obtaining the second relic.

"You're not angry that I went behind your back to look for the relics?" Assumpta asked.

Father Tony turned rueful eyes to hers. "Yes, I'm still angry. You'll find out just how much when you come to confession tomorrow night." He smiled then. "But I must admit I'm very pleased that you found them."

"About her touch breaking the demon's spell…" Greg ventured.

"A miracle!" Father Tony said. "From eating the hosts. It could be nothing less."

"All hail Saint Assumpta," Greg said, bowing.

"We mustn't be hasty," Father Tony said, grinning at Greg. "It's *Blessed* Assumpta first. We need another miracle before we can elevate her to sainthood."

CHAPTER 38

"J ESUS, MARY AND JOSEPH!" FATHER TONY SAID, hurrying toward Father Hughes, and kneeling by his side. All signs of his earlier mirth vanished. "I didn't like the man, but I certainly didn't wish him dead."

"It's not your fault," Assumpta said, arriving more slowly at the body.

"I know that, child, but it doesn't make me feel any less sorry for his death." Father Tony made the sign of the cross on Father Hughes' chest, over his heart, and then made another on his forehead, reciting a prayer under his breath.

"Last rites?" Greg asked.

"Nothing so formal, I'm afraid," Father Tony said, rising. "Father Hughes is beyond my help. The rites aren't given once the soul is departed. I offered but a simple blessing for him." He sat down in a pew beside the body, then pulled a cell phone out of his pocket. "I'll call the police and wait here with Father Hughes for someone to come for him. You two go home. You look like you need the rest."

"They'll have questions," said Assumpta.

"Not as many as you think," said Father Tony, "unless they look at the two of you. You look guilty. Go home."

"He's right," Greg said.

"But—"

"We'll talk tomorrow, Assumpta." Father Tony stood and ushered them to the rear of the church.

Greg grabbed her hand and tugged her down the granite steps of the church and to the car.

"We've got to talk, too," Greg said. "About us." He opened the door and let her in. "But that, too, can wait until morning. I want to shower and go right to sleep."

Us? She thought, *is there an us?* She didn't know if there could be, after Jak. But Jak was gone, and she was alone. And Greg wasn't bad, for a rich guy. She could do worse.

"You know," she said, thinking of the church, cleansed of any sign of their supernatural fight, "you'd think the demons would want to prove their existence. Why wouldn't they want to show their power, and the damage they can do? Leave this place looking like a battle was fought?"

"That would tip their hand," Greg said, stepping back into his element. "Proving they exist also proves the existence of God."

"Not necessarily."

He smiled. "Good and evil, black and white, Heaven and Hell. We do love our opposites. The concept built into every nation, every people, from time immemorial. Without one, there can be no other. Even if God isn't real, who would believe it, faced with the existence of demons? Besides, maybe it's God who cleaned up the mess."

"Wouldn't He want to prove His own existence, then?"

"He's not that type," Greg said. "He demands utter faith."

CHAPTER 39

ASSUMPTA RAPPED HER KNUCKLES HARD ON THE paned glass door of her father's house and waited for him to answer. Rain dripped over the edge of her umbrella, and she was soaked from the walk from the bus stop. She tapped her foot on the marble stoop, waiting. Finally, she heard the footsteps of booted feet and saw the curtain inch back. A single, bleary eye stared at her. He'd been drinking again, of course.

The curtain fell and another few seconds passed before she heard the scrape of the key in the lock and the door open a few inches. His footsteps moved away. She pulled the storm door open herself and pushed her way into the living room.

"You just missed your mother," her father said, sitting down hard on the sofa and propping his feet on the coffee table. "She got a call and said she had to run out for a moment."

"I caught her on the walk. She's going to call me later," Assumpta said, shaking her umbrella and leaning it against the storm door. "I'm here to see you, not her."

"I'm flattered."

"You won't be, when I'm finished," she said.

"Might as well sit down and get on with it." He cracked open a fresh beer. "You're wasting my time."

"I won't take but a minute."

"You've got my cash, then," he said, dropping his feet to the floor and leaning forward. "You can leave it on the mantle on your way out."

"Not a cent," she said. "I'm here to let you know I won't be paying any more of your guilt extortion."

"Well, you know the deal, then: out goes your mother."

She smiled. Taking on her father was child's play after kicking demon butt. His threats didn't scare her anymore.

"That's where you're wrong, Father," she said, "because extortion is illegal. No court would ever side with you against me." She dropped her purse and sat. "You kick Mom out—though God only knows why she wants to stay with you—and we'll have you divorced and paying alimony so fast you won't know what hit you. You'll be the one looking for an apartment and scrounging to put food on your table."

"I won't hear that kind of talk from my daughter—"

"You have no idea what it's like to lose your home and worry about where your next meal is going to come from. Trust me when I tell you that the courts won't care, either, just as long as half your paycheck goes to Mom and you keep out of her way. Maybe if you're lucky, she'll invite you over once in a while for a free meal and to reminisce."

"Why, you little—" He stood and tottered, reeling around the coffee table toward her.

Assumpta jumped up and grabbed her purse, hurrying for the door.

"Try it," she said, "and I'll have you arrested for assault."

That stopped him. His shoulders drooping; he looked defeated. "Ungrateful bit—"

"Don't say anything you'll regret later, Father."

Something in her tone must have put the steel back in his spine, because he stood up straight and said, "After all I've done for you."

"You haven't done anything you didn't expect to get paid back for later. With interest. Had you shown a little love, you might have been repaid in kind. What kid doesn't expect to help out an aging parent?" She ran a shaking hand through her hair. Saying what had to be said was harder than she thought it would be. "Consider this your interest: I'm done with you. I hope you find it easier to get along than I do. At least you'll have Mom by your side, unless you mess that up, too. Treat her right, or we'll file the divorce papers anyway. I've got them all filled out and ready to go." She didn't—*what good Catholic did?* But her dad couldn't know that.

She grabbed her umbrella, then pushed through the storm door and bounced down the marble steps, feeling lighter than she had in a long time.

She walked to the bus stop, arriving just as the bus had pulled up. An elderly woman with a cane approached the doors before her, taking her time getting on, and took a seat in front, just behind the driver. Assumpta dropped her fare into the slot, then took a seat in the rear of the bus and leaned her head back against the hard plastic.

She smiled. She'd done it. Gotten her dad off her back and made sure he wouldn't throw her mother into the streets. She exhaled, suddenly sleepy, and closed her eyes.

Through closed eyes, she sensed a brightness in front of her...

At the next stop, a guy in a leather jacket got on. He walked down the aisle, ignoring all the empty seats, and sat next to Assumpta. He wore cologne, tangy and cool, and a secret smile like he knew something she didn't.

She'd smelled that cologne only once before in her life.

"Jak?" she asked.

He slid his hand under her small one and twined his fingers with hers.

"I thought I'd never see you again," she said.

"I'm only here for a moment," said Jak. "I have to go back, but I'm out on good behavior."

"How long?" *A lifetime*, she hoped.

"Not long enough." He jabbed his chin upward. "*He* gave me only a few minutes to say goodbye."

"So, I'll never see you again?"

"I can't say."

"Can't, or won't?" *Why did this conversation sound so familiar?*

"Can't, definitely," Jak said. "Free will and all that."

She smiled. "So there's always the possibility."

"Always."

He leaned toward her and brushed his lips against hers. It wasn't enough for her. She disentangled her hand from his and reached up for the collar of his leather jacket. She pulled him tightly against her and opened her mouth to his.

She felt the smile against her lips before he opened his own mouth, his tongue searching for hers.

And then she was standing on the sidewalk in front of the university chemistry department, looking at a help wanted sign in the window of the front office.

Wanted: Chemistry Technician to moderate lab and experiments, perform inventory. General bottle washer and chief dogsbody.

She looked up, smiling. *I can do that,* she thought.

The job with Greg probably wouldn't last long now that the demon problem had been solved. She would need work, anyway. And she would have to move out, although from last night's conversation, Greg seemed to be interested in something more. Did they have a future? She had no idea, but she wasn't sure she wanted to entertain it if there was the slightest possibility of her sharing something with Jak. Could she even have a relationship with a spirit? Time would tell.

She shrugged her purse up higher on her shoulder, then walked to the building and opened the door.

Thanks, Jak, she thought, pulling the sign out of the window.

A peal of thunder split the air, but sunlight pierced the gloom, streaming down from between two dark clouds in the sky.

EPILOGUE

A SSUMPTA WAS ASLEEP WHEN HE CAME TO HER again.

No soft touches this time. No tentative licks in sensitive places to caress her to wakefulness. Now wasn't the time, no matter how much he desired it. He found it hard to believe he desired it, even in this form.

"Can you hear me?" he asked. Then, a little louder, "Assumpta, I have something to tell you."

She rolled over onto her back, awake, kicking the covers to the foot of the bed, and blinked in the darkness of the room, looking puzzled.

Jak knew she couldn't hear him when she was awake, so he waited. In a few seconds, her eyes fluttered closed and she drifted off once more.

In a soft voice, he said, "I didn't mean to wake you. I can't talk to you when you're awake."

In her sleep, she smiled. "Jaaaaaak," she said, husky and long. "Miss you." The words were tinged with sadness.

He smiled unhappily, believing her. He felt her sorrow—all her emotions, in fact. And her physical pains. Worse, he could feel her arousal, mirrored within himself. He hadn't anticipated that, though the other was all part of the job.

"Why do we have to talk?"

"There are things you need to know—"

"So tell me. " She was smiling again, reaching toward him, though he was there only in spirit.

He hadn't realized how hard it would be to admit all this to her. And she didn't make it any easier. He took a deep breath—at least it felt like he took a deep breath—and said, "I accidentally broke an urn. An urn containing Lord knows what. It was my duty to protect it. I'd sworn to do so, but I'd been distracted."

"By what?"

"By a sloe-eyed nymph, sent by the enemy to tempt me." His words were gruff. A millennium had passed, and he was still mad at himself. No amount of time's passage could cure him of the embarrassment. "She promised me a good time."

"And was she?"

"Was she *what?*" Jak asked.

"A good time?" asked Assumpta, smiling again in her sleep. "Did you get what you bargained for?"

"I got less," he said, the words clipped. "And I lost the urn to boot. Not only that, I lied about it, and when I was killed in battle, there was but one place for my soul to go."

"Where?"

"To Hades, of course. Brought up in the Roman Empire, I believed that everyone who dies go to Hades. Here and now, that name's a euphemism for Hell. Wish I'd known that then."

"But you're not in Hell now, Jak." She rolled over onto her belly again, sliding one hand under her down pillow and the other on top. "Thanks to me."

"Yes, thanks to you, I'm no longer in Hell. But that's what I came to talk to you about."

"We're talking."

"Yes, but we're not getting very far. That's the problem with talking in dreams. Things don't move along fast enough."

"I could use a back rub, Jak."

And he wanted to give her one. But he didn't have the time. It would have been forbidden anyway.

He said, "For being so kind to help me—"

"My pleasure, Jak." She practically purred those words, and he felt a tightening in the area of his groin, though he had no groin.

"For being so kind to help me," he repeated, "I won't spend an eternity in Hell, but things are worse for you. Because of me, you've been demon-marked."

"Doesn't matter," Assumpta said. "Already marked. Minions."

"You misunderstand. You're literally marked: somewhere on your body—"

She smiled, and Jak felt her excitement three-fold through the dream. If he'd had a body, he'd be just as hot as she right now.

"Hide and seek, Jak. You can find it for me."

He felt his insides curl—but he had no insides. How could he *feel*, when he had nothing to feel with? Yet, he felt more for this woman than he had felt about anything in more than a thousand years.

"You're not grasping the seriousness of this," he said, relocating his essence. He would appear to sit down on the bed beside her. She reached for him, for clearly she was seeing something in her dream, and patted through his ethereal self, her hand finding only the cotton texture of the bedspread. She frowned.

"Assumpta," he said with a sigh, "you've been marked. That means you're fair game for the Dark One. Consorting with me, apparently, was a mortal sin, but only because I was under his influence at the time. You're destined for Hell unless you can erase the mark."

"What's it look like?"

"The mark? I don't know."

"Then look."

He bent to her, and instinctively tried to lift a hand to brush the hair away from her face. Her own hand lifted, and moved the hair so he could see on the side of neck. *Not there.*

"I can feel you," Assumpta said.

But I can't feel you, he thought, though in the darkness a curious thing happened. Where his hand would have touched her, if he had a hand, a glowing silhouette of a hand appeared. He leaned forward and brushed the soft cotton of her tank top upward with a sweep of his glowing palm. Now he could feel the warm satin of her skin, revealed inch by inch as he pushed the shirt upward.

She sighed. Her body whispered to him, stronger than her words. He could smell her musk, a heavy perfume in the room.

"Feels good, Jaaaak," Assumpta whispered, pulling one knee to her chest and tilting her hips at an inviting angle. He could see the moisture between her thighs. It wouldn't take much effort, he thought, to coax her to her knees, and thrust forward to bury himself in her.

He remained formless, but surely with the way he felt now, he could bring them both to climax one last time. He could make it good.

But he wouldn't. He couldn't take advantage of her that way, even if she begged—not while she slept.

He needed to find the mark. In the past, the Dark One hid them away in birthmarks, but he grew increasingly more clever, and more daring. Assumpta didn't have a birthmark that he recalled, but then, he hadn't looked for one. Even if she did, Jak was certain he wouldn't find the Dark One's taint there. It would be somewhere more…in vogue.

He brushed her long mane of hair away from her back and he found it. In the middle of her shoulder blades, about the size of a quarter, it could easily be mistaken for a tattoo or a sorority brand, with its brown mottling: an upside-down cross, surrounded by a circle. It wasn't unlike crosshairs, seen through the scope of a rifle.

He caressed the mark with his thumb, feeling the warmth of her skin beneath his phantom hand. Grimly, he smiled, then closed his eyes and cursed himself for the danger he had put her in.

And yet, he couldn't help feeling the tiniest bit glad, because this mark enabled him to remain close to her, even if it were only long enough to help her erase it from her soul. Only then would they both be eligible for Paradise.

But would he go when the time came? Or would he remain with her?

AUTHOR'S NOTE

Baltimore has been known as Charm City since the mid-1970s. Lovers of fable will tell you that journalist H.L. Mencken was the first to dub it so (Mencken died in 1956), but it was really the brainchild of four of the leading ad-men in Baltimore, brought together by then-mayor William Donald Schaefer to do something about Baltimore's poor image. (This was a Baltimore before Harbor Place, Oriole Park, or the Ravens.)

It took only five full-page ads in local newspapers, each with a charm bracelet depicted at the bottom, to cement the name "Charm City."

While I strived to be accurate in my description of the city, I'll admit that some of the scenery and locations of Baltimore depicted in *Stoned in Charm City* come from the rosy recollections of my childhood. And some do not exist at all: I'm sorry to say that Assumpta's favorite coffee shop, The Charm City Brewery is completely fictitious.

ABOUT THE AUTHOR

Kelly A. Harmon used to write truthful, honest stories about authors and thespians, senators and statesmen, movie stars and murderers. Now she writes lies, which is infinitely more satisfying, but lacks the convenience of doorstep delivery.

Her short fiction appears in many acclaimed and award-winning anthologies including Deep Cuts: Mayhem, Menace, & Misery, Triangulation: Dark Glass, Bad Ass Fairies 3: In All Their Glory, and Hellbore and Rue. Her story Lies short-listed for the Aeon, Ireland's Science Fiction, Fantasy and Horror Award.

Her award-winning novella, Blood Soup, is available electronically, re-released by Pole to Pole Publishing.

Ms. Harmon is a former magazine and newspaper reporter and editor. She has published articles at SciFi Weekly, eArticles, and many other magazines and newspapers in the U.S. and abroad.

Read more about Ms. Harmon at her Web site: http://kellyaharmon.com.

A THANK YOU TO DEAN KOONTZ

A quick story: long ago and far away when I was a young writer, I wrote to best-selling author Dean Koontz to ask him how I might get a copy of his out-of-print book, *Writing Popular Fiction*. I was then, and remain, a huge fan. Mr. Koontz, busy as he is, might have ignored me. He didn't.

Instead, he wrote me back and told me to forget about his book. Additionally, he sent me photocopies of some articles on how to write, and advised me to pick up a few other books, all written by other authors.

I took his advice to heart and honed my writing, but I did the worst thing imaginable: I never wrote back to thank him (despite the fact that his letter still sits on my desk all these years later, mocking my inconsideration).

I want to acknowledge Mr. Koontz here. His letter has been a source of inspiration for many years. Thank you!

ACKNOWLEDGMENTS

In my last book, I did not have the opportunity to thank my family who support me in my writing endeavors. I'd like to do that now. They have been there to bounce ideas off of, listen to me gripe, offer suggestions, make me martinis, and eat many a dinner burned to a crisp while I was off playing in make believe. Thank you all.

I must also thank the authors in my face-to-face writers group who scrutinize the early drafts of my work and tell me what I'm doing wrong. Margery Ritchie, Steven R. Southard, and Andrew Gudgel: thank you for the many dinners and great conversation, and most of all for the suggestions that improve my manuscripts.

Thank you also to the many wonderful folks I first met virtually on line, and have become special friends through our shared love of writing. I appreciate your input and your expertise. Thank you to authors: Trisha J. Wooldridge, Jennifer Allis Provost, Justine Graykin and Terri Bruce. I raise a glass of single-malt scotch to you all.

On the business side, I'd like to thank Dean Wesley Smith and Kristine Kathryn Rusch who go out of their way to educate authors who want to learn the business. I've attended their classes on the Oregon Coast, and on line, and found each and every one of them invaluable. They've created a strong network of authors helping authors which is supportive in so many ways. Thank you!

And, finally, very big thank you to my copy editor Dayle Dermatis, and proofreader Justine Graykin, who were instrumental in cleaning up the final manuscript. Any remaining mistakes are completely my own.

Other Novels by Kelly A. Harmon

A Favor for a Fiend, Charm City Darkness, #2
- Coming Soon

Blood Soup

A girl child must rule or the kingdom will fall, said the prophesy. The stubborn king commits murder to thwart it, but prophesies can be stubborn, too. Which triumphs in this blood tale?

Other Stories by Kelly A. Harmon

Lies

Crippled and bitter, Beresh is ordered to save the life of his queen. But the medicine isn't working, and the magic...well, that's complicated. He needs to craft the proper lie to save her, but time is running out. Can he save the queen's life before the king takes his?

Sky Lit Bargains

Refusing to befome her new brother-in-law's plaything, Sigrid leaves home the day of her twin's wedding. In search of her mother's jewels, she finds more than she bargained for at her Uncle's keep. One set of jewels is as good as another, right, even if she has to fing a wyvern to get them?

SELK SKIN DEEP

1967. Vietnam. Not just a Navy SEAL, but a selkie, too. When the bombs start to explode on deck, can Cade owen save the aircraft carrier the USS Livingstone, and himself, as well?

THE DRAGON'S CLAUSE

Each year the citizens of San Marino pay tribute to their dragon. Though a contract exists between them, no one has seen the dragon in hundreds of years. They people are certain they're throwing their money away. What happens when the residents renege on their contract with the dragon?

ON THE PATH

When Tan's soul engine explodes, the half-reincarnated souls flee to the nearby woods. Tan learns the hard way that honoring ancestors and walking the path sometimes conflict. Ghostly ancestors might not stink after three days, but they're a lot harder to throw out with the trash.

BY MORNING'S LIGHT

Washed up on shore after her family's boat is caught in a storm, Lukia wakes to find her mother dead, and by tribal law, herself evicted from the tribe. Determined to earn her place, she finds a way to exact her revenge and become part of the tribe once more, but is that what she really wants?

A Sneak Peak at Book 2 in the Charm City Darnkess Series...

A Favor for Fiend

A Charm City Darkness Novel

by

Kelly A. Harmon

Chapter 1

The bus pulled to the curb in front of Baltimore City Community College with a squeal of hydraulic brakes and the odor of diesel exhaust. Assumpta Mary Magdalen O'Connor cleared the plexiglass shelter, felt the brief, delicate touch of November snowflakes on her head and shoulders, then climbed aboard wearily, dropping her quarters into the fare box, and headed to the back of the bus. She brushed her long, whispy bangs off her forehead, now damp with snow, and held her voluminous purse more tightly to her as she swept past the other passengers.

Thank God no one sat in the back row. She hated having to sit anywhere else. From the rear, she could see all the comings and goings.

And she could be reasonably circumspect when Jak decided to visit. She didn't need people thinking she was crazy. But when she talked to the dead, it looked like she talked to herself–and that looked a little nuts. People could think what they wanted–they'd do as they pleased anyway–she just didn't need the guys in the white coats chasing her down to take her to her own private, padded room.

Maybe all those crazy people weren't crazy, she thought Maybe they chatted with the dead, too.

She sighed heavily, letting out a pent up breath as if she'd been storing it all day, then breathed in deeply, trying to relax, then regretted it. The back of the bus smelled like urine with high notes of vomit. No relaxing here, but at least she was on her way home: the home she was going to have to move out of soon.

Her back itched, right between her shoulder blades. She twisted her arm up behind her to scratch it.

I refuse to take advantage of Greg any longer, she thought.

"He won't mind if you stay," said a voice beside her.

She flinched. The bus hadn't stopped again, so this guy had materialized, not walked on board. Just what I need, she thought, another damn demon. She couldn't stop the gallop of her heart if she wanted to. A sheen of sweat broke out on her brow.

His blue eyes twinkled in a way that let her know he knew much more about the situation than she did, and enjoyed it. His blond hair look sun-dyed and windswept, as if he'd just come off the beach, but his nose had been broken more than once, giving him a rakish, rather than boyish appearance.

He'd be attractive, if she thought she could trust him. But he already knew more about her than she liked – or he'd read her mind. She didn't care for either scenario.

She detected the faintest whiff of sulfur. Then she sneezed.

"Who are you?" she asked, pulling a tissue from her purse, but keeping an eye on the creature.

"Friend of Jak's. Dan." He held out his hand. Assumpta ignored it.

"Oh, really?" Jak never mentioned anyone. Not that he'd had time to. "How'd you meet?" She offered him a look that said, I don't believe a word of your bull.

The smile in his eyes dimmed. "We were introduced by a mutual...acquaintance." He put the hand he'd previously held out to her on her knee. She slapped it away, but her hand went right through his and slapped her own thigh. Still, she still felt the warmth of his palm as it traveled up her knee to her hip.

"Jak!"

A few passengers from the front of the bus looked in her direction, then turned away.

"He can't come right now," Dan said in a soft voice, leaning toward her ear. "He's busy."

He'd always come before, immediately, she thought. What could keep him away?

"I can't imagine why you're here," Assumpta said, sliding over one seat, she pressed into the wall of the bus, trying to get as far away as possible. Dan slid along with her, trapping her in the corner seat.

"Please leave," she said.

He looked down at her lap, his hand on her thigh, and chuckled. His hand smoothed down to her knee again and fingered the edge of her hunter-green tartan skirt. Thank God, for thick woolen stockings, she thought.

"I'm not leaving until I get a little taste of what Jak's been getting." He leaned into her, curling his fingers under the edge of her skirt, pushing it higher. His lips touched her neck, hot and burning. She could smell the sulfur more strongly now, enveloping him like a cheap cologne.

Assumpta twisted away. Pushing was useless. Her hands went right through him.

His hands searched for the buttons to release the skirt, fingers fumbling at the closure. She couldn't imagine what the other passengers on the bus were seeing.

"Ah!" he screamed, suddenly, pulling his hand from her waist. A terrible odor filled the air. "You bitch!"

He shook his hand as if it burned, and pulled away from her entirely.

Thank you, Grandma, she thought. Dan must have touched the religious medals she kept pinned to the hem of her skirt—medals that had originally belonged to her grandmother. Nearly all of them had been blessed at one point or another. She new from firsthand experience that demons could not touch blessed things.

The bus stopped, making its familiar wheeze of breaks and exhaust. Assumpta jumped up from the seat, torpedoed through Dan, and jumped out the rear exit of the bus. She took off running, slinging the long handle of her purse over her head so she wouldn't lose it as she ran.

Snow fell harder now, and a breeze pushed the snowflakes across the sidewalk in front of her. It seemed to insulate the city, muffling the road noise from Cold Spring Lane.

She sprinted down Kenwood, passing the topiary trees and high wrought-iron fences that signaled she was closer to Greg's apartment than she thought. She turned left at the corner and saw the covered portico of the apartment building.

"Where do you think you're going?" Dan materialized right next to her, running beside her at her pace. Still, she ran.

He showed her his burned hand, a spherical shape, blackened the palm of his hand. Still, she ran.

Tendrils of blackness radiated out from the center of Dan's palm, blackening his skin. "Do you see this?" He pushed his hand right into her face. She lost her footing and stumbled, but caught herself on a lamp post, and kept running.

"I will get you for this, just as soon as I take care of it."

And then he was gone.

She slowed to a quick walk, breathing heavy, but hot under the corduroy coat, despite the falling snow. She typed the code into the keypad by the front door, and let herself in, heading toward the elevator.

Good lord, what had she gotten herself into?

The elevator dropped her off in front of Greg's door. Her door, but not for much longer.

She unlocked the door and stepped into the marble foyer, still holding the doorknob in her hand. She hated entering this place alone ever since she'd been attacked by demons right here in the doorway. She looked around, seeing nothing out of place: ashes in the marble fireplace, pillows stacked neatly on the leather couches, tiny herbal wreathes still hanging in all the windows she could see.

She closed the door behind her and locked it, then knelt to the threshold for her bottle of blessed oil and salt. She poured a little on a rag, than swiped it across the floor where she'd crossed over the threshold. Then, she checked the other rooms in the apartment to make certain all the windows were closed and wreathed.

Finally, she could relax.

She headed to her bedroom, pulling her pendulum from her purse and tossing it to the night stand. She bent to untie her leather ankle boots, then kicked them under the bed.

She needed answers, and she needed them fast.

But first, she needed to look at her demon mark.

25778864R00186

Made in the USA
Middletown, DE
09 November 2015